THE GHOST SHIP

A MYSTERY OF THE SEA

THE GHOST SHIP

A MYSTERY OF THE SEA

John C. Hutcheson

CONTENTS

The Star of the North

The sun sank below the horizon that evening in a blaze of ruby and gold.

It flooded the whole ocean to the westward, right up to the very zenith, with a wealth of opalescent light that transformed sea and sky alike into a living glory, so grand and glorious was the glowing harmony of kaleidoscopic colouring which lit up the arc of heaven and the wide waste of water beneath, stretching out and afar beyond ken. Aye, and a colouring, too, that changed its hue each instant with marvellous rapidity, tint alternating with tint, and tone melting into tone in endless succession and variety!

Throughout the day the weather had looked more than threatening. From an early hour of the morning the wind had been constantly veering and shifting, showing a strong inclination to back; and now the sea was getting up and the white horses of Neptune had already begun to gambol over the crests of the swelling billows, which heaved up and down as they rolled onward with a heavy moaning sound, like one long, deep-drawn sigh!

It looked as if the old monarch below, angered by the teasing of the frolicsome zephyrs, was gradually working himself up into a passion, which would vent itself, most probably, ere long in a much more telling fashion than by this melancholy moan, so different to the sea-god's usual voice of thunder!

Yes, it looked threatening enough in all conscience!

A brisk breeze had been blowing from the nor'-east before breakfast, but this had subsequently shifted to the nor'ard at noon, veering back again, first to the nor'-east and then to due east in the afternoon. The wind freshened as the hours wore on, being now accompanied towards sunset by frequent sharp gusts, a sign betokening plainly enough to a seaman's eye that something stiffer was brewing up for us by-and-by.

Glancing over the side, I noticed that our brave vessel, the Star of the North, was becoming very uneasy.

She was running under her jib and foresail, with fore-topsail and fore-topgallantsail, being only square rigged forwards, like most ocean steamers; but, in order to save coals and ease the engines, the skipper had set the fore and main trysails with gaff-topsails and staysails as well, piling on every rag he could spread.

With this press of canvas topping her unaccustomed hull, the poor old barquey heeled over more and more as the violent gusts caught her broadside-on at intervals, rolling, too, a bit on the wind fetching round aft; while, her stern lifting as some bigger roller than usual passed under her keel, the screw would whiz round aimlessly in mid air, from missing its grip of the water, "racing," as sailors say in their lingo, with a harsh grating jar that set my teeth on edge, and seemed to vibrate through my very spinal marrow as I stood for a moment on the line of deck immediately over the revolving shaft.

At the same time also that the afterpart of the vessel rose up on the breast of one billowy mountain, her forefoot in turn would come down with a resonant "thwack" into the valley intervening between this roller and the next, the buoyant old barquey dipping her bows under and giving the star-crowned maiden with golden ringlets, that did duty for her figurehead, an impromptu shower bath as she parted the indignant waves with her glistening black hull, sending them off on either hand with a contemptuous "swish" on their trying in mad desperation to leap on board, first to port and then to starboard, as the ship listed in her roll.

It was, however, but a vain task for these mad myrmidons of Neptune to attempt, strive as recklessly as they might in their wrath, for the good ship spurned them with her forefoot and the star-crowned maiden bowed mockingly to them from her perch above the bobstay, laughing in her glee as she rode over them triumphantly and sailed along onward; and so the baffled roysterers were forced to fall back discomforted from their rash onslaught, swirling away in circling eddies aft, where, anon, the cruel propeller tossed and tore them anew with its pitiless blades—ever whirling round with painful iteration to the music of their monotonous refrain, "Thump-thump, Thump-thump," and ever churning up the already seething sea into a mass of boiling, brawling, bubbling foam that spread out astern of us in a broad shimmering wake in the shape of a lady's fan, stretching backward on our track as far as the eye could see and flashing out sparks of fire as it glittered away into the dim distance, like an ever-widening belt of diamonds fringed with pearls.

The SS Star of the North was a large schooner-rigged cargo steamer, strongly built of iron in watertight compartments, and of nearly two thousand horsepower, but working up, under pressure, of nearly half as much again on a pinch, having been originally intended for the passenger trade.

She belonged to one of the great ocean lines that run between Liverpool and New York, and was now on her last outward trip for the year and rapidly nearing her western goal—the Fastnet light—and, according to our reckoning when we took the sun at noon, in latitude 42° 35 minutes North, and longitude 50° 10 minutes West, that is, just below the banks of Newfoundland, our course to our American port having been a little more southerly than usual for the season. This was in consequence of Captain Applegarth, our skipper, wishing, as I said before, to take advantage of the varying winds of the northern ocean as much as possible, so as to economise his steam-power and limit our consumption of fuel; for freights "across the herring-pond," as the Yankees call it, are at a very low ebb nowadays, and it is naturally a serious consideration with shipowners how to make a profit out of the carrying trade without landing themselves in the bankruptcy court. So, they have to cut down their working expenses to the lowest point practicable with efficiency, where "full speed" all the way is not a vital necessity—as in the case of the mail steamers and first-class passenger ships of enormous steam-power and corresponding speed, which, of course, run up a heavy coal bill, for they always "carry on" all they can to and fro across the Atlantic, accomplishing the passage now between Queenstown and Sandy Hook, veritable greyhounds of the ocean that they are, within the six days, all told, from land to land. Aye, and even this "record" promises to be beaten in the near future.

Prior to our leaving Liverpool on this voyage, the very day before we sailed, in fact, greatly to my surprise and satisfaction, as may be imagined, I was made fourth officer, the owners having unexpectedly promoted me from the position of "apprentice," which I had filled up to our last run home without any thought of so speedy a "rise." Of course I had to thank my old friend Captain Applegarth for my good fortune, though why the skipper thus spoke up for me I'm sure I cannot say, for I was very young to hold such a subordinate post, having only just turned my seventeenth year, besides being boyish enough in all conscience, and beardless, too, at that! But, be that as it may, fourth officer I was at the time of which I write.

I recollect the evening well enough.

It was on the seventh of November, the anniversary of my birthday, a circumstance which would alone suffice to imprint the date on my memory were I at all disposed to forget it. But that is not very likely.

No, I can assure you.

It would be impossible for me to do that, as you will readily believe when you come to know my story; for, on this eventful evening there happened something which, somehow or other, thenceforth, whether owing to what visionary folk term "Destiny," or from its arising through some curious conjuncture of things beyond the limits of mere chance, appeared to exercise a mysterious influence on my life, affecting the whole tenor and course of my subsequent career.

I had better tell you, however, what occurred, and then you will be able to judge for yourself.

Sail Ho!

Away forward, I remember, the ship's bell under the break of the forecastle, or "fo'c's'le," as it is pronounced in nautical fashion, was just striking "two bells" in the first day watch.

In other words, more suited to a landsman's comprehension, it was five o'clock in the afternoon when I came on deck from my spell of leisure below, to relieve Mr Spokeshave, the third officer, then on duty, and the sight I caught of the heavens, across the gangway, was so beautiful that I paused a moment or two to look at the sunset before going up on the bridge, where Mr Spokeshave, I had no doubt, was anxiously awaiting me and, equally certainly, grumbling at my detaining him from his "tea!"

This gentleman, however, was not too particular as to time in relieving others when off watch, and I did not concern myself at all about Master "Conky," as all of us called him aboard, on account of a very prominent, and, so to speak, striking feature of his countenance.

Otherwise, he was an insignificant-looking little chap, as thin as threadpaper and barely five feet high; but he was always swelling himself out, and trying to look a bigger personage than he was, with the exception that is, of his nose, which was thoroughly Napoleonic in size and contour. Altogether, what with the airs he gave himself and his selfish disposition and nasty cantankerous temper, Master Spokeshave was not a general favourite on board, although we did not quarrel openly with the little beggar or call him by his nickname when he was present, albeit he was very hard to bear with sometimes!

Well, not thinking of him or his tea or that it was time for me to go on watch, but awed by the majesty of God's handiwork in the wonderful colouring, of the afterglow, which no mortal artist could have painted, no, none but He who limns the rainbow, I stood there so long by the gangway, gazing at the glorious panorama outspread before me, that I declare I clean forgot Spokeshave's very existence, all-important though he considered himself, and I was only recalled to myself by the voice of Mr Fosset, our first officer, who had approached without my seeing him, speaking close beside me.

Ah, he was a very different sort of fellow to little Spokeshave, being a nice, jolly, good-natured chap, chubby and brown-bearded, and liked by every one from the skipper down to the cabin boy. He was a bit obstinate, though, was Mr Fosset; and "as pigheaded as a Scotch barber," as Captain Applegarth would say sometimes when he was arguing with him, for the first mate would always stick to his own opinion, no matter if he were right or wrong, nothing said on the other side ever convincing him to the contrary and making him change his mind.

He had caught sight of me now leaning against the bulwarks and looking over the side amidships, just abaft the engine-room hatch, as he passed along the gangway towards the bridge which he was about to mount to have a look at the standard compass and see what course the helmsman was steering, on his way from the poop, where I had noticed him talking with the skipper as I came up the booby-hatch from below. "Hullo, Haldane!" he cried, shouting almost in my ear, and giving me a playful dig in the ribs at the same time; this nearly knocked all the breath out of my body. "Is that you, my boy?"

"Aye, aye, sir," I replied, hesitating, for I was startled, alike by his rather too demonstrative greeting as well as his unexpected approach. "I—I—mean, yes, sir."

Mr Fosset laughed; a jolly, catching laugh it was—that of a man who had just dined comfortably and enjoyed his dinner, and did not have, apparently, a care in the world. "Why, what's the matter with you, youngster?" said he in his chaffing way. "Been having a caulk on the sly and dreaming of home, I bet?"

"No, sir," I answered gravely; "I've not been to sleep."

"But you look quite dazed, my boy."

I made no reply to this observation, and Mr Fosset then dropped his bantering manner.

"Tell me," said he kindly, "is there anything wrong with you below? Has that cross-grained little shrimp, Spokeshave, hang him! been bullying you again, like he did the other day?"

"Oh no, sir; he's on the bridge now, and I ought to have relieved him before this," I replied, only thinking of poor "Conky" and his tea then for the first time. "I wasn't even dreaming of him; I'm sure I beg his pardon!"

"Well, you were dreaming of some one perhaps 'nearer and dearer' than Spokeshave," rejoined Mr Fosset, with another genial laugh. "You were quite in a brown study when I gave you that dig in the ribs. What's the matter, my boy?"

"I was looking at that, sir," said I simply, in response to his question, pointing upwards to the glory in the heavens. "Isn't it grand? Isn't it glorious?"

This was a poser; for the first mate, though good-natured and good-humoured enough, and probably a thinking man, too, in his way, was too matter-of-fact a person to indulge in "dreamy sentimentalities," as he would have styled my deeper thoughts! A sunset to him was only a sunset, saving in so far as it served to denote any change of weather, which aspect his seaman's eye readily took note of without any pointing out on my part; so he rather chilled my enthusiasm by his reply now to me.

"Oh, yes, it's very fine and all that, youngster," he observed in an off-hand manner that grated on my feelings, making me wish I had not spoken so gushingly. "I think that sky shows signs of a blow before the night is over, which will give you something better to do than star-gazing!"

"I can't very well do that now, sir," said I slily, with a grin at catching him tripping. "Why, the stars aren't out yet."

"That may be, Master Impudence," replied Mr Fosset, all genial again and laughing too; "but they'll soon be popping out overhead."

"But, sir, it is quite light still," I persisted. "See, it is as bright as day all round, just as at noontide!"

"Aye, but it'll be precious dark soon! It grows dusk in less than a jiffey after the sun dips in these latitudes at this time o' year," said he. "Hullo! I say, though, that reminds me, Haldane—"

"Of what, sir?" I asked as he stopped abruptly at this point. "Anything I can do for you, Mr Fosset?"

"No, my boy, nothing," he replied reflectively, and looking for the moment to be in as deep a brown study as he accused me of being just now. "Stop, though, I tell you what you can do. Run forwards and see what that lazy lubber of a lamp-trimmer is about. He's always half an hour or so behind time, and seems to get later every day. Wake him up and make him hoist our masthead lantern and fix the side lights in position, for it'll soon be dark, I bet 'ee, in spite of all that flare-up aloft over there, and we're now getting in the track of the homeward-bounders crossing the Banks, and have to keep a sharp look-out and let 'em know where we are, to avoid any chance of collision."

"Aye, aye, sir," I cried, making my way along the gangway by the side of the deckhouse towards the fo'c's'le, which was still lit up by the afterglow as if on fire. "I'll see to it all right, and get our steam lights rigged up at once, sir."

So saying, in another minute or so, scrambling over a lot of empty coal sacks and other loose gear that littered the deck, besides getting tripped up by the tackle of the ash hoist, which I did not see in time from the glare of the sky coming right in my eyes, I gained the lee side of the cook's galley at the forward end of the deckhouse. Here, as I conjectured, I found old Greazer, our lamp-trimmer. This worthy, who was quite a character in his way, was a superannuated fireman belonging to the line, whom age and long years of toil had unfitted for the rougher and more arduous duties of his vocation in the stoke-hold, and who now, instead of trimming coals in the furnaces below, trimmed wicks and attended to the lamps about the ship, on deck and elsewhere. He managed, I may add, to make his face so dirty in the carrying out of the lighter duties to which he was now called, probably in fond recollection of his byegone grimy task in the engine-room, that his somewhat personal cognomen was very appropriate, his countenance being oily and smutty to a degree!

He was a very lazy old chap, however; and, in lieu of attending to his work, was generally to be found confabulating with our mulatto cook, Accra Prout, as I discovered him now, more bent on worming out an extra lot of grog from the chef of the galley in exchange for a lump of "hard" tobacco, than thinking of masthead lanterns or the ship's side lights, green and red.

"What are you about, lamp-trimmer?" I called out sharply on catching sight of him palavering there with the mulatto, the artful beggar furtively slipping the tin pannikin out of which he had been drinking into the bosom of his jumper. "Here's two bells struck and no lights up!"

"Two bells, sir?"

"Aye, two bells," I repeated, taking no notice of his affected air of surprise. "There's the ship's bell right over your head where you stand, and you must have heard it strike not five minutes ago."

"Lor', Master Dick, may I die a foul death ashore if I ever heard a stroke," he replied as innocently as you please. "Howsomdever, the lamps is all right, sir. I ain't 'ave forgot 'em."

"That's all right, then, Greazer," I said, not being too hard on him, and excusing the sly wink he gave to Prout as he told his barefaced banger about not hearing the bell, in memory of his past services. "Come along now and rig them up smart, or you'll have Mr Fosset after you."

Making him hoist our masthead light on the foremast, twenty feet above the deck, according to the usual Board of Trade regulations for steamers under way at sea, I then marched him before me along the deck and saw him place our side lights in their proper position, the green one to starboard and the red on our port hand.

Old Greazer then mounted the bridge-ladder, in advance of me, with the binnacle lamp in his hand to put that in its place, and, as I followed slowly in his slow footsteps, for the ex-fireman was not now quick of movement, an accident in the stoke-hold having crippled him years ago, I half-turned round as I ascended the laddering to have a look again at the horizon to leeward over our port quarters, when I fancied, when advancing a foot with the lamp-trimmer, I had seen something to the southward.

In another instant my fancy became a certainty.

Yes, there, in the distance, sailing at an angle to our course, right before the wind, was a large full-rigged ship. Everything, though, was not right with her, as I noted the moment I made her out, with her white canvas all crimson from a last expiring gleam of the afterglow; for I could see that her sails were tattered and torn, with the ragged ends blowing out loose from the boltropes in the most untidy fashion, unkempt, uncared for!

Besides, she was flying a signal of distress, patent to every sailor that has ever crossed the seas.

Her flag was hoisted half-mast high from the peak halliards. Half-mast high!

I did not wait, nor did I want, to see anything further. No, that was enough for me; and, springing on to the bridge with a bound that nearly knocked poor old Greazer down on his marrowbones as he stopped to put the lantern into the binnacle, I shouted out in a ringing voice that echoed fore and aft, startling everybody aboard, even myself, "Sail ho! A ship in distress! Sail ho!"

Did I Dream It?

"Where away, Haldane?" cried Mr Fosset, the first to notice my shout, catching up a telescope that lay handy on the top of the wheel-house of the bridge; and, in his hurry, eagerly scanning every portion of the horizon but the right one. "I don't see her!"

"There she is, sir, away to the right!" said I, equally flurried, pointing over the lee rail in the direction where I had observed the ship only a second before as I mounted the bridge-ladder, although I could not actually make her out distinctly at the moment now, on account of the smoke from our funnels, which, just then, came belching forth in a thick, black cloud that streamed away to leeward, athwart our starboard beam, obscuring the outlook.

"There away, sir; out there!"

"Well, I can't see anything!" ejaculated Mr Fosset impatiently, rising to his feet after stooping down to the level of the bridge cloth, trying to get a sight of the strange vessel as best he could under the cloud of smoke, which was now trailing out along the horizon, blown far away to leeward by the strong wind across our beam. "I'm sure I can't see anything over there, youngster; you must have dreamt it!"

"Yes, when you were lolling about in the waist below there, just now," put in my friend, Master Spokeshave, who had been pretending to look-out from his end of the bridge because he thought he ought to do so as Mr Fosset was there, although he really couldn't possibly see anything aft from that position on the port side, on account of the wheel-house and funnel, which were of course abaft the bridge, blocking the view. The cantankerous little beggar sniffed his beak of a nose in the air as if trying to look down on me, though he was half a head shorter, and spoke in that nasty sneering way of his that always made me mad. He did enjoy growling at any one when he had the chance; and so he went on snarling now, like a cat behind an area railing at a dog which couldn't get at it to stop its venomous spitting. "I saw you, my joker, star-gazing down there, instead of coming up here to relieve me at the proper time! I believe you only sang out about the ship to cover your laziness and take a rise out of us!"

"I did nothing of the sort, Mr Spokeshave," I answered indignantly, for the little beast sniggered away and grinned at Mr Fosset as if he had said something uncommonly smart at my expense. I saw, however, where the shoe pinched. He was angry at my having kept him waiting for his tea, and hence his spiteful allusion to my being late coming on watch; so I was just going to give him a sharp rejoinder, referring to his love for his little stomach, a weak point with him and a common joke with us all below at meal-times, when, ere I could get a word out of the scathing rebuke I intended for him, the smoke trail suddenly lifted a bit to leeward and leaving the horizon clear, I caught sight again of the ship I had seen over the rail. This, of course, at once changed the current of my thoughts; and so, without troubling my head any further about "Conky," I sang out as eagerly as before to the first mate, all the more anxious now to prove that I had been right in the first instance, "There she is, Mr Fosset, there she is!"

"Where on earth are you squinting now, boy?" said he, a bit huffy at not making her out and apparently inclined to Spokeshave's opinion that I had not really seen her at all. "Where away?"

"There, sir, away to leeward," cried I, almost jumping over the bridge rail in my excitement. "She's nearly abreast of our mizzen chains and not a mile off. She seems coming up on the port tack, sir!"

For, strangely enough, although we were going ten knots good by the aid of the wind that had worked round more abeam, so that all our fore and aft sail drew, while the ship, which, when I saw her before, seemed to be running with the nor'-easter and sailing at a tangent to our course so that she ought really to have increased her distance from us, now, on the contrary, appeared ever so much nearer, as if she had either altered her helm or drifted closer by the aid of some ocean current in the interim; albeit, barely five minutes at the best, if that, had only elapsed since I first sighted her.

But, stranger still, Mr Fosset could not see her, when there she was as plain as the sun setting in the west awhile ago—at least to my eyes; and, as she approached nearer yet in some unaccountable way, for her bows were pointed from us and the wind, of course, was blowing in the opposite direction, she being on our lee, I declare I could distinctly see a female figure, like that of a young girl with long hair, on the deck aft; and beside her I also noticed a large black dog, jumping up and down!

"I'm sure I can't see any ship, youngster," said Mr Fosset at the moment. Even while he was actually speaking, I observed the sailing vessel to yaw in her course, her ragged canvas flattening against the masts as if she were coming about, although from the way her head veered about, she did not seem to be under any control. "There's nothing in sight, Haldane, I tell you. What you perhaps thought was a ship is that big black cloud rising to the southward. It looks like one of those nasty sea fogs working up, and we'll have to keep a precious sharp look-out to-night, I know."

"There's no ship there," echoed my friend "Conky," tapping his forehead in a very offensive way to intimate that I had "a screw loose in the upper storey," as the saying goes, grinning the while as I could see very well in the dim light and poking his long nose up in the air in supreme contempt. "The boy is either mad, or drunk, or dreaming, as you say, sir. It is all a cock and a bull yarn about his sighting a vessel, and he only wants to brave it out. There's no ship there!"

"Can you see anything, Atkins?" asked Mr Fosset of the man steering. "There away to leeward, I mean."

"No, sir," answered the sailor; "not a speck, sir."

"Do you see anything, lamp-trimmer?"

"No; can't say I does, sir," replied old Greazer, after a long squint over our lee in the direction pointed out, "Not a sight of a sail, nor a light, nor nothink!"

It was curious.

For, at that very moment, when the first mate and Spokeshave and the helmsman and lamp-trimmer, standing on the bridge beside me, one and all said they could see nothing, I declare to you I saw not only the ship and the figures on her deck, but I noticed that the girl on the poop waved a scarf or handkerchief, as if imploring our assistance; and, at the same time, the dog near her bounded up against the bulwarks, and I can solemnly assert from the evidence of my ears that I heard the animal distinctly bark, giving out that joyous sort of bark with which a well-dispositioned dog invariably greets a friend of his master or mistress.

I could not make it out at all.

It was most mysterious.

"Look, look, Mr Fosset!" I cried excitedly. "There she is now! There she is, coming up on our lee quarter! Why, you must be all blind! I can not only see the ship distinctly, but also right down on to her deck!"

"Nonsense, boy; you'd better go below!" said the first mate brusquely, while Spokeshave sniggered and whispered something to the lamp-trimmer and man at the wheel that made them both laugh out right. "There's something wrong with you to-night, Haldane, for you seem quite off your chump, so you'd better go below and sleep it off. There's no ship near us, I tell you! What you imagined to be a sailing vessel is that dark cloud there, coming up from the leeward, which is fast shutting out the horizon from view. It's a sea fog, such as are frequently met with hereabouts below the Banks, as we are now!"

It was true enough about the cloud, or mist, or fog, or whatever it was; for, as Mr Fosset spoke, the darkness closed in around us like a wall and the ship that I swear I had seen the moment before vanished, sky and sea and everything else disappearing also at the same instant, leaving us, as it were, isolated in space, the veil of vapour being impenetrable!

A Conflict of Authority

Just then Captain Applegarth appeared on the scene.

He had gone down by the companion-way into the saloon below, after Mr Fosset had left the poop, to look at the barometer in his cabin, and now came along the upper deck and on to the bridge amidships, startling us with his sudden presence.

The skipper had a sharp eye, which was so trained by observation in all sorts of weather that he could see in the dark, like a cat, almost as well as he could by daylight.

Looking round and scanning our faces as well as he could in the prevailing gloom, he soon perceived that something was wrong.

"Huh!" he exclaimed. "What's the row about?"

"There's no row, sir," explained the first mate in an off-hand tone of bravado, which he tried to give a jocular ring to, but could not very successfully. "This youngster Haldane here swears he saw a full-rigged ship on our lee quarter awhile ago, flying a signal of distress; but neither Mr Spokeshave, who was on the watch, nor myself, could make her out where Haldane said he saw her."

"Indeed?"

"No, sir," continued Mr Fosset; "nor could the helmsman or old Greazer here, who came up with the binnacle lamp at the time. Not one of us could see this wonderful ship of Haldane's, though it was pretty clear all round then, and we all looked in the direction to which he pointed."

"That's strange," said Captain Applegarth, "very strange."

"Quite so, sir, just what we all think, sir," chimed in Master Spokeshave, putting in his oar. "Not a soul here on the bridge, sir, observed anything of any ship of any sort, leastways one flying a signal of distress, such as Dick Haldane said he saw."

"Humph!" ejaculated the skipper, as if turning the matter over in his mind for the moment; and then addressing me point blank he asked me outright, "Do you really believe you saw this ship, Haldane?"

"Yes, sir," I answered as directly as he had questioned me; "I'll swear I did."

"No, I don't want you to do that; I'll take your word for it without any swearing, Haldane," said the skipper to this, speaking to me quietly and as kindly as if he had been my father. "But listen to me, my boy. I do not doubt your good faith for a moment, mind that. Still, are you sure that what you believe you saw might not have been some optical illusion proceeding from the effects of the afterglow at sunset? It was very bright and vivid, you know, and the reflection of a passing cloud above the horizon or its shadow just before the sun dipped might have caused that very appearance which you took to be a ship under sail. I have myself been often mistaken in the same way under similar atmospheric surroundings and that is why I put it to you like this, to learn whether you are quite certain you might not be mistaken?"

"Quite so," shoved in Spokeshave again in his parrot fashion; "quite so, sir."

"I didn't ask your opinion," growled the skipper, shutting him up in a twinkling; and then, turning to me again, he looked at me inquiringly. "Well, Haldane, have you thought it out?"

"Yes, captain, I have," I replied firmly, though respectfully, the ill-timed interference of the objectionable Mr Spokeshave having made me as obstinate as Mr Fosset. "It was no optical illusion or imagination on my part, sir, or anything of that sort, I assure you, sir. I am telling you the truth, sir, and no lie. I saw that ship, sir, to leeward of us just now as clearly as I can see you at this moment; aye, clearer, sir!"

"Then that settles the matter. I've never had occasion to doubt your word before during the years you've sailed with me, my boy, and I am not going to doubt it now."

So saying, Captain Applegarth, putting his arm on my shoulder, faced round towards the first mate and Spokeshave, as if challenging them both to question my veracity after this testimony on his part in my favour.

"This ship, you say, Haldane," then continued the skipper, proceeding to interrogate me as to the facts of the case, now that my credulity had been established, in his sharp, sailor-like way, "was flying a signal of distress, eh?"

"Yes, sir," I answered with zest, all animation and excitement again at his encouragement. "She had her flag, the French tricolour, I think, sir, hoisted half-mast at her peak; and she appeared, sir, a good deal battered about, as if she had been in bad weather and had made the worst of it. Besides, cappen—"

I hesitated.

"Besides what, my boy?" he asked, on my pausing here, almost afraid to mention the sight I had noticed on the deck of the ill-fated ship in the presence of two such sceptical listeners as Mr Fosset and my more immediate superior, the third officer, Spokeshave. "You need not be afraid of saying anything you like before me. I'm captain of this ship."

"Well, sir," said I, speaking out, "just before that mass of clouds or fog bank came down on the wind, shutting out the ship from view, she yawed a bit off her course, and I saw somebody on her deck aft."

"What!" cried the skipper, interrupting me. "Was she so close as that?"

"Yes, sir," said I. "She did not seem to be a hundred yards away at the moment, if that."

"And you saw somebody on the deck?"

"Yes, cap'en," I answered; "a woman."

He again interrupted me, all agog at the news.

"A woman?"

"Yes, sir," said I. "A woman, or rather, perhaps a girl, for she had a lot of long hair streaming over her shoulders, all flying about in the wind."

"What was she doing?"

"She appeared to be waving a white handkerchief or something like that, as if to attract our attention—asking us to help her, like."

The skipper drew himself up to his full height on my telling this and turned round on Mr Fosset, his face blazing with passion.

"A ship in distress, a woman on board imploring our aid," he exclaimed in keen, cold, cutting tones that pierced one like a knife, "and you passed her by without rendering any assistance,—a foreigner too, of all. We Englishmen, who pride ourselves on our humanity above all other nations. What will they think of us?"

"I tell you, sir, we could not see any ship at all!" retorted the first mate hotly, in reply to this reproach, which he felt as keenly as it was uttered. "And if we couldn't see the ship, how could we know there was a woman or anybody aboard?"

"Quite so," echoed Spokeshave, emphasising Mr Fosset's logical argument in his own defence. "That's exactly what I say, sir."

"I would not have had it happen for worlds. We flying the old Union jack, too, that boasts of never passing either friend or foe when in danger and asking aid."

He spoke still more bitterly, as if he had not heard their excuses.

"But hang it, cap'en," cried Mr Fosset, "I tell you—"

Captain Applegarth waved him aside.

"Where did you last sight the ship, Haldane?" he said, turning round abruptly to me. "How was she heading?"

"She bore about two points off our port quarter," I replied as laconically. "I think, sir, she was running before the wind like ourselves, though steering a little more to the southwards."

The skipper looked at the standard compass in front of the wheel-house on the bridge, and then addressed the helmsman.

"How are we steering now, quartermaster? The same course as I set at noon, eh?"

"Aye, aye, sir," replied Atkins, who still stood by the steam steering gear singlehanded. If it had been the ordinary wheel, unaided by steam-power, it would have required four men to move the rudder and keep the vessel steady in such a sea as was now running. "We've kept her pretty straight, sir, since eight bells on the same course, west by south, sir, half south."

"Very good, quartermaster. Haldane, are you there?"

"Yes, sir," said I, stepping up to him again, having moved away into the shadow under the lee of the wheel-house whilst he was speaking to Atkins. "Here I am, sir."

"Was that vessel dropping us when we passed her, or were we going ahead of her?"

"She was running before the wind, sir, at a tangent to our course, and more to the southwards, moving through the water quicker than we were, until she luffed up just before that mist or fog bank shut her out from view. But—"

"Well?"

"I think, sir," I continued, "that was done merely to speak us; and if she bore away again, as she was probably forced to do, being at the mercy of the gale, she must be scudding even more to the southwards, almost due south, I should fancy, as the wind has backed again more to the nor'ard since this."

"I fancy the same, my boy. I see you have a sailor's eye and have got your wits about you. Quartermaster?"

"Aye, aye, sir?"

"Let her off a point or two gradually until you bring her head about sou'-sou'-west, and keep her so."

"Aye, aye, sir," responded Atkins, easing her off as required. "Sou'-sou'-west it shall be, sir, in a minute."

"That will bring us across her, I think," said the skipper to me. "But we must go a little faster if we want to overtake her. What are we doing now, eh?"

"I don't quite know, sir," I answered to this question. "I was only just coming up on the bridge to relieve Mr Spokeshave when I sighted the ship and have not had time to look at the indicator. I should think, though, we're going eight or nine knots."

This didn't satisfy the skipper, so he turned to the first mate, who had remained moodily aloof with Spokeshave at the end of the bridge.

"Mr Fosset," he sang out abruptly, "what are the engines doing?"

"About thirty revolutions, sir; half speed, as nearly as possible."

"How much are we going altogether?"

"Ten knots, with our sails," replied the other. "The wind is freshening, too."

"So I see," said Captain Applegarth laconically.

"And it'll freshen still more by-and-bye if I'm not mistaken!"

"Yes, it looks as if we're going to have a bit of a blow. The scud is flying all over us now that we are running before the wind. I really think we ought to ease down, sir, for the screw races fearfully as she dips and I'm afraid of the shaft."

"I'm responsible for that, Mr Fosset," answered the skipper as, moving the handle of the gong on the bridge communicating with the engine-room, he directed those in charge below to put on full speed ahead. "I never yet abandoned a ship in distress, and I'm not going to do so now. We're on the right course to overhaul her, now, I think, eh, Haldane?"

"Yes, sir," I replied. "I hope, though, we won't pass her in the fog, sir, or run into her, perhaps."

"No fear of that, my boy: The fog is lifting now and the night will soon be as clear as a bell, for the wind is driving all the mists away. Besides, we'll take precautions against any accident happening. Mr Fosset?"

"Aye, aye, sir?"

"Put a couple of lookouts on the fo'c's'le."

"Aye, aye, sir."

"Perhaps, too, we'd better send up a rocket to let 'em know we're about. Mr Spokeshave? Mr Spokeshave?"

No answer came this time, however, from my friend, Master "Conky," though he had been ready enough just now with his aggravating "quite so."

"I think, sir," said I, "Mr Spokeshave has gone below to his tea."

"Very likely," replied the skipper drily; "he's precious fond of his breadbasket, that young gentleman. I don't think he'll ever starve where there's any grub knocking about. Fancy a fellow, calling himself a man, thinking of his belly at such a moment! Go, Haldane, and call him up again and tell him I want him."

I started to obey Captain Applegarth's order, but I had hardly got three steps down the ladder when Spokeshave saved me further trouble by coming up on the bridge again of his own accord, without waiting to be summoned.

The skipper, therefore, gave him instructions to let off, every quarter of an hour, a couple of signal rockets and burn a blue light or two over our port and starboard quarter alternately as we proceeded towards the object of our quest.

"All right, sir; quite so!" said "Conky," as well as he could articulate, his mouth being full of something he had hurriedly snatched from the steward's pantry when he had gone below, and brought up with him to eat on deck, knowing that the skipper would be sure to sing out for him if he remained long away at so critical a juncture. "All right, sir; quite so!"

The skipper laughed as he went down again to get the rockets and blue lights which were kept in a spare cabin aft for safety.

"He's a rum chap, that little beggar," he observed to Mr Fosset, who had been forward to set the look-out men on the forecastle and had returned to the bridge. "I think if you told him he was the laziest loafer that ever ate lobscouse, he couldn't help saying 'Quite so!'"

"You're about right, sir. I think, though, he can't help it; he's got so used to the phrase," replied the other, joining in the skipper's laugh. "But, hullo, here comes old Stokes, panting and puffing along the gangway. I hope nothing's wrong in the engine-room."

"I hope not," said the skipper. "We want to go all we can just now, to overhaul that ship Haldane saw."

"If he saw it," muttered the first officer, under his breath and glowering at me. "A pack of sheer nonsense, I call it, this going out of our course on a wild-goose chase and tearing away full speed on a wild night like this, in a howling sea, with a gale, too, astern; and all because an ass of a youngster fancies he saw the Flying Dutchman!"

I daresay the captain heard him, but the appearance just then of Mr Stokes, our chief engineer, who had now reached the bridge, panting and puffing at every step, as Mr Fosset had said, he being corpulent of habit and short-winded, stopped any further controversy on the point as to whether I had seen, or had not seen, the mysterious ship.

"Cap'en, Cap'en Applegarth!" cried out the chief engineer asthmatically as soon as he got within hail, speaking in a tearful voice and almost crying in his excitement. "Are you there, sir?"

"Aye, here I am, Mr Stokes, as large as life, though not quite so big a man as you," answered the skipper jocularly.

"I am here on the bridge, quite at your service."

Mr Stokes, however, was in no jocular mood.

"Cap'en Applegarth," said he solemnly, "did you really mean to ring us on full speed ahead?"

"I did," replied the skipper promptly. "What of that?"

"What of that?" repeated the old engineer, dumbfounded by this return shot. "Why, sir, the engines can't stand it. That is all, if you must have it!"

"Can't stand what?"

"They can't stand all this driving and racing, with the propeller blades half out of water every second revolution of the shaft. No engines could stand it, with such a heavy sea on and the ship rolling and pitching all the time like a merry-go-round at Barnet Fair. The governor is no good; and, though Grummet or Links have their grip on the throttle valve all the while to check the steam, and I've every stoker and oiler on duty, the bearings are getting that heated that I'm afraid of the shaft breaking at any moment. Full speed, sir? Why, we can't do it, sir, we can't do it!"

"Nonsense, Stokes," said the skipper good-humouredly. "You must do it, old fellow."

"But, I tell you, Cap'en Applegarth, the engines can't stand it without breaking down, and then where will you be, I'd like to know?"

"I'll risk that."

"No, cap'en," snorted the old chief, doggedly. "I'm responsible to the owners for the engines, and if anything happened to the machinery they'd blame me. I can't do it."

The skipper flew up to white heat at this.

"But, Mr Stokes, recollect I am responsible for the ship, engines and all, sir. The greater includes the less, and, as captain of this ship, I intend to have my orders carried out by every man-jack on board. Do you hear that?"

"Yes, sir, I hear," replied Mr Stokes grumblingly as he backed towards the bridge-ladder. "But, sir—"

The skipper would not give him time to get out another word.

"You heard what I said," he roared out in a voice that made the old chief jump down half a dozen steps at once. "I ordered you to go full speed ahead and I mean to go full speed ahead whether the boilers burst, or the propeller races, or the screw shaft carries away; for I won't abandon a ship in distress for all the engineers and half-hearted mollicoddles in the world!"

"A ship in distress?" gasped old Mr Stokes from the bottom rung of the ladder. "I didn't hear about that before."

"Well, you hear it now," snapped out the skipper viciously, storming up and down the bridge in a state of great wrath. "But whether it's a ship in distress or not, I'll have you to know, Mr Stokes, once for all that if I order full speed or half speed or any speed, I intend my orders to be obeyed; and if you don't like it you can lump it. I'm captain of this ship!"

The Gale Freshens

Presently a cloud of thick black smoke again pouring forth from the funnels showed that Mr Stokes had set the engine-room staff vigorously to work to carry out the skipper's orders; while the vibration of the upper deck below our feet afforded proof, were such needed, that the machinery was being driven to its utmost capacity, the regular throbbing motion caused by the revolving shaft being distinctly perceptible above the rolling of the vessel and the jar of the opposing waves against her bow plates when she pitched more deeply than usual and met the sea full butt-end on.

The surface fog, or mist, which had lately obscured the view, rising from the water immediately after the last gleams of the sunset had disappeared from the western sky, had now cleared away, giving place to the pale spectral light of night, an occasional star twinkling here and there in the dark vault overhead, like a sign-post in the immensity of space, making the wild billowy waste, through which we tore with all the power of wind and steam, seem all the wilder from contrast.

We had carried on like this for about an hour, steering steadily to the southwards, without catching sight again of the strange ship, though Spokeshave and I had continued to let off signal rockets and burn blue lights at intervals, the gale increasing in force each instant, and the waves growing bigger and bigger, so that they rose over the topsail as we raced along, when, all at once, a great green sea broke amidships, coming aboard of us just abaft of the engine-room hatchway, flooding all the waist on either side of the deckhouse and rolling down below in a regular cataract of tumid water, sweeping everything before it.

"That's pretty lively," exclaimed Captain Applegarth, clutching hold of the rail to preserve his balance as he turned to the quartermaster at the wheel. "Steady there, my man! Keep her full and by!"

"Aye, aye, sir," answered Atkins. "But she do yaw so, when she buries her bows. She's got too much sail on her, sir."

"I know that," said the skipper. "But I'm going to carry on as long as I can, all the same, my man."

Even as he spoke, however, a second sea followed the first, nearly washing us all off the bridge, and smashing the glass of the skylight over the engine-room, besides doing other damage.

By Captain Applegarth's directions, a piece of heavy tarpaulin was lashed over the broken skylight, securing the ends to ringbolts in the deck; but hardly had the covering been made fast ere we could see the chief engineer picking his way towards us, struggling through the water that still lay a foot deep in the waist and looking as pale as death.

"Hullo, Mr Stokes," cried the skipper, when the old chief with great difficulty had gained the vantage of the bridge-ladder. "What's the matter now, old fellow?"

He was too much exhausted at first to reply.

"What's the matter?" he echoed ironically when able at last to speak. "Oh, nothing at all worth mentioning; nothing at all. I told you how it would be, sir, if you insisted on going ahead full speed in such weather as we're having! Why, Cap'en Applegarth, the stoke-hold's full of water and the bilgepump's choked, that's all; and the fires, I expect, will be drowned out in another minute or two. That's what's the matter, sir, believe me or not!"

With that the poor old chap, who was quite overcome with the exertions he had gone through and his pent-up emotion, broke down utterly, bursting into a regular boohoo.

"Dear me, Mr Stokes; Mr Stokes, don't give way like that," said the skipper soothingly, patting him on the back to calm him down, being a very good-hearted man at bottom, in spite of his strict discipline and insistence on being "captain of his own ship," as he termed it. "Don't give way like that, old friend! Things will come all right by-and-bye."

"O-o-h, will they?" snivelled the old chap, refusing to be comforted, like a veritable Rachel mourning for her children. "We may possibly get rid of the water below, but the crosshead bearings are working loose, and I'd like to know who's going to give me a new gudgeon pin?"

"Hang your gudgeon pin!" cried the skipper irascibly, not perhaps for the moment attaching the importance it demanded to this small but essential part of the engines, uniting the connecting rod of the crank shaft with the piston which he thus irreverently anathematised; and then, struck by the comic aspect of the situation, with the waves breaking over us and the elements in mad turmoil around us, while the fat old chief was blubbering there like a boy about his gudgeon pin as if bewailing some toy that had been taken from him, that he burst out with a roar of laughter, which was so contagious that, in spite of the gloomy outlook and our perilous surroundings, Mr Fosset and all of us on the bridge joined in, even the quartermaster not being able to prevent a grin from stealing over his crusty weatherbeaten face, though the man at the wheel on board ship, when on duty, is technically supposed to be incapable of expressing any emotion beyond such as may be connected with the compass card and the coursing of the ship. "Wha—wha—what's the matter with that now, old chap? One would think it was a whale and not a gudgeon, you make such a fuss about it."

Of course the captain's joke set us all off cackling again; Mr Spokeshave's "he-he-he" sounding out, high in the treble, above the general cachination.

This exasperated Mr Stokes, making the old fellow quite furious.

"This is no laughing matter, Cap'en Applegarth," said he with great dignity, standing up as erectly as he could and puffing his corpulent figure out to such an extent that I thought he would burst. "I'll have ye to know that, sir. Nor did I come on deck, sir, at the peril of my life almost, to be made a jeer block of, though I'm only the chief engineer of the ship and you're the ca'p'en."

He spoke with so stately an air that I confess I felt sorry I had given away to any merriment at his expense, while the others grew serious in a moment; and as for Atkins, his whilom grinning face seemed now to be carved out of some species of wood of a particularly hard and fibrous nature.

"Now, don't get angry, Stokes, old fellow," cried the skipper shoving out his fist and gripping that of the chief in the very nick of time, for the vessel gave a lurch just then and, still "standing on his dignity," as the poor old chap was, without holding on to anything, he would have been precipitated over the rail to the deck below, but for the skipper's friendly aid. "Don't be angry with me, old chum. I'm sorry I laughed; but you and I have been shipmates too long together for us to fall out now. Why, what the devil has got over you, Stokes? You've never been so huffy since I first sailed with you, and I should have thought you one of the last in the world to take offence at a little bit of harmless chaff."

"Well, well, Cap'en Applegarth, let it bide, let it bide," replied the old chief, coming round at once, his rage calming down as quickly as it had risen. "I don't mind your laughing at me if you have a mind too. I daresay it all seemed very funny to you, my being anxious about my engines, but I'm hanged if I can see the fun myself."

"But it was funny, Stokes; deuced funny, I tell you, 'ho-ho-ho!'" rejoined the skipper, bursting out into a regular roar again at the recollection of the scene, his jolly laugh causing even the cause of it to smile against his will.

"However, there's an end of it, gudgeon pin and all. Now, about that stoke-hold of yours. It's flooded, you say?"

"Aye; there's eighteen inches of water there now, right up to the footplates," said the engineer with a grave air. "The bilge-pumps won't act, and all my staff of stokers are so busy keeping up the steam that I can't spare a man to see to clearing out the suctions, though if the water rises any higher, it will soon be up to the furnace bars and put out the fires."

"Humph, that's serious," answered the skipper meditatively. "I'll see what I can do to help you. I say, Fosset?"

"Aye, aye, sir! Want me?"

"Yes," replied the skipper. "Mr Stokes is shorthanded below and says the bilge-pumps are choked. Can you spare him a man or two to help clear the suctions? I daresay there's a lot of stray dunnage washing about under the stoke-hold plates. You might go down and bear a hand yourself, as I won't leave the bridge."

"Certainly, sir; I'll go at once with Mr Stokes and take some of the starboard watch with me. It's close on seven bells and they'd soon have to turn out, anyway, to relieve the men now on deck."

"That'll do very well, Fosset," said the skipper, and, raising his voice, he shouted over the rail forwards—

"Bosun, call the watch!"

Bill Masters, who had been waiting handy on the deck amidships, immediately below the bridge, expecting some such order with the need, as he thought, of the skipper reducing sail, at once stuck his shrill boatswain's pipe to his lips and gave the customary call: Whee-ee-oo-oo—whee-ee-ee.

"Starboard watch, ahoy!"

The men came tumbling out of the fo'c's'le at the sound of the whistle and the old seadog's stentorian hail; whereupon the first mate, selecting six of the lot to accompany him, he followed Mr Stokes towards the engine-room hatchway.

Before disappearing below, however, the engineer made a last appeal to the skipper.

"I say, cap'en," he sang out, stopping half-way as he toddled aft, somewhat disconsolately in spite of the assistance given him, "now won't you ease down, sir, just to oblige me? The engines won't stand it, sir; and it's my duty to tell you so, sir."

"All right, Stokes; you've told me, and may consider that you've done your duty in doing so," replied the skipper, grimly laconic. "But I'm not going to ease down till seven bells, my hearty, unless we run across Dick Haldane's ship before, when we'll go as slow as you like and bear up again on our course to the westwards."

"Very good, sir," answered the old chief as he lifted his podgy legs over the coaming of the hatchway, prior to burying himself in the cimmerian darkness of the opening, wherein Mr Fosset and his men had already vanished.

"I'll make things all snug below, sir, and bank the fires as soon as you give the signal."

With that, he, too, was lost to sight.

The skipper, I could see, was not very easy in his mind when left alone; for he paced jerkily to and fro between the wheel-house and the weather end of the bridge as well as he was able, the vessel being very unsteady, rolling about among the big rollers like a huge grampus and pitching almost bows under water sometimes, though the old barquey was buoyant enough, notwithstanding the lot of deadweight she carried in her bowels, rising up after each plunge as frisky as a cork, when she would shake herself with a movement that made her tremble all over, as if to get rid of the loose spray and spindrift that hung on to her shining black head, and which the wind swept before it like flecks of snow into the rigging, spattering and spattering against the almost red-hot funnels up which the steam blast was rushing mingled with the flare of the funnels below.

After continuing his restless walk for a minute or two, the skipper stopped by the binnacle, looking at the compass card, which moved about as restlessly as the old barquey and himself, oscillating in every direction.

"We ought to have come up with her by now, Haldane," he said, addressing me, as I stood with Spokeshave on the other side of the wheel-house. "Don't you think so from the course she was going when you sighted her?"

"Yes, sir," I answered, "if she hasn't gone down!"

"I hope not, my boy," said he; "but I'm very much afraid she has, or else we've passed ahead of her."

"That's not likely, sir," I replied. "She looked as if crossing our track when I last saw her; and, though we were going slower then, we must be gaining on her now, I should think."

"We ought to be," said he. "We must be going seventeen knots at the least with wind and steam."

"Aye, aye, sir, all that," corroborated old Masters, the boatswain, who had come up on the bridge unnoticed. "Beg pardon, sir, but we can't carry on much longer with all that sail forrad. The fore-topmast is a-complainin' like anythink, I can tell ye, sir. Chirvell, the carpenter, and me's examinin' it and we thinks it's got sprung at the cap, sir."

"If that's the case, my man," said Captain Applegarth to this, "we'd better take in sail at once. It's a pity, too, with such a fine wind. I was just going to spare the engines and ease down for a bit, trusting to our sails alone, but if there's any risk of the spars going, as you say, wrong, we must reduce our canvas instead."

"There's no help for it, sir," returned the boatswain quickly. "Either one or t'other must go! Shall I pass the word, sir, to take in sail?"

"Aye, take in the rags!"

"Fo'c's'le, ahoy there!" yelled Masters instantly, taking advantage of the long-desired permission. "All hands take in sail!"

We had hauled the trysails and other fore and aft canvas, which was comparatively useless to a steamer when running before the wind at the time we had altered course towards the south, in quest of the ship in distress, the Star of the North speeding along with only her fore-topsail and fore-topgallantsail set in addition to her fore-topmast staysail and mizzen staysail and jib.

The gale, however, had increased so much, the wind freshening as it shifted more and more to the north that this sail was too much for her, the canvas bellying out, and the upper spars "buckling" as the vessel laboured in the heavy sea, the stays taut as fiddle-strings and everything at the utmost tension.

The skipper perceived this now, when almost too late.

"Let go your topgallant bowline, and lee sheet and halliards," he roared out, holding on with both hands to the rail and bending over the bridge cloth as he shouted to the men forward who had tumbled out of the forecastle on the boatswain's warning hail. "Stand by your clewlines and by your boat lines!"

The men sprang to the ropes with a will, but ere they had begun to cast them off from the cleats an ominous sound was heard from aloft, and, splitting from clew to earring, our poor topgallantsail blew clean out of the boltropes with a loud crack as if a gun had been fired off, the fragments floating away ahead of us, borne on the wings of the wind like a huge kite, until it disappeared in the dark chiaraoscura of the distant horizon, where heaven and sea met amid the shadows of night.

Just then a most wonderful thing happened to startle us further!

While all of us gazed at the wreck aloft, expecting the topsail to follow suit before it could be pulled, though the hands were racing up rigging for the purpose, the halliards having been at once let go and the yard lowered, a strange light over the topsail made us look aft, when we saw a huge ball of fire pass slowly across the zenith from the east to the west, illuminating not only the northern arc of the sky, but the surface of the water also, immediately beneath its path, and making the faces of the men in the rigging and indeed any object on board, stand out in relief, shining with that corpse-like glare or reflection produced by the electric light, the effect being weird and unearthly in the extreme!

At the same instant one of the lookouts in the bows who had still remained at his post and had probably been awakened from a quiet "caulk" by the awful portent, suddenly shouted out in a ringing voice, that thrilled through every heart on board—

"Sail Ho!"

Captain Applegarth and the rest of us on the bridge faced round again at once.

"Where away, where away, my man?" cried the skipper excitedly. "Where away?"

"Right ahead of us, sir," replied the man in an equally eager tone. "And not half a cable's length away!"

"My God!" exclaimed old Masters, the boatswain, whose grey hair seemed to stand on end with terror as we all now looked in the new direction indicated and saw a queer ghost-like craft gliding along mysteriously in the same direction as ourselves, and so close alongside that I could have chucked a biscuit aboard her without any difficulty. "That there be no mortal vessel that ever sailed the seas. Mark my words, Cap'en Applegarth, that there craft be either The Flying Dutchman, as I've often heard tell on, but never seen meself, or a ghost-ship; and—Lord help us—we be all doomed men!"

A Chapter of Accidents

"Nonsense, man!" cried Captain Applegarth. "Don't make such an ass of yourself! Flying Dutchman indeed! Why, that cock and bull yarn was exploded years ago, and I didn't think there was a sailor afloat in the present day ass enough to believe in this story!"

"I may be a hass, sir; I know I am sometimes," retorted old Masters, evidently aggrieved by the skipper speaking to him like this before the men. "But, sir, seein' is believin'. There's this ship an' there's that there craft a-sailin' alongside in the teeth o' the gale. Hass or no hass, I sees that, captain!"

"Hang it all, man, can't you see that it is only the mirage or reflection of our own vessel, produced by the light of the meteor throwing her shadow on to the mass of cloud leeward? Look, there are our two old sticks and the funnels between, with the smoke rushing out of them! Aye, and there, too, you can see this very bridge here we're standing on, and all of us, as large as life. Why, bo'sun, you can see your own ugly mug reflected now opposite us, just as it would be in a looking glass. Look, man!"

"Aye, I sees, sir, plain enuff, though I'm a hass," said Masters at length. "But it ain't nat'rel, sir, anyhow; an' I misdoubts sich skeary things. I ain't been to sea forty years for nothin', Captain Applegarth, an' I fears sich a sight as that betokens some danger ahead as 'ill happen to us some time or other this voyage. Even started on a Friday, sir, as you knows on, sir!"

"Rubbish!" cried the skipper, angry at his obstinacy. "See, the mirage has disappeared now that the meteor light has become dispersed. Look smart there, aloft, and furl that topsail! It's just seven bells and I'm going to ease down the engines and bear up on our course again. Up with you, men, and lay out on the yard!"

The hands who had stopped half-way up the fore-rigging, spell-bound at the sight of the mirage, now bestirred themselves, shaking off their superstitious fears; old Masters, in the presence of something to be done, also working, and soon the sail was furled, the bunt stowed, and the gaskets passed.

"It's no use our keeping on any longer after that ship of yours, Haldane," observed the skipper, turning to me when the men had all come in from the topsail yard and scrambled down on deck again after making everything snug aloft. "If she were still afloat we must have overhauled her before this.

I really think, youngster, she must have been only a sort of will-o'-the-wisp, like that we saw just now—an optical illusion, as I told you at the time, recollect, caused by some cross light from the afterglow of the sunset thrown upon the white mist which we noticed subsequently rising off the water. Eh, my boy?"

"Ah, no, captain," I replied earnestly. "The ship I saw presented a very different appearance to that reflection of ours! She was full-rigged, I told you, sir, and though her canvas was torn and she looked a bit knocked about in the matter of her tophamper, she was as unlike our old Star of the North as a sailing vessel is unlike a steamer!"

"She might have been a derelict."

"I saw a girl on her deck aft, sir, with a dog beside her, as distinctly as I see you, sir, now!"

"Well, well, be that as it may, my lad, though I'm very sorry for the poor young thing, if she is still in the land of the living, I can't carry on like this for ever! If she were anywhere in sight it would be quite another matter; but, as it is, not knowing whether we're on her right track or not, we might scud on to the Equator without running across her again. No, no; it wouldn't be fair to the owners or to ourselves, indeed, to risk the ship as well as the lives of all on board by continuing any longer on such a wild-goose chase."

"Very good, sir," said I, on his pausing here, as if waiting for me to say something. "We've tried our best to come up with her, at any rate."

"We have that, and I daresay a good many would call us foolhardy for carrying on as we've done so long. However, I'm going to abandon the chase now and bear up again on our proper course, my boy, and the devil of a job that will be, I know, in the teeth of this gale!"

So saying, the skipper, grasping the handle of the engine-room telegraph, which led up through a tube at the end of the bridge, signalled to those in charge below to slow down to half speed.

"Down with the helm, quartermaster!" he cried to the man at the wheel, and, at the same moment holding up his hand to attract the attention of old Masters, who had returned to his station on the fo'c's'le, greatly exercised in his mind by what had recently occurred, he sang out in a voice of thunder that reached the knightheads and made the boatswain skip: "Haul in your jib sheet and flatten those staysails sharp! I want to bring her round to the wind handsomely, to prevent taking in another of those green seas aboard when we get broadside-on. Look smart, bo'sun, and keep your eye on her. Keep your eye on her, d'you hear? It's ticklish work, you know. Look-out sharp or she'll broach to!"

Far as the eye could reach, the storm-tossed surface of the deep was white with foam, white as a snowfield, and boiling with rage and fury.

The bank of blue-black cloud that had rested along the horizon to leeward had now melted away in some mysterious fashion or other, and the sky became as clear as a bell, only some wind-driven scrap of semi-transparent white vapour sweeping occasionally across the face of the pale, sickly-looking moon that looked down on the weird scene in a sort of menacing way; while, in lieu of the two or three odd sentinels that had previously peeped out from the firmament, all the galaxies of heaven were, at this moment, in their myriads above, spangling the empyrean from zenith to pole.

But the gale!

While running before the wind, the wind, although it had ballooned our sails out to bursting point, brushing us along at a wild, mad-cap rate, and buffeting the boisterous billows on either hand, scooping them up from the depths of the ocean and piling them in immense waves of angry water that rolled after us, striving to overwhelm us, we could hardly, even while taking advantage of it, appreciate its awful and tremendous force.

On coming about, however, and facing it, the case was vastly different, the wind increasing tenfold in its intensity.

Where it had sung through the rigging it now shrieked and howled, as if the air were peopled with demons, while the waves, lashed into fury, dashed against our bows like battering rams, rising almost to the level of our masthead where their towering crests met overhead.

Round came the old barquey's head slowly, and more slowly still as she staggered against the heavy sea, until, all at once, she stopped in stays, unable apparently, though struggling all she could, to face her remorseless foe.

"Luff up, quartermaster!" roared the skipper to the top of his voice and dancing up and down the bridge in his excitement. "Luff, you beggar, luff!"

"I can't, sir," yelled the man in desperation—a fresh hand who had come on duty to relieve Atkins at six bells. "The steam steering gear has broken-down, sir, and I can't make her move."

"By Jingo, that's a bad job," cried the skipper, but he was not long at a nonplus. "Run aft, Haldane, and you too, Spokeshave. Loosen the bunt of the mizzen-trysail and haul at the clew. That'll bring her up to the wind fast enough, if the sail only stands it!"

To hear was to obey, and both Spokeshave and I scuttled down the bridge-ladder as quickly as we could and away along the waist of the ship aft, the urgency of our errand hastening our movements if we had needed any spur beyond the skipper's sharp, imperative mandate.

But, speedily as we had hurried, on mounting the poop-ladder and rushing towards the bitts at the foot of the mizzenmast to cast off the bunt-lines and clewlines of the trysail we found we had been already forestalled by an earlier arrival on the scene of action.

This was Mr O'Neil, the second officer, whom I had left below asleep in his cabin when I came up at two bells from the saloon, he having been on duty all the afternoon and his services not being required again until night, when he would have to go on the bridge to take the first watch from eight to midnight.

Feeling the bucketing-about we were having in the trough of the sea when we came about, and probably awakened by the change of motion, just as a miller is supposed to be instantaneously roused by his mill stopping, though he may be able to sleep through all the noise of its grinding when at work, Garry O'Neil had at once shoved himself into his boots and monkey jacket and rushed up on the poop through the companion and booby-hatch that led up directly on deck from the saloon.

Arrived here, he had evidently noted the vessel's insecurity, and, seamanlike, had hit upon the very same way out of the difficulty that had suggested itself to the skipper, having, ere we reached his side, cast off the ropes confining the folds of the trysail and trying singlehanded to haul out the clew.

"Begorrah, me bhoys, ye've come in the very nick o' time!" he exclaimed on seeing us. "Here, Spoke, me darlint, hang on to the end of this sheet and you, Dick, step on to the tail of it, whilst I take a turn of the slack round that bollard! Faith, it's blo'in' like the dievle, and we'll have our work cut out for us, me bhoys, to git a purchase on it anyhow. Now, all together, yo-heave-ho! Pull baker, pull dievle!"

With that, bending our backs to it, we all hauled away at the sheet, succeeding by a great endeavour in stretching the clew of the sail to the end of the boom, which we then secured amidships as best we could, though the spar and sail combined jerked to such an extent that it seemed as if the mizzenmast would be wrenched out of the ship each instant, the heavy fold of the canvas that hung loosely under the jaws of the gaff shaking and banging about with a noise like thunder.

Even the small amount of canvas exposed to the wind, however, was sufficient to supply the additional leverage required aft; and the engines working at half speed, with the headsails flattened, the ship's bows were presently brought up to the wind, when we lay-to under easy steam.

"Well done, my lads!" sang out the skipper from the bridge, when the ship's head was round and the peril of her broaching-to in the heavy seaway been fortunately averted; the wind was blowing aft, of course, and bringing his voice to us as if he stood by, and shouting in our very ears, "Now look sharp and come here under the bridge; I want you to cast off the lashings of the big wheel amidships and see that the yolk lines run clear. We shall have to manhandle the helm and steer from below, as the steam gear up here in the wheel-house is hopelessly jammed and will take a month of Sundays to get right!"

"Aye, aye, sir," we made answer, under his nose, having been scurrying forwards while he was speaking, the Irish mate adding in his native vernacular, "Begorrah, we'll rig up the whole, sir, in the twinkling of a bedpost, sure!"

"Hullo!" exclaimed the skipper, "is that you, O'Neil?"

"Faith, all that's lift of me, sir!"

"How's that?—I was just going to send down to your cabin to rouse you out."

"Begorrah, its moighty little rousin' I want, sor! The ould barquey's that lively that she'd wake a man who'd been d'id for a wake, sure! I've been so rowled about in me burth and banged agin' the bulkheads that my bones fell loike jelly and I'm blue-mouldy all over. But what d'ye want, cap'en? Sure, I'm helping the youngster with this whale here."

"By jingo!" cried the skipper, "you're the right man in the right place!"

"Faith, that's what the gaolor s'id to the burghlor, sor, when he fixed him up noicely on the treadmill!"

The skipper laughed.

"Well, you fix up your job all right, and you'll be as good as your friend the gaoler," he said. "When we have the helm all alaunto again, we can bear up on our course and jog along comfortably. I think we are lucky to have got off so lightly, considering the wind and sea, with this steering gear breaking down at such an awkward moment!"

"Ah, we ain't seed the worse on it yet, and you'd better not holler till ye're out o' the wood!" muttered old Masters under his breath, in reply to this expression of opinion of the skipper, the boatswain having come to our assistance with all the hands he could muster, so as to get the wheel below the bridge in working order as soon as possible. "I knowed that this ghost-ship meant sumkin' and we ain't come to the end o' the log yet!"

Almost as he uttered the words, Mr Fosset came up the engine-room hatchway and made his way hurriedly towards us.

"By jingo, Fosset, here you are at last!" exclaimed the skipper on seeing him. "I thought you were never coming up again, finding it so jolly warm and comfortable below! Are things all right there now, and are the bilge-pumps working?"

Captain Applegarth spoke jocosely enough, everything being pretty easy on deck and the ship breasting the gale like a duck, but Mr Fosset's face, I noticed, looked grave and he answered the other in a more serious fashion than his general wont, his mouth working nervously in the pale moonlight that lent him a more pallid air as the words dropped from his lips, making his countenance, indeed, almost like that of a corpse.

"But what, man!" exclaimed the skipper impatiently, interrupting his slow speech before Mr Fosset could get any further. "Anything wrong, eh?"

"Yes, sir, I'm sorry to say something is very wrong, I fear—very wrong below," replied the other sadly. "There has been a sad accident in the stoke-hole!"

Old Masters, whose ears had been wide open to the conversation, here nudged me with his elbow as I stood beside him, and at the same time giving forth a grunt of deep and heartfelt significance.

"I knowed summet 'ud happen," he whispered in a sepulchral voice that sounded all the more gruesome from the attendant circumstances, the shrieking wind tearing through the riggings, the melancholy wash of the waves alongside, the moaning and groaning of the poor old barquey's timbers as if she were in grievous pain, while at that very moment the bell under the break of the fo'c's'le struck eight bells slowly, as if tolling for a passing soul. "You seed the ghost-ship, Mr Haldane, the same as me, for I saw it, that I did!"

Disaster on Disaster

"Accident in the stoke-hold!" repeated the skipper, who of course did not overhear the old boatswain's aside to me. "Accident in the stoke-hold!" again repeated the skipper; "anybody hurt?"

"Yes, sir," replied the first mate in the same grave tone of voice. "Mr Stokes and two of the firemen."

"Seriously?"

"Not all, sir," said the other, glancing round as if looking for some one specially. "The chief engineer has one of his arms broken and a few scratches, but the firemen are both injured, and one so badly hurt that I fear he won't get over it, for his ribs have been crushed in and his lower extremities seem paralysed!"

"Good heavens!" exclaimed the skipper. "How did the accident happen?"

"They were searching under the stoke-hold plates to get out some cotton waste that had got entangled about the rosebox of the suctions, which, as we found out, prevented the bilge-pumps from acting, when, all in a moment, just when all the stray dunnage had been cleared out, the ship gave a lurch and the plates buckled up, catching the lot of them, Mr Stokes and all, in a sort of rat trap. Mr Stokes tumbled forwards on his face in the water and was nearly drowned before Stoddart and I could pull him out, the poor old chap was so heavy to lift, and he nearly squashed Blanchard, the stoker, by falling on top of him as we were trying to raise him up, cutting his head open besides, against the fire bars. Poor Jackson, however, the other fireman, was gripped tight between two of the plates and it was all we could do to release him, Stoddart having to use a jack-saw to force the edges of the plates back."

"My God! horrible, horrible!" ejaculated the skipper, terribly upset and concerned. "Poor fellows; Jackson, too, was the best hand Stokes had below!"

"Aye, sir, and as good a mechanic, too, I've heard them say, as any of the engineers," agreed Mr Fosset, with equal feeling. "But, sir, I'm losing time talking like this! I only came up for assistance for the poor fellows and the others who are wounded. Where's Garry O'Neil?"

"Why, he was here under the bridge a moment ago," cried the skipper eagerly. "Hullo, O'Neil? Pass the word up, men, for Mr O'Neil. He's wanted at once! Sharp, look alive!"

Our second officer, it should be explained, was not only a sailor but a surgeon as well. He had run away to sea as a boy, and, after working his way up before the mast until he had acquired sufficient seamanship to obtain a mate's certificate, he had, at his mother's entreaty, she having a holy horror of salt water, abandoned his native element and studied for the medical profession at Trinity College, Dublin. Here, after four years' practice in walking the hospitals, he graduated with full honours, much to his mother's delight. The old lady, however, dying some little time after, he, feeling no longer bound by any tie at home, and having indeed sacrificed his own wishes for her sake, incontinently gave up his newly-fledged dignity of "Doctor" Garry O'Neil, returning to his old love and embracing once more a sea-faring life, which he has stuck to ever since. He had sailed with us in the Star of the North now for over a twelvemonth, in the first instance as third officer and for the last two voyages as second mate, the fact of his being a qualified surgeon standing him in good stead and making him even a more important personage on board than his position warranted, cargo steamers not being in the habit of carrying a medical man like passenger ships, and sailorly qualities and surgical skill interchangeable characteristics!

Hitherto we had been fortunate enough to have no necessity for availing ourselves of his professional services, but now they came in handy enough in good sooth.

"Mr O'Neil?" sang out the men on the lower deck, passing on his name in obedience to the skipper's orders from hand to hand, till the hail reached the after hatchway, down which Spokeshave roared with all the power of his lungs, being anxious on his own account to be heard and so released from his watch so that he could go below. "Mr O'Neil?" he again yelled out.

Spokeshave must have shouted down the Irishman's throat, for the next instant he poked his head up the hatchway.

"Here I am, bedad!" he exclaimed, shoving past Master "Conky," to whom he had a strong dislike, though "Garry," as we all called him, was friendly with every one with whom he was brought in contact, and was, himself, a great favourite with all the hands on board. Now, as he made his way towards the bridge, where some of the men were still singing out his name, he cried out, "Who wants me, sure? Now, don't ye be all spaking at once; one at a time, me darlints, as we all came into the wurrld!"

"Why, where did you get to, man?" said the skipper, somewhat crossly. "We've been hunting all over the ship for you!"

"Sure, I wint down into the stowage to say if the yolklines and chains for the wheel were all clear, and to disconnect the shtame stayrin' gear," replied our friend Garry. "But you'll find it all right now, with the helm amidships, and you can steer her wheriver you like; only you'll want four hands at least to haul the spokes steady if she breaks off, as I fear she will, in this say!"

"That's all right," cried the skipper, appeased at once, for he evidently thought that Garry had gone back to his cabin and left us in the lurch. "But I've bad news, and sorry to say, O'Neil, we want your services as a doctor now. There's been a bad accident in the stoke-hold and some of the poor fellows are sadly hurt."

"Indade, now!" ejaculated the other, all attention. "What's the matter? Any one scalded by the shtame, sure?"

"No, not that," said Mr Fosset, taking up the tale. "Mr Stokes has had his arm broken and another poor fellow been almost crushed to death. He's now insensible, or was when I came on deck so you'd better take some stimulant as well as splints with you."

"Faith, I understand all right and will follow your advice in a brace of shakes," replied the second mate, as he rushed off towards the saloon. "You'd better go on ahead, Fosset, and say I'm coming!"

With these parting words both he and the first officer disappeared from view, the latter hastening back to the engine-room, while the captain slowly mounted the bridge-ladder again and resumed his post there by the binnacle, after placing four of the best hands at the wheel amidships with old Masters, the boatswain, in charge.

"Ah, what d'ye think o' that now?" observed the latter to me, as I stood there awaiting my orders from the skipper, or to hear anything he might have to say to me. "I said as how summut was sure to happen. That there ship—the ghost-ship—didn't come athwart our hawser for nothink, I knowed!"

Just then there was a call up the voicepipe communicating between the wheel-house on the bridge and the engine-room.

The skipper bent his ear to the pipe, listening to what those below had to say, and then came to the top of the ladder.

"Below there!" he sang out. "Is Mr Spokeshave anywhere about?"

"No, sir," I answered. "He went off duty at eight bells."

"The devil he did, and me in such a plight, too, with that awful accident below!" cried Captain Applegarth angrily. "I suppose he's thinking of his belly again, the gourmandising little beast! He isn't half a sailor or worth a purser's parings! I'll make him pay for his skulking presently, by Jingo! However, I can't waste the time now to send after him, and you'll do as well, Haldane—better, indeed, I think!"

"All right, sir," said I, eager for action. "I'm ready to do anything."

"That's a willing lad," cried the skipper. "Now run down into Garry O'Neil's cabin and get some lint bandages he says he forgot to take with him in his hurry, leaving them on the top of his bunk by the doorway; and tell Weston, the steward, to have a couple of spare bunks ready for the injured men—in one of the state rooms aft will be best."

"All right, sir," said I, adding, as he seemed to hesitate, "anything else, sir?"

"Yes, my boy; take down a loose hammock with you, and some lashings, so as to make a sort of net with which to lift and carry poor Jackson. He's the only chap badly hurt and unable to shift for himself, so O'Neil says. Look sharp, Haldane, there's no time to lose; the poor fellow's in a very ticklish state and they want to get him up on deck in order to examine his injuries better than they can below in the stoke-hold!"

"Aye, aye, sir!" I answered, darting aft immediately, to avoid further debation, towards the saloon door under the poop. "I'm off, sir, at once!"

Here I soon got what the Irishman had asked for out of his cabin, and, giving Weston his order about the state room, unslinging the while my own hammock from its hooks and rolling it up, blankets and all, in a roll, I kicked it before me as I made my way down the engine-room hatchway as quickly as I could.

The machinery, I noticed when passing through the flat to the stoke-hold, which was, of course, on a still lower level, was working away pretty easily, the piston in the cylinder moving steadily up and down, and the eccentric, which always appeared to me as a sort of bandy-legged giant, executing its extraordinary double-shuffle in a more graceful fashion than when we were going at full speed, as it performed its allotted task of curvetting the up-and-down motion of the piston into a circular one, thus making the shaft revolve; while Grummet, the third engineer, who was still watching the throttle valve, hand on lever, had a far easier job than previously, when we were running with full power before wind and sea, and rolling and pitching at every angle every minute.

But even in the fleeting glance I had passing by, the screw still went round in a dangerous way when the stern of the vessel lifted, as some big wave passed under her keel, in spite of all Grummet's precautions in turning off steam and I could not help wondering how long the engines would stand the strain, which was all the more perilous from being intermittent.

On reaching my destination below, however, all thought of the machinery and any possible damage to the ship was instantly banished from my mind by the sight that met my gaze.

In the narrow stoke-hold, lit up by the ruddy glare of the furnace fires, the light from which enabled me to see the brackish bilge water washing about beneath the hole in the flooring and gurgling up through the broken portplates there, I saw that a group of half-naked firemen, and others, were bending over a pile of empty coal sacks heaped up against the further bulkhead, dividing the occupied apartments from the main hold, as far away as possible from the blazing fires, on which one of the stokers on duty pitched occasionally a shovelful of fuel, or smoothed the surface of the glowing embers with a long-toothed rake.

I couldn't distinguish at first any one in particular, the backs of all being towards me as I came down the slippery steel ladder, carrying the hammock, for I had taken the precaution of hoisting it on my shoulders on leaving the engine-flat above, in order to prevent its getting wet, while the noise of the machinery overhead and the roar of the furnaces, coupled with the washing of the water, prevented my hearing any distant sound.

Presently however, I recognised Garry O'Neil's voice above the general din.

"Clear off, ye murthorin' divvles!" he cried, waving his arms above the heads of the crowd of onlookers, as I could now see. "The poor chap wants air, and ye're staylin' the viry br'ith out of his nosshrils! Away wid ye all, ye spalpeens! or by the powers, it's a-pizening the howl batch of ye I'll be doin' the next toime ye comes to me for pill or powdher!"

The men clustering round him spread out, moving nearer to me; and they laughed at his comical threat—which sounded all the more humorous from the Irishman's racy brogue, which became all the more prominent when Garry was at all excited. God knows, though, their merriment, untimely as it might have sounded to outside ears, betrayed no want of sympathy with their comrade. They laughed, as sailors will do sometimes, holding their lives in their hands, as is the practice of those who have to brave the manifold dangers of the deep below and aloft on shipboard, even when standing on the brink of eternity.

As they moved away, the fierce light from one of the open furnace doors was beating on their bare bodies and making them look, indeed, the very devils to whom the Irishman had jocularly likened them; the latter looked up quickly, saw me, and beckoned me to approach nearer.

"Arrah, come along, man, with those bandages!" he said. "Sure ye moight have made 'em in the toime since I called up to the skipper. Where are they now, me darlint?"

I produced the roll of lint at once from the pocket of my monkey jacket.

"Hullo!" said he as he took and deftly proceeded to unroll the bundle of bandages, "what's that you've got on your shoulders—a rick?"

"A hammock, sir," I replied. "Cap'en Applegarth told me to bring one down for lifting the poor chap who's so hurt, and so I took my own, which had blankets already in it, thinking it would be warmer for him, sir."

"Begorrah, the skipper's got his head screwed on straight, and you the same, too, Haldane," said he approvingly, with a sagacious nod as he bent over the pile of sacks in the corner. "Come and see the poor fellow, me bhoy. There doesn't seem much loife lift in him, sure, hay?"

There certainly did not; to me he looked already dead.

Stretched out on the pile of dirty sacking, in a half-sitting, half-reclining position, lay the recumbent figure, or rather form, of the unfortunate fireman Jackson, his face as ghastly as that of a corpse, while his rigid limbs and the absence of all appearance of respiration tended to confirm the belief that the spark of life had fled.

Stoddart, the second engineer, was kneeling beside the poor fellow, rubbing his hands and holding every now and then to his nose what seemed to me a bottle of ammonia or some very pungent restorative, the powerful fumes of which overcame the foetid atmosphere of the stoke-hold, Mr Stokes, looking almost as pale as the unconscious man, assisting with his unwounded arm, with which he lifted Jackson's head, his broken one being already set in splints by our doctor-mate.

Blanchard, the other sufferer from the accident, was sitting down on a bench near by, evidently recovering from the shock he had experienced, which really was not so serious as at first anticipated, a rather stiff glass of brandy and water which Garry had given him, having pretty soon brought him to himself.

All our attention, therefore, concentrated on Jackson, who, as yet, made no sign of amendment, in spite of every remedy tried by O'Neil.

"By George!" exclaimed Mr Stokes, a few minutes later when we all began to despair of ever bringing him back to life again. "I'm sure I felt his head move then!"

"Aye, sir," corroborated Stoddart, pressing his hand gently on Jackson's chest, to feel his heart, where a slight convulsive movement became perceptible, at first feeble and uncertain enough, as you may suppose, but then more and more sustained and regular, as if the lungs were getting to work again. "Look alive! he's beginning to breathe again—and—yes—his heart beats, I declare, quite plain!"

"Hurray!" shouted Garry O'Neil, hastily putting to his patient's lips a medicine glass, into which he dropped something out of a small vial, filling up the glass with water. "I've got something here shtrang enough, begorrah, to make a dead man spake!"

The effect of the drug, whatever it was, seemed magical. In an instant the previously motionless figure moved about uneasily, the pulsation of his chest grew more rapid and pronounced, and then, stretching out his clenched hands with a jerk, as if he were suddenly galvanised into life, thereby displaying the magnificent proportions of his torso, he being stripped to the waist, Jackson opened his eyes, drawing a deep breath the while, a breath something between a sob and a sigh!

"Where—where am I?" he said, looking round with a sort of far-away, dreamy stare, but meeting Mr Stokes' sympathetic gaze, he at once seemed to recover his consciousness. "Ah, I know, sir. I found out what was the matter with the suction before that plate buckled and gripped me. I have cleared the rose box, too, sir, and you can connect the bilge-pumps again as soon as you like, sir."

Of course all this took him some time to get out.

"All right, my man," answered the old chief, greatly overcome at the fact of the old sailor, wounded to the death, thinking of his duty in the first moment of his recovery. "Never mind that, man! How do you feel now, my poor fellow—better, I trust?"

"Why, just a little pain here, sir," said Jackson, pressing his hand to his right side. "I'm thankful, though, my legs escaped, sir. I've no pain there."

Garry O'Neil looked grave and shook his head at this, and looking too as he cast down his eyes over the lower part of the unfortunate man's body, I saw that the cruel edges of the iron plates had torn away part of his canvas overalls from the thigh to the knee of one leg, peeling off with the covering, the flesh from the bone; while the foot of the other—boot and all—was crushed into a shapeless bloody mass horrible to behold, the sight making one feel sick.

"It's a bad sign his having no fayling there, Haldane," whispered the Irishman to me very low, so that Jackson could not hear. "It's jost what I thought, sure. God may help him, but I can't. He'll niver recover, do what we moight for him, niver in this worruld. The poor misfortunate fellow has his spoine injured, and he can't live forty-eight hours, if as long as that, sure!"

He did not tell him this, however; nor did he lead any of the others to understand, either, that Jackson's case was hopeless!

On the contrary, when he spoke aloud, as he did immediately afterwards, he seemed in the best of spirits, as if everything was going on as well as possible, though I noticed a tear in his eye and a quiver in his voice that touched me to the heart, making me turn away my head.

"Now you mustn't talk now, old fellow, for we want you to husband all your strength to get up the hatchway to a foine cabin of yer own on the upper deck, where we're goin' to nurse ye, me darlint, till ye're all roight, sure!" he said cheerfully. "Here, now, just dhrink another drop of the craythur, me bhoy, to kape yer spirits up, and you, Master Haldane, jist hand over that hammock ye've got storved away on ye shulder, so that we can fix up Jackson comfortable like for his trip to the upper reggins!"

So saying, the good-hearted Irishman busied himself, with the help of Stoddart, who was equally gentle in handling the poor fellow, getting him ready for removal; and when he had been carefully placed in the hammock and covered with the blanket, the two of them, both being strong and powerful men, they lifted their burden with the utmost tenderness and carried him upward to the main deck, where he was put into a berth in one of the state rooms that the steward had prepared, and every attention paid him.

Mr Fosset and I helped up Blanchard, the other fireman, he, luckily, not requiring to be carried; and we then went down for Mr Stokes, who had refused to leave the stoke-hold until his men had been attended to.

Propping up the stout old chap behind so that he could not slip back down the slippery steel ladder, as he only had the one arm now to hold on by, the three of us reached the level of the engine-room all right, the chief, resting here a moment to give a look round and a word to Grummet, who of course was still in charge, telling him to slow down still further and use all his spare steam for clearing the bilge, as the sluice valves had been opened to prevent the fires being flooded out, and the pumps were in good working order again.

Grummet promised to attend carefully to these directions, and a host of others I cannot now recollect, poor Mr Stokes being as fussy and fidgetty as he was fat, and in the habit of unintentionally worrying his subordinates a good deal in this way, and the three of us again started on our way upwards, the old chief leading, as before, and Mr Fosset and I bringing up the rear very slowly, so as to prevent accident, when all at once there was a fearful crash that echoed through my brain, followed by a violent concussion of the air which nearly threw us all down the engine-room ladder, though Mr Fosset and I were both hanging on to it like grim death and supporting the whole weight of Mr Stokes between us.

At the same instant, too, the crank shaft stopped revolving, all motion of the machinery ceased, and the hatchway, with all the space around us, was filled by a dense cloud of hot steam!

Anchored

Nor was this the worst, for hardly had we begun to draw breath again in the stifling vapour-bath-like atmosphere surrounding us, ere we could utter a cry, indeed, or exchange a word of speech with reference to what had just occurred, there arose a sudden and violent oscillation of the vessel, which pitched and rolled, and then heeled over suddenly to port, while an avalanche of water came thundering down the hatchway on top of our heads.

"Good Lord, we're lost!" gulped out Mr Stokes as we all floundered together on the grating forming the floor of the engine-room, where fortunately the flood had washed us, instead of hustling us down the stoke-hold below, where all three of us would most inevitably have been killed by the fall. "A boiler's burst and the ship broached-to!"

"Not quite so bad as that, sir," sang out the voice of Grummet in the distance, the thick vapour lending it a far-away sound. "The vessel is recovering herself again, and the cylinder cover's blown off, sir—that's all!"

"All, indeed!" exclaimed the old chief in a despairing tone as he staggered to his feet, enabling Mr Fosset and myself to rise up too—an impossibility before, as he was right on top of us, and had served us out worse than the water had done. "Quite enough damage for me, and all of us, I think!"

"How's your arm, Mr Stokes?" asked Mr Fosset as the atmosphere cleared a little and the engine-room lights glimmered through the misty darkness that now enveloped the place. "I hope it hasn't been hurt by your tumble?"

"Oh, damn my arm!" cried the other impatiently, evidently more anxious about the machinery than his arm. "Have you shut off the steam?"

"Yes, sir," replied his subordinate calmly. "I closed all the stop valves up here the moment I knew what had happened; and the men below in the stoke-hold have cut off the supply from the main pipe, while Mr Links has gone into the screw well to disconnect the propeller."

"Very good, Grummet. So they be all right down below?"

"All right, sir."

"Thank God for that! How about the fires?"

"Drowned out, sir, all but the one under the fire boiler on the starboard side."

"You'd better look after that, to keep the bilge-pumps going, or else it'll be all drowned out, with this lot of water coming down the hatchway every time the ship rolls! I do hope the skipper will lie-to and keep her head to sea until we can get the engines going again, though I'm afraid that'll be a long job!"

Before Grummet could reply to this, Stoddart, the second officer, or rather engineer, came scrambling down from the saloon, where he had been assisting Garry O'Neil in making poor Jackson comfortable, the escape of the steam having evidently told its own tale to an expert like himself.

Although a younger man than Mr Stokes, his brains were considerably sharper and he was a better mechanic in every way; so now, when, after examining the damage done to the cylinder, he made light of the accident, instead of groaning over it like the old chief. Mr Fosset, I could see, and with him myself also, who shared his belief, saw that the injury was not irreparable and that it might certainly have been worse.

"Of course it can't be done in a day!" Stoddart said; "still it can be patched up."

"That's all very well," interposed Mr Stokes, holding to his despondent view of the situation. "But I'd like to know how you're going to get that cracked cover off the cylinder with the vessel rolling like this!"

"Oh, I'll manage that easy enough," said the energetic fellow in his confident way. "I've done worse jobs than that in a heavy sea. Why, I'll lash myself to the cylinder if it comes to the worse and unscrew the cover nut by nut, shifting my berth round till I have it off. Then if Grummet will see to getting the portable forge ready, and some old sheet iron or boiler plates for working and making into a patch, and if Links will turn out some new bolts and screws with the lathe, we'll have everything in working order before we know where we are!"

"Bravo, my hearty!" cried Mr Fosset, lending Stoddart a hand to lash himself to the cylinder, while Grummet held a screw-wrench and other tools up to him. "You ought to be a sailor, you're so smart!"

"I prefer my own billet," retorted the other with an air of conscious power. "I am an engineer!"

Mr Fosset laughed.

"All right!" said he good-humouredly. "Every one to his trade!"

"Humph!" groaned Mr Stokes, who was leaning against the bulkhead, "looking very white about the gills," as Grummet whispered to me. The steam gradually dispersing and the lights burning more brightly, enabled us to see his face better. "I suppose there's nothing I can do?"

"No, nothing, sir," answered Stoddart, busy at the moment with the first nut of the cylinder cover. "You can very safely leave matters to Grummet and me! And Mr O'Neil told me as I left the maindeck that you ought to go to your cabin and lie down, so as to rest your arm, or it might mortify, he says, when he would not answer for the consequences, you understand, sir?"

"Ah, that settles the matter; I won't give our amateur sawbones a chance of lopping it off, as I daresay he'd like!" said poor Mr Stokes, with a feeble attempt at a joke. "Yes, I'd better go to my cabin, for I see I'm not wanted here; and, to tell the truth, I've an aching all over me, and feel rather tired and faint."

"Then off you go to the doctor at once," cried Mr Fosset, catching hold of him by his uninjured arm and leading him towards the hatchway again, the ship being pretty steady for the moment.

"You and I, too, Haldane, ought to be on deck helping the skipper and the rest, instead of stopping here, hindering these smart fellows at their work. Come along with me, my lad!"

Leaving Mr Stokes at the door of the saloon in charge of Weston, the steward, the first mate and I proceeded along the waist to the bridge, where we found Captain Applegarth pacing up and down in his customary jerky, impatient way, like the Polar bear in the Zoological Gardens, as I always thought.

"Well," he said to Mr Fosset, bringing himself up short in front of the rail on our approach, "how are matters getting on below—badly, I'm afraid?"

The first mate explained. Spokeshave, who was at the other end of the bridge, coming up to listen, as usual, to the conversation.

"That's good news, indeed!" said the skipper on hearing how Stoddart had set to work to repair the damage. "I thought the engines were completely broken-down. If it weren't for poor Jackson, who, O'Neil told me just now, was in a bad way, I think we'd got out of the scrape pretty well, for the old barquey is comfortable enough now, and, though there's a heavy sea running and it is still blowing stiff from the north'ard and the west'ard, the sky is clearer than it was, and I fancy we've seen the worst of the gale, eh?"

"I'm sure I hope so, sir," replied Mr Fosset, not committing himself to any definite expression of opinion in the matter. "It has given us a rare good doing all round while it was about it, at an rate!"

"Aye, it has that," said the skipper. "The old barquey, though, has come through it better than any one would have supposed, with all that deadweight amidships, considering that she broached-to awhile ago and got caught in the trough of the sea the very moment the machinery below gave out. By George, Fosset, we had a narrow squeak then, I can tell you!"

"I can quite believe that, sir," said the other, looking round about and aloft, sailor-like, as he spoke. "For my part I feared the worst, I'm sure. However, all's well that ends well, and the old barquey looks first rate, as you say, sir, in spite of all she's gone through. She rides like a cork."

She certainly was a capital seaboat and lay-to now as easily as if she were at anchor in the Mersey, though the wind was whistling through the rigging and the ocean far and wide white with foam, bowing and scraping to the big waves that rolled in after her like an old dowager duchess in a ball room, curtseying to her partner.

During the long time the first mate and I had been down below in the stoke-hold, the skipper had lowered the upper yards and housed her top-masts, getting her also under snugger canvas, the fore and mizzen topsails being set "scandalised," as we call it aboard ship, that is, with the heads of the sails hauled up, and their sheets flattened taut as boards, so as to expose as little surface as possible to the wind, only just sufficient to keep the vessel with her head to sea, like a stag at bay.

Opportunity had also been taken, I noticed, to secure the broken engine-room skylight in a more substantial way than formerly, and so prevent any more green seas from flooding the hold, the opening having been planked over by the carpenter, and heavy bars of railroad iron, which formed part of our cargo, laid across, instead of the tarpaulin that was deemed good enough before and had given way when Mr Stokes—poor man—and the first mate and myself got washed down the hatchway by a wave that came over the side, crumpling the flimsy covering as if it were tissue paper.

Altogether, the outlook was more reassuring than when I had gone below; for although a fierce northerly gale was howling over the deep, making it heave and fret and lashing it up into wild mountainous billows, the heaven overhead was clear of all cloud, and the complaisant moon, which was at the full, but shining with a pale, peaceful light, while numerous stars were twinkling everywhere in the endless expanse of the firmament above, gazing down serenely at the riot of the elements below.

It was now close on midnight and Garry O'Neil came on deck to take the middle watch, it being his turn of duty.

"Well, doctor," said the skipper, anxious to hear something about the invalids, "how're your patients?"

"Both going on capitally; Jackson sleeping quietly, sir, though he can't last out long, poor fellow!"

"And Mr Stokes?"

"Faith, he's drivin' his pigs to market in foine stoil; you should only hear him, cap'en!" answered the Irishman, looking out to windward. "Begorrah, ain't it blowin', though, sir! Sure, as we used to say at ould Trinity, de gustibus non est disputandum, which means, Mister Spokeshave, as yo're cockin' up your nose to hear what I'm after sayin', it's moighty gusty, an' there's no denyin' it!"

The skipper laughed, as he generally did at Garry's nonsensical, queer sayings.

"By George, O'Neil! I must go down and have a glass of grog to wash the taste of that awful pun out of my mouth!" he cried, turning to leave the bridge for the first time since he had come up there at sunset. "You can call me if anything happens or should it come to blow worse, but I shall be up and down all night to see how you're getting on."

"Och! the divvle dout ye!" muttered the Irishman in his quizzing way, as the skipper went down the ladder, giving a word to the boatswain and man at the wheel below as he passed them on his way up. "Ye niver give a chap the cridit of keeping a watch to himself!"

Soon after this I, too, left the deck and turned in, Garry O'Neil telling me he did not want me on the bridge and that I had better sleep while I could, a permission I readily availed myself of, tired out with all I had gone through and the various exciting episodes of the evening.

There was no change in the weather the following morning, the wind even blowing with greater force and the sea such as I had never seen it before, and such a sea as I hope never to experience again; so, in order that the ship might ride the more easily and those below in the engine-room better able to go on with the repair of the cylinder than they could with the old barquey pitching her bows under and then kicking up her heels sky high, varying her performances by rolling side to side violently, like a pendulum gone mad, the skipper had all our spare spars lashed together, and attaching a stout steel wire hawser to them, launched the lot overboard through a hole in the bulwarks, where one of the waves had made a convenient clean sweep, veering the hawser ahead with this "jetsam" to serve as a floating anchor for us, and moor the ship.

By this means we all had a more comfortable time of it, the old barquey no longer shipping water in any considerable quantity and there being less work below in the way of clearing it, all of the bilge-pumps, fortunately for us all, Stoddart and the engine-room staff were able to keep going; otherwise we must have foundered long since!

The gale continued without abatement all that day and the next, the second since our mishap, when, late in the afternoon the wind began to go down, veering from the north-west to the north, and so on, back to the eastern quadrant.

Soon after this, just before it got dark, an English man-of-war hove in sight, and, seeing our disabled condition, signalled to ask whether we required any assistance.

Through the clumsiness of Mr Spokeshave, who had charge of our signal department and showed his cleverness by hoisting the very numbers of the flags giving the skipper's reply, that, though our engines were temporarily broken-down, they were fast being repaired, the captain of the man-of-war could not understand him; and so, fearing the worst, ranged up under our stern to see what help he could render in what he evidently considered, from Spokeshave's "hoist," to be a pressing emergency.

"Ship ahoy!" he shouted through a speaking trumpet from his quarter-deck aft, which was on a level with our bridge, the vessel, a splendid cruiser of the first-class, towering over the comparatively puny dimensions of the poor, broken-down Star of the North. "Shall I send a boat aboard with assistance?"

"No, thank you very much," replied our skipper, taking off his cap and returning the greeting of the naval officer. "We've got over the worst of it now, sir, and will be soon under weigh again, as the weather is breaking."

"Glad to hear it," returned the other, who could read our name astern as she lay athwart us. "Where are you bound to?"

"New York, sir," sang out the skipper. "Twelve days out from England. We've been disabled forty-eight hours."

"Hope your engines will soon be in working order," sang out the handsome officer from the deck of the man-of-war, giving some other order at the same minute, for I heard the shrill sound of a boatswain's pipe and the rattle of feet along her deck. "Please report us when you reach your destination."

"What name, sir?"

"Her Majesty's ship Aurora, on passage from Bermuda to Halifax."

With that he waved his hand, and her white ensign, whose blood-red cross of Saint George stood out in bold relief, dipped in parting salute to our vessel, which reciprocated the compliment as the man-of-war bore away on her course to the northward, a group of officers rollicking round their captain on her deck aft and gazing at us as she moved off rapidly under a full pressure of steam, evidently admiring our skipper's wonderful sea anchor.

As the noble ship glided away through the still tempestuous sea against a strong headwind, a thing of beauty and of might—such a contrast to us lying there, almost at the mercy of the seas—I could not help thinking of the wondrous power of mind over matter displayed in our grand ocean steamers, and what a responsibility rests upon their engineers!

How little do the thousands of passengers who yearly go to and fro across the Atlantic know, or, indeed, care to know, that their comfort and the rate at which they travel through the water—they who talk so glibly of making the passage in such and such a time, be the sea smooth or rough, and the wind fine or contrary—that all this depends on the unceasing vigilance of the officers in charge of the vessel in which they voyage!

Do they even think, I wondered, that while they are sleeping, eating, enjoying themselves and doing what they please on board, even grumbling at some little petty defect or shortcoming which they think might be prevented, the engineers below, in an atmosphere in which they could not breathe, are incessantly watching the movements of the machinery and oiling each part at almost every instant of time, moving this slide and that, adjusting a valve here and tightening a nut there, ever cooling the bearings and raking at the furnaces and putting on fresh coal, this being done every hour of the day and night through the passage from land to land? Have any of them realised the fact that these same engineers and their able assistants, the firemen and oilmen and trimmers, the whole stoke-hold staff, so to speak, run a greater risk of their lives, in the event of an accident happening, than any one else in the ship, as, should a boiler or cylinder burst they may be scalded to death before the noise of the explosion could reach those above? Or again, should the vessel strike on a rock, the compartment below in which perforce they are compelled to work deep down in the vessel's bowels will fill, from the very weight of the engines, quicker than any other part of the ship, most probably, when those confined below must necessarily be liable to be drowned, like rats in a hole, without the chances of escape possessed by the passengers and hands on board.

"No, I don't suppose any one even thinks of such things," said I to myself as I left the bridge and went towards the saloon to ask how poor Jackson was, uttering my thoughts unconsciously aloud as I reflected, and now that I considered their responsibility, thought how much poor old Mr Stokes, with his broken arm, and Stoddart and the others must have on their minds! "Hullo, who is that?"

It was Weston, the steward, who spoke.

"I wish you'd come and look at Jackson, sir," he said. "The poor chap wore all right when Mr O'Neil comed down jist now, and a sleepin' still as when you seed him awhile ago. But all of a suddink he starts up as he hears you a comin' down the companion-way, sir, and is jabbering away like anythink!"

"Oh, but," I exclaimed, "why did you leave him?"

"I wor afeard he'd jump overboard, or try to do somethink awful!"

"Nonsense! the very thing you are there for to prevent," said I, going into the cabin, where I saw the poor fellow trying to get out of the cot. Turning angrily to Weston I repeated again, "You shouldn't have left him for one moment in this state!"

"But, sir, I wanted to hail Mr O'Neil or somebody; I thought I oughter 'ave summun by to 'elp me, in case he becomed desperate-like, and I couldn't make no one hear on deck, and that's why I comed when I knowed you was a-passing along, sir."

This was unanswerable logic, though Weston always had an answer for anything and everything.

Poor Jackson, though, did not look as if he would be "desperate" again in any shape or form.

That he was delirious I could see at a glance, for his eyes, great wild eyes, were wide open, staring at vacancy, fixed on the bulkhead that divided the cabin from the captain's, which was just beyond; and he was very much excited, sitting up in the cot and, gesticulating violently with both his hands, and waving his arms about as he repeated some unintelligible gibberish over and over again, that I could not make out.

Presently he looked at me very straight as if he recognised me, and afterwards spoke a little more coherently.

"Ah, yes, sir, I recollect now," he said at last. "You're Mr Haldane, I know; but—where's the little girl and the—the—dog?"

"Why, Jackson, old man," I said, speaking soothingly to him, "what's the matter with you? There's no girl or dog, you know, here. Don't you know where you are, my poor fellow?"

He got quite savage at this. There's no reason in delirium!

"Of course I know where I am," he screamed out, making a grab at Weston, as he writhed in torture from the internal and violent inflammation which must have set up. "I'm in—hell. I—can—feel—I—am—I am—burning—all over—inside me—here. And you? Oh, yes—I know you!"

This paroxysm left him again after a moment, and he lay back on his pillows, only to sit up the next minute again, however.

He now pointed his finger in the direction of the sea through the porthole, gazing earnestly as if he saw something there.

"The ship has come for me again—as—it did t'other night—you know—you know?" he said in agonised whispers. "There—there,—can't you see it now? sailing—along—as—Mister—Haldane—said,—there with a—a—signal—of—distress—flying—the—flag—half-mast high! Why,—there it is,—now, as plain as—plain—can be; and, see—see they're—lowering—a—boat,—look,—for me,—to take me aboard. Lend us a hand,—mate. I wants to halloo—to 'em and I—feels so bad—and—I can't, I can't—move myself. Hi,—there!—Ship ahoy! Wait—a—minute—can't you? Ship ahoy!—I'm—coming—I'm—comi-ing. I'm—"

Then, raising his eyes to heaven, and drawing a long deep breath, something between a sob and a sigh, a breath that was his last, poor Jackson fell back on the pile of pillows behind him, stone dead!

We Sight the Strange Craft Again

"That's number one!" said old Masters, the boatswain, meeting me at the door of the saloon as I came out on deck, Weston having already told him the sad news. "Master Stokes'll foller next, and then you or hi, Master Haldane, for we be all doomed men, I know, arter seein' that there ghost-ship!"

I made no reply to the superstitious old seaman's ominous prediction, but as I made my way forward to the bridge to inform Captain Applegarth and the others of what had happened, I could not help thinking how strange it was that poor Jackson should have recalled, at the very moment the spirit was quitting his crippled body, the fact of my sighting the ship in distress and the account I had given the skipper of what I had seen on board that mysterious craft!

Mr Fosset, or some of the hands who accompanied him, must have taken down the yarn to the stoke-hold, only just before the unfortunate man met with his terrible accident, though I had no doubt that he must have seen the man-of-war through the port hole of the cabin, which was right opposite his bunk, as she brought up under our stern to speak to us earlier in the afternoon, and the sight of HMS Aurora had, somehow or other, amid the wanderings of his unconscious brain, got mixed up with the remembrance of what he had previously heard concerning the vessel I had seen at sunset the two days prior.

It was now getting dark, the evening closing in quickly, and, what with the dying man's queer talk and the boatswain harping on the same theme immediately afterwards, I confess I felt far from comfortable, my nerves being in a state of constant tension from the painful scene in the cabin that I had just witnessed, while the gloomy shades of the night that were fast enwrapping us, the dull roar of the ever-breaking sea and the groaning of the ship as she rolled, like a living creature in pain, all worked on my overtried fancy and made me almost afraid of my own shadow as I slipped and stumbled along the sloppy deck, my mind being in a complete whirl till I reached my goal—the bridge.

"What's the matther, me bhoy?" asked Garry O'Neil, who was speaking to the skipper, the two examining a chart in the wheel-house, the light from the doorway of which fell on my face. "Faith, ye look quite skeared, Haldane, jist as if ye'd sane a ghoast, sure!"

I mentioned what had happened, however, and he at once dropped his chaffing manner, looking as grave as a judge.

"Begorrah, it's moighty sorry I am to hear that, now!" said he in a more serious tone. "Sure, and he was a foine, h'ilthy man entirely, barrin' that accident, bad cess to it! He moight have lived till a hundred, an' then aunly died of auld age; for he'd the constitution of an illiphent. Faith, I never saw such a chist and thorax on a chap in me loife before!"

"Poor fellow!" observed the skipper. "He seems to have gone off awfully sudden at the last. I thought you said he was getting on well when you went down to see him awhile ago?"

"Bedad, I did that, sir; father's no denyin' it," answered the Irishman, off-hand. "But I niver s'id he'd git over it, cap'en. I tuld ye from the first he couldn't reciver, for he was paralysed, poor craytur', from the waist downwards, and had a lot of internal injury besides. It was aunly bekase he was sich a shtrang man that he's lasted so long, sir. Any one else would have died directly outright afther the accident, for he was pretty well smashed to pieces!"

"Strange!" muttered Captain Applegarth, who, although hasty of temper sometimes, was a man of deep feeling. "Sunday night again and that man dead! Only a week ago, this very evening, he came up to me here as I was standing by the binnacle to ask about some carpenter's stores that were wanted in the engine-room. He and I then got talking, I recollect, it being Sunday, I suppose, of religious matters. He imagined himself—poor chap—a 'materialist,' as they call themselves, but his arguments on the point were very weak. He argued that there was no hereafter, no future state; the heaven and hell spoken of in Scripture, he suggested, being the happiness or punishment we meet with below here, while living, in accordance with our own lives."

"Faith!" said Garry O'Neil, who was not a deep thinker, not troubling himself much about anything beyond the present. "That's a puzzling question; but I, for one, wouldn't care to be of that way of thinkin', sure, sir."

"That question however, poor Jackson has solved, long ere this!"

As Captain Applegarth uttered these words, solemnly enough, the fireman's ravings, when in the agonies of death, came back to me, and I thought that, if confident in his materialism when in health and strength, his creed had not altogether eased his mind at the last, when I saw him raise his eyes, for a few minutes, to heaven in prayer.

That night the gale, which had moderated considerably during the afternoon, assailed us again with renewed vigour, as if old Boreas had put a fresh hand to the bellows, as sailor folk say.

It began in the middle watch, when the wind suddenly veered to the southwards, and it came on to blow great guns, causing the skipper the utmost uneasiness, as he feared we would break away from our spar anchor, when, disabled as we were, a steamer in a storm without the use of the engines being no better off than a baby in arms deprived of its nurse, it seemed almost impossible to prevent the vessel from broaching-to, in which case she would more than likely founder with all hands.

Consequently, not a soul turned in the livelong night, the port and starboard watches both remaining on duty, with Captain Applegarth and Mr Fosset on the bridge, while Garry O'Neil relieved the boatswain, who now had eight men under him in charge of the wheel, where the utmost caution and the greatest vigilance were necessary to keep the old barquey's head to the sea. I had fearfully hard work, too, for the big waves ever and anon leapt up over her bows, burying the fo'c's'le in clouds of spray and spent water that came pouring down into the waist and rushing aft, flooding the whole deck almost up to the gunwhales taking everything movable overboard, the boats being lifted off the chocks amidships even and swept away, and the cook's galley in the forward part of the deckhouse got badly damaged.

This was in the height of the storm, just before daybreak, about two bells in the morning watch, or five o'clock AM.

Our poor old barquey then rolled so much that the skipper thought the wire hawser attached to the spars had parted and that we were at the very mercy of the tempest. So certain, indeed, was he, that he yelled out for all hands to make sail, with the idea of trying one last desperate venture and beard the winds with our puny canvas.

Fortunately, however, there was no need for us to essay this futile expedient, breaking the force of the billows as they reared up in their colossal grandeur to annihilate us and keeping us steadily facing their attack; and presently, shortly after six bells, when we really experienced pretty nearly the worst of it, there was a muttered growl of thunder, accompanied by a lightning flash that illuminated the whole of the heavens from pole to pole, and then rain came down in a deluge, the wind dropping, as suddenly, with a wild, weird shrill shriek of disappointed rage that wailed and whistled through the rigging, and then quietly died away.

Of course the sea did not quiet down all at once, old Neptune not being easily pacified after being stirred up to so great an extent, and the waves ran high most of the day, while the sky was overcast and the ocean of a dull leaden colour; but towards evening it cleared up and, the water being a bit calmer, the captain thought it a fitting time to bury poor Jackson.

All the hands were mustered on deck, the engineers and stokers stopping their busy repairing work below, which they had kept at night and day without intermission ever since our breakdown, and coming up with the rest of the crew to pay the last tribute of respect to their departed comrade, even Mr Stokes, though he was still in a very weak state of health and had his head and broken arm bandaged up, insisting on being present, Garry O'Neil and Stoddart supporting him between them for the purpose.

Then the body of the unfortunate fireman, enclosed in a hammock covered by the ship's ensign and having a pig of ballast tied to the feet to ensure its submersion, was brought up from the cabin where he had died, and placed on a plank by the gangway where the waves had washed away our bulwarks, leaving a wide open space.

Captain Applegarth read over the remains the beautiful prayers of the Church Service appointed for the burial of those who die at sea, all of us standing bareheaded around.

A faint gleam of light from the setting sun, away on our port bow, shone through a mist of cloud that obscured the horizon to windward; and, as this disappeared, the skipper came to the end of the viaticum, when, at a signal from the boatswain, the plank was tipped and poor Jackson's body was committed to the deep with a sigh of regret at his untimely end, and the devout hope that though his earthly voyage had been cut short, he might yet reach that haven where there are no accidents nor shipwrecks, and where seas swallow not up, or stormy winds blow!

Some little while after this a slight breeze sprang up from the southward and westward, bringing a cool feeling with it, and I shivered as I stood on the bridge looking out over the dark waste of waters, feeling rather melancholy, if the truth be told.

"That's a bad sign, Master Haldane," said old Masters close to my ear, making me jump, for I did not know he was there. "They say that when a ship chap shivers like that there, it be meaning that somebody or summit be a-walking over his grave!"

"Stave that, bo'sun!" I cried impatiently. "You're a regular old Jonah, and enough to give a fellow the creeps!"

"Ah, you may try to laugh it off, Mister Haldane," he retorted in his lugubrious way. "But, as I says to ye last night, says I, when that poor chap kicked the bucket as we've just been a-burying on, we ain't seen the end on it yet. I misdoubts the weather, too, sir. There's a great bank of cloud now rising up to win'ard, and I fancies I heard jist now the sound o' thunder ag'in."

"Thunder?" I exclaimed. "Nonsense!"

"No, Mister Haldane, it ain't no nonsense," said the old fellow solemnly. "You ain't known me to croak afore without re'sin, and I tells ye I don't likes the look o' things to-night. There's summit a-brewin' up over there, or I'm a Dutchman!"

"What's that, bo'sun?" cried the skipper, coming up on the bridge at the moment to look for the chart of the North Atlantic, which he had left in the wheel-house the night before, and overheard the old growler's remark. "Got the Flying Dutchman on the brain again?"

"No, sir, I weren't talking o' that," replied Masters. "I was a-saying to Master Haldane that it were precious misty and thick to win'ard and I feared thunder over there."

"Thunder! thunder your grandmother!" cried the skipper testily. "I've pretty sharp ears, bo'sun, and I have heard none to-night. Have you, Haldane?"

"N–n–o, sir, not thunder," I answered, listening attentively for a moment. "Stay, sir, though. I do hear something now, but the sound seems more like firing in the distance."

"What, guns?"

"No sir, more like rifle shots, or the discharge of a revolver firing quickly at intervals."

Captain Applegarth thereupon listened attentively, too, in his turn, while Masters went out to the end of the bridge and peered out over the side to windward with rapt gaze.

"By George, yes, you're right, boy!" cried the skipper the next moment. "I can hear the shots quite plainly, I do believe. Hullo, there! What the deuce is going on over there, I wonder?"

There was reason for exclamation.

At that instant the dark mass of cloud on the horizon, towards which we were all looking, was rent by a flash, and we could see, standing against the black background in vivid relief, the masts and spars of a large full-rigged ship.

She was evidently burning a "flare-up" to attract attention, and, ere the light waned, I noticed that her yards were all a cock-bill and her sails and rigging torn and disordered; while, stranger still, she had her flag astern hoisted half-mast high—the French tricolour, too!

Both the boatswain and I, simultaneously, involuntarily, uttered a cry of dismay.

The vessel in sight was the very identical ship I had seen three nights before, flying the same signal of distress; and here she was now, sailing, as then, four points off our weather bows and eight before the wind, which was, as I've already said, blowing a light breeze from the southward and westward.

What new calamity did this second appearance of the "ghost-ship," as the old boatswain called her, portend to all of us?

Aye, what, indeed!

Time alone could tell.

Mystification

Old Masters turned his face towards me as the fleeting vision became swallowed up in the darkness that now obscured the sky to the westwards, and I saw that he looked horror-struck, staring into space spell-bound.

As for me, I cannot express what I felt, because I am unable to describe it fully.

"There, there!" I exclaimed, clutching Captain Applegarth's arm in nervous horror. "There she is again!"

But the skipper, although startled by the sudden appearance of the mysterious vessel in the first instance, as his ejaculation on catching sight of her showed, evidently did not regard her in the same light as the boatswain and myself.

"Why, Haldane, what's the matter with you, my lad?" he said in a joking way, "You seem all of a tremble; and, by George, you grip tight!"

"I beg your pardon, sir, I'm sure," I stammered out, trying to pull myself together as I released his arm. "But—but—did you—did you—see her, sir?"

"See that ship just now? Yes, of course I did. I suppose she sighted us lying here like a log and wanted us to report her or something, though why they lit that flare-up over her stern I am sure I can't imagine. They couldn't expect us to read her name at that distance. She must have been close on five miles off!"

"But, sir," I cried out quickly. "She's the same!"

"The same what, Haldane?"

"Why, the ship in distress, sir, that I sighted at sunset on Friday night just before our breakdown."

Captain Applegarth whistled through his teeth.

"My good lad," he said incredulously, "that's simply impossible!"

"Well, sir, you may not believe me," I urged, rather nettled that he should put me down in this way, "but I declare to you she is the identical vessel I saw that evening, as I told you at the time, and of which we went in chase till the gale stopped us and our machinery gave out! I cannot doubt the evidence of my own eyes, sir."

"My dear boy," replied the skipper, in kinder tones than I expected to this outburst, for he was a hot-tempered man generally, and disliked anything like argument from his officers when he had once said his say, being of the opinion that his word should be last. "Just reflect a moment and let your own natural good sense decide the point. How can it be likely that the vessel you asserted you saw on Friday night, hundreds of miles away from here, should come across us now under precisely similar circumstances, considering all that has happened since?"

"She's the same ship, sir, nevertheless," I maintained stubbornly, though I was a bit puzzled on my own account, mind, by his putting the case so strongly. "The vessel I saw on Friday night was a full-rigged ship, with her sails knocked about and had her ensign hoisted half-mast high at the peak, and this one seemed the same in every particular. I did not notice all that when she burnt the flare-up just now. The light only lasted an instant."

"There is something in that, certainly, Haldane," answered the skipper, wavering a little, I thought, in his ideas. "Still, when one is inclined to believe in a thing, the imagination is often a great aid in turning a wish into a certainty."

"Besides, sir," I continued, wishing to clench my argument, "if we were driven out of our course by the gale, she might have been similarly affected, and the winds and currents might have brought us together again."

"That's possible, but not probable," he rejoined. "I've known two bottles of the same weight dropped overboard from the same ship at the same hour, and—"

"Well, sir?"

"One was found landed on the Lofoden Isles, off the coast of Norway: the other came ashore at Sandy Point, in the Straits of Magellan!"

He laughed when he said this, apparently thinking he had utterly settled the matter, but I checkmated him with his own theory.

"The very uncertainty of the action of the currents of the Atlantic which you instance, sir," I said, "shows that what you think impossible might be very possible, and the strange, weird vessel that I saw three nights ago might have come within sight of us again."

"That's one for you, Haldane," acknowledged the skipper very good-naturedly, for he was a fair man when anything was laid clearly before him. "But, recollect, no one saw this ship distinctly but yourself. I couldn't say of my own knowledge what rig she was, and I certainly didn't see any flag or sign of distress. I only saw something that looked like a ship burning a flare-up in the distance—that's all."

"Beg pardon, sir," whispered old Masters, stepping up and touching his cap ere he addressed the skipper, "but I seed the ghost-ship, too, sir, the same as Master Haldane, sir."

The skipper wheeled round and stared at him.

"Ghost-ship, man! What do you mean?"

"I means that there ghost-ship that hove in sight jist now and which have passed us afore, sir. She be sent as a warning to us, I knows, and as a Christian man, Cap'en Applegarth, I takes it as sich!"

The old seaman spoke so earnestly that the skipper, although he had hard work to keep himself in, answered him without ridiculing his extraordinary delusion, as he held it to be.

"I am a Christian man, too, I hope, bo'sun," he said. "I believe in a divine power above, and put my trust in a merciful providence; but I can't believe in any of your queer supernatural visitations, whether as warnings or what not!"

"Not if you seed the same blessed thing three times?"

"No; not if I saw it a hundred times!" he roared out impatiently.

"Ah, seein' is believin', I says," whined old Masters, not a whit shaken on the point, in spite of the skipper's scepticism. "Master Haldane seed it, and I seed it, and poor Jackson seed it."

"Indeed?" cried the skipper. "I did not know he had been on deck before the accident."

"It wore arter that, sir, that he seed the ghost-ship," said the old boatswain in reply to the implied question. "It were jist afore he died."

"Just before he died!" repeated Captain Applegarth indignantly, as if he thought he was being made a fool of. "Why, man, the poor fellow was out of his mind then, and besides, never stirred out of his cabin!"

"Ah, but he had the warnin' jist the same, for Weston, it was, told me as how Jackson seed the ship and cried out when he lay there a-dyin'. Bulkheads can't keep sperrits out, sir."

"Nor in, either, as I know to my cost," returned the skipper drily. "Your friend Weston is pretty familiar with them, if they come in his way, I fancy! Stuff and nonsense, bo'sun; how can you believe such rubbish? The other night you imagined the reflection of our own vessel, when that meteor came by, to be a ghost-ship, as you call it in your absurd folly; and to-night, when that craft to win'rd passed and lit a flare-up, hanged if you aren't at it again with your ghost-ship! By George, it makes me sick, Masters, to think that a grown man and a good seaman like yourself should be such a confounded ass!"

"Hass or no hass, there she wer'," said the old fellow doggedly. "But here comes Mr Fosset, sir. He were on the poop aft when that vessel passed as I speaks on. Ax him what he thinks of her and if she weren't the same full-rigged ship as Master Haldane and all of us seed?"

"I will," replied Captain Applegarth promptly; and on the first mate approaching nearer, he hailed him. "I say, Fosset, what did you think of that ship just now?"

The other's answer, however, bewildered the skipper more than Masters and I had done previously.

"Ship!" said the first mate. "What ship?"

"That vessel that lit the flare-up awhile ago."

"I didn't see any flare-up!" replied Mr Fosset, "and certainly no ship has passed us to my knowledge since I've been on deck."

"By George, I don't know who or what to believe," exclaimed Captain Applegarth, looking from the one to the other of us. "You've set my very brains wool-gathering between you, with your 'vessels in distress' and 'ghost-ships'; I'm hanged if I won't go down to the engine-room and have a little practical common sense knocked into me, as well as see how they're getting on with the repairs to the machinery!"

So saying, the skipper went below, and, as there was nothing particular for me to do on deck, I followed his example. Instead of proceeding down to the engine-room, however, I only went as far as my bunk and turned in, wondering what the morrow would bring forth. I was haunted, though, by strange dreams all through the night, continually waking up and then getting to sleep again in snatches, only to wake up again immediately after I had dropped off.

In the Gulf Stream

"It's a dead calm, sir!" I heard Mr Fosset sing out next morning outside the door of the skipper's state room, which opened out of the saloon, close to my berth, when he went to call him at four bells, in obedience to orders given overnight. "The gale has completely blown itself out, and there's only a little cat's-paw of a breeze from the south'ard."

"Humph!" yawned the skipper from within. "That's a good job, Fosset. I think we've had enough wind to last us for a blue moon!"

"So say I, sir," agreed the other with much heartiness. "I wouldn't like to go through the same experiences again, by Jingo!"

"Nor I," came from the other, evidently about to turn out from his bunk. "I'll be on deck in five minutes or so, Fosset."

The first mate, however, would not take this for a dismissal, having apparently further important information to give and which he at once proceeded to disclose.

"Do you know, sir, I think we're in the Gulf Stream," he said in an impressive tone. "There's a lot of the weed knocking about round the ship."

"Gulf-weed?" exclaimed the skipper's voice again from the cabin, sounding a bit muffled as if he were in the act of pulling his shirt over his head. "Are you certain?"

"Aye," affirmed the other. "There's not the slightest doubt about it. It's as plain as a pike staff, sir."

"The deuce it is!" said the skipper in a louder key, showing that my surmise had been correct as to the progress of his toilet, and that his head was now unloosed from its bag-like envelope. "By George, I can't make it out at all!"

"There's no getting over the fact, sir," persisted the first mate. "We're quite surrounded by the weed. I saw it well the first streak of light at two bells, on suddenly looking over the side, sir. There's Mr O'Neil up on the bridge now, and he has noticed it too!"

The skipper, to judge from the voice that came from his cabin and the way he was banging his boots and other things about, was as much mystified by Mr Fosset's unexpected announcement as he had been the previous evening by the sight he and I and the boatswain had seen.

He was also angry, I know, so I thought it good for me to turn out likewise from my bunk as speedily as possible, it not being advisable under the circumstances to be "caught napping."

"By George, I can't understand it!" repeated Captain Applegarth crossly. "If we're in the Gulf Stream, all I can say is, we must have drifted a wonderful distance in the last two or three days. Why, man, the current is seldom perceptible above the fortieth parallel!"

"I know that, sir," replied the first mate; "but if you recollect, sir, from the lunar observation Mr O'Neil took on the night of the breakdown, we were then as far south as 41° 30 minutes, and we've been drifting south-east by east ever since."

"Well, Fosset, I'm hanged if I know where we are, after the bucketting-about we've had since last Friday!" said the skipper, who now came into the saloon, where I, already dressed, was hurriedly having a cup of cocoa and bite of biscuit Weston had just brought me in from the pantry. "I feel half inclined to believe now in the old superstition about it being an unlucky day, though I always used to laugh at the notion!"

"There are plenty aboard who believe queerer things than that!" said Mr Fosset drily, with a meaning glance in my direction, eyeing my cocoa as if he rather fancied a cup himself. "I say, Haldane, that cocoa smells good!"

"It's not half bad, sir," I replied grinning. "Perhaps you would like some too, sir. Weston's got a lot more inside here, hot, just fetched from the galley!"

"I don't mind if I do have a cup," said he. "Will you join me, cap'en?"

"No, thanks; I'm too worried. I'll wait till breakfast," said the skipper, turning to go up on deck by the companion-way and hitching his cap off the hook by his cabin door. "You won't be long, I hope, eh?"

"I'll follow you up in a jiffey, sir, as soon as I have swallowed a toothful of this warm stuff to keep out the cold. Hi, steward?"

"Aye, aye, sir?" answered Weston, promptly putting his head out of his pantry, where he had been listening. "Cup of cocoa, sir?—yezzir."

"I say, Fosset," said the captain, who had lingered near awhile, as if in deep thought, as he stood with one foot on the lower step of the companion as if he were trying to recollect something, "I say, we must make some points to-day on the chart, you know!"

"Yes, sir. I don't think there'll be any difficulty about that. Do you?"

"No; the sun ought to be pretty clear at noon with a morning like this—clear enough, at all events, for us to find out the latitude and longitude."

"Just what I said to Spokeshave, sir, before I came down to call you awhile ago."

"Quite so."

"Aye, 'quite so,' sir."

Whereupon both sniggered at the skipper's apt mimicry of Master Conky's pet phrase, which Captain Applegarth pronounced in the little beggar's exact tone of voice, so like indeed being the imitation that I nearly choked myself while swallowing the balance of my cocoa, as I hastily drained my cup and rose to follow the skipper up the companion-ladder to the deck.

As Mr Fosset had said, there was a dead calm on the bosom of the deep, for the slight swell that remained after the gale on the previous evening, even up to the time of my going down below, had quite disappeared, the surface of the water being as smooth as glass as far as the horizon line and all aflash now with the rosy hue of sunrise to the eastward. The sky still preserved, however, the pale neutral tints of night in the west, and up to the zenith, where it merged into a faint and beautiful seagreen that lost itself imperceptibly in the warm colouring of the orient, which each moment became more and more intense in hue, heralding the approach of morn.

At last, up jumped the glorious orb of day, proudly, from his ocean bed, came with one bound as it were, a veritable globe of liquid fire, flooding the vast distant heaven and sea with a wealth of light and radiance that seemed to give life to everything around.

"There, Haldane," said Captain Applegarth, pointing over the taffrail at a lot of straggling masses of quasi-looking stringy stuff that came floating on top of the water close by the ship, resembling vegetable refuse discarded from Neptune's kitchen garden. "That's the gulf-weed Mr Fosset was just speaking about to me."

"Indeed, sir, I can't say much for its appearance. It looks more like a parcel of cauliflowers run to seed than anything else, sir!"

"Yes, that's not a bad simile of yours, my lad," he replied, moving nearer to the side and sending his keen sailorly glance alow and aloft, examining our old barquey to see how she fared after the storm. "If I can remember rightly, I think one of our best naturalists has given a similar description of it. Yes, that's the gulf-weed, or sargassum, or fucus natans, as the big guns variously call it in their Latin lingo. A rum sort of tackle, isn't it?"

"Yes, it does look funny, queer stuff, sir," said I, for I had never had the opportunity of noticing it before, all my voyages hitherto backwards and forwards across the Atlantic having been outside the limits of the uncanny looking gulf-weed. "Does it grow in the sea, sir? It looks so fresh and green."

"Well, that depends how you take it, my lad," returned the skipper rather absently, his attention being fixed on something forward, about which he evidently could not quite make up his mind, as there was a slight puzzled expression on his face. "You see, it is all through those long-winded chaps who won't be content with what the Creator gives them, but must put a cause and reason for everything beyond God's own will and pleasure, and who lay down arbitrary rules of their own for the guidance of Dame Nature, though, between you and I and the binnacle, Haldane, the old lady got on well enough for a good many scores of years—I'd be sorry to say how many—without their precious help! Now these gentlemen, who know everything, will have it that the gulf-weed grows deep down at the bottom of the sea and that only the branches and tendrils, or leaves, so to speak, float on the top and are visible to us."

"How strange, sir," said I. "Just like an aquarium plant. It is strange!"

"It would be, if true, for they would have to possess uncommonly long stems, as, in the Sagossa Sea, in the centre of the Gulf Stream, where the weed is most plentiful and to be seen at its freshest and most luxuriant growth, the recorded depth of the water is over four miles!"

"That is not likely, then," I observed in reply to this—"I mean, sir, the fact of its growing up from the bottom of the sea."

"Certainly not, my boy. Another wise man, of the same kidney as the long-winded chap of the theory I've just explained, says that the gulf-weed in its natural and original state grows on the rocky islets and promontories of the Florida coast and that it is torn thence by the action of the great Atlantic current that bears it many miles from its home; though, strangely enough, I have never seen any gulf-weed growing on rocks in the Gulf of Florida or in any of the adjacent seas, nor has any one else to my knowledge!"

"Then you do not believe it grows to anything at all, do you, sir?"

"No, I don't. My opinion is that it is a surface plant of old Neptune's rearing and that the warm water of the Gulf Stream breeds it and nourishes it, for at certain times it seems partly withered, and this could not be due to accident. The weed, I believe, is a sailor, like you and I, my lad, and lives and has its being on the sea, no matter what your longshore naturalists, who don't know much about it from personal observation, may say to the contrary. Hullo! though, my boy, look forrad there! Where has our spar anchor gone? I thought I noticed something and could not make out at first what it was. Look, youngster, and see whether you can see it!"

I was equally puzzled for the moment, for although our good ship rested as peacefully on the bosom of the deep as if she were moored, the raftlike bundle of spars, to which she had been made fast the night before, was now no longer to be seen bobbing up ahead, athwart our hawser as then.

Where could our wonderful floating anchor have gone?

The next moment, however, I saw what had happened, the mystery being easily explained by the calm.

"They've floated alongside, sir," I said. "I can see them under the counter on the port side, sir."

"Yes, of course, there they are, exemplifying the attraction of gravitation or some other long-winded theory of your scientific gentlemen," replied the skipper, who seemed to have got science on the brain this morning, being violently antagonistic to it, somehow or other. "Ah, Fosset, see, our anchor's come home without weighing. I think you'd better have the spars hauled on board and rig up the sticks again, now that they've served our time in another way—aye, and served it well, too."

"Aye, aye, sir," said the first mate, who had come up after us on the poop, looking, I couldn't help noticing, all the better for the good and early breakfast he had just finished. "I thought of getting them in just now, but waited to call you first."

"Well, you needn't wait any longer, Fosset," rejoined the skipper. "Pass the word for the bo'sun forrad."

"Yes, yes, sir. Quartermaster, call Masters!"

"Bo'sun, pipe all hands to hoist spars aboard!" These orders were roared out by Mr Fosset in rapid succession, and then in equally rapid sequences came the boatswain's whistle and hail to the men down the hatchway just along the deck.

All had a rare time of it, and an amount of "yoho-hoes-hoing" went round that it would have done anybody's heart good to hear; the first mate was bellowing out his orders and old Masters seeing to their proper execution by the busy hands and active feet, the skipper meanwhile standing on the poop, superintending matters with his keen eye, and woe to the lubber who bungled at a hitch or left a rope's end loose or brace slack!

Boat Ahoy!

By the time the sun was near the meridian our top-masts were up and the upper yards swayed aloft and crossed, making the old barquey all ataunto again and pretty nearly her old self, our broken bulwarks and smashed skylight betraying the only damage done by the storm, on deck, at all events.

"I 'calculate,' Fosset, as our Yankee friends would say, we may now cry spell O!" observed the skipper, who was highly pleased with the progress made in refitting the ship. "Tell the bo'sun to pipe the hands to dinner, and you and I had better go up on the bridge and see what we can do in the way of determining our position on the chart. That gulf-weed must have lost its bearings, I'm sure. It seems impossible to me that we could have drifted so far to the south as to bring us in the Stream!"

"An observation will soon settle the point, sir," replied the first mate, passing the word to Masters to knock off work. "Run down, Haldane, and get my sextant for me, there's a good chap! I left it on the cabin table, all ready. You'll find it there!"

"Belay, there!" sang out the skipper, as I started off towards the companion-way. "You may as well bring mine, too, while you're about it. Two heads are better than one, eh, Fosset?"

"Yes, sir, perhaps so," rejoined the other, before I got out of earshot. "It seems, though, as if we're going to have three on the job; for here comes Mr O'Neil with his sextant under his arm, evidently bent on the same errand!"

I soon was back with the instruments for the other two, and presently all three were at work taking the sun's altitude and measuring off the angle made by the luminary with the horizon.

A short delay ensued from our clocks being fast on account of our having drifted to the eastward of where they had last been set.

Then all at once Mr Fosset sang out.

"It's just noon, sir, now. The sun's crossing the meridian!"

"All right, make it so," replied the skipper. "Bos'un, strike eight bells."

"Aye, aye, sir," came back from old Masters away forward, and then followed the melodious chime of the ship's bell that hung immediately under the beak of the fo'c's'le. "Ting-ting, ting-ting, ting-ting, ting-ting."

"Now," going into the wheel-house, "let us look at the chronometer and see what Greenwich time says, and then tot up our reckonings!"

The two others followed him into the little room on the bridge, sitting down to a table in which the track chart of the ship's course lay, and all were busy for some few moments calculating and working out our latitude and longitude.

I was standing by the doorway after bringing up the correct time of the chronometers, which the skipper kept locked up in his own cabin to prevent their being meddled with, and I could see he looked puzzled, adding up and subtracting his figures over and over again, as if he thought he must have made some error, though he found that he invariably came to the same result.

"Well, Fosset," he cried at length, unable to restrain himself any longer. "What do you make it?"

"39° 20 minutes north latitude sir, and 47° 15 minutes west longitude."

"Faith, an' I make it the same, sir," also put in Garry O'Neil, the twain having worked out the reckoning long before the poor skipper. "Both of us agree to the virry minnit, sure, lavin' out the sicconds, sir!"

"By George!" exclaimed the skipper. "It's even worse than I thought."

"How, sir?" asked Mr Fosset with a smile on his face, no doubt chuckling to himself at being cleverer and wiser than Captain Applegarth, who would not believe we were in the Gulf Stream. "Don't you think us right, sir?"

"Oh, yes, Fosset; I agree with you myself. The reckoning is right enough, but father's the devil to pay!"

The skipper couldn't sacrifice the joke, though he was terribly put out.

"See here," he continued, "jabbing," with great noise and force the compasses with which he was measuring off our position, into the chart, as if that was in fault, while Fosset and O'Neil laughed. "Look where we are! I shouldn't have thought it possible for us to have been driven so far south, right into the Gulf Stream, as we are, for the current generally runs to the nor'-east'ards below the Banks."

"The stream has done it, though, sure enough," said Mr Fosset; "that and the gale, for the one has drifted us to the coast and the other pressed us down southwards; and between the two we're just fetched where we are, sir!"

"Well," replied the skipper, shrugging his shoulders, "you were right, Fosset, and I was wrong this morning. Let me see, though, how we have fetched here, if we can trace our course so far, from when we last took the sun."

"Sure, an' that was Friday, that baste of a day!" interposed Garry O'Neil, pointing to a place on the chart. "I worked at the rickonin' and I put it down meself, marking it with a red pencil."

"Yes; here it is, 42° 35 minutes north latitude, and longitude 50° 10 minutes west," said the skipper. "I worked it out also, on my own hook, and you and I tallied, if you recollect?"

"Of course we did, the divvil doubt it, sir," answered the second mate in his usual Irish fashion. "Thin, sor, we ran for five hours from that p'int on a west by south course, going between ten and twelve knots; for, though I didn't say it meself, Mister Fosset tould me the wind was freshinin' all the toime, so that we must have travelled about sixty miles, more or less."

"So that brings us to this blue mark here?"

"Yes, sor, to 42° 28 minutes north, and 51° 12 minutes west."

"Then we sailed right before the wind, due south?"

"Sure, an' we did that same afther Mister Haldane's will-o'-the-wisp for three hours, bedad!"

"Oh, Mr O'Neil," I pleaded, "please leave me out of it. I'm sure I've seen and heard enough of the ship already!"

"Be aisy, me darlint! It's only me fun, sure; and I mean ye no harrum," said he in his jocular way. "Arrah how can I lave ye out of the story when ye're the howl h'id and tail of it, sure, and without ye there'd be none to tile. Yes, cap'en, dear, sure, an' as I was a-saying when Haldane broke in upon me yarn, thray hours on this southerly course brought us here right where ye see me little finger, now!"

"About 51° 5 minutes west longitude and 41° 40 minutes north latitude. How did you get this, eh?"

"Faith, sor, the ould moon looked so moighty plisint that night that I took a lunar or two, jist to divart mesilf with, when Spokeshave wint below and there was nobody lift to poke fun at, sure!"

"A very useful sort of amusement," said the skipper drily. "And I see, too, you've put in the distance we've run, by dead reckoning, as about another fifty miles or so?"

"Yes, sor. The bo'sun hove the log ivery half hour till the engines stopped, an' he made out we were going sixteen knots an' more, bedad, so he s'id, whin we were running before the wind with full shtame on."

"That was very likely, O'Neil," replied the skipper, "but, after that, we altered course again, you know!"

"In course we did, sor, an' you'll say it marked roight down there on that line! We thin sailed west, a quarter south by compass, close-hauled on the starboard track, for two hours longer after you altered course ag'in an' bore up to the west'ard, keeping on till the ingines bhroke down, bad cess to 'em!"

"When was that?" asked the skipper slowly. "I was so worried and flurried at the moment that I forgot to take the time."

"Four bells in the first watch, sor," replied the Irishman quickly. "It was after we'd brought up poor Jackson from below, as Stoddart, the engineer, faith, was a sittin' near, jist before me, attindin' on the poor chap in the cabin, whin the rush of shtame came flyin' up the hatchway, faith, an' the sekrew stopped. We both of us looked at the saloon clock on the instant, sure, an' saw the toime, sor."

"That is the last mark on the chart, then?" said the old skipper meaningly, pencil and compass in hand, and still bending over the tell-tale track map spread out on the wheel-house table. "Since that, nobody knows how we've drifted!"

"Faith, no one, sor," returned Garry O'Neil, thinking the question was addressed to him. "Only, perhaps, the Pope, God bless him, or the Imporor of Chainy!"

All laughed at this, Captain Applegarth now losing his preoccupied air as if there were nothing to be gained, he thought, by dwelling any longer on the past.

It was wonderful, though, how we had drifted in the short interval, comparatively, that had elapsed since we became disabled!

As Mr Fosset had been the first to find out in the morning the Gulf Stream—that great river that runs a course of some two thousand miles in the middle of the ocean, keeping itself perfectly distinct from the surrounding water through which it flows, from its inception as a current in the Caribbean Sea to its final disposal in the North Atlantic—had first carried us in an easterly direction after we had broken-down so utterly; while the strong nor'-westerly gale, aided probably by the Arctic current, running due south from the Polar regions and which disputes the right of way with the Gulf Stream some little distance to the southwards of the great Banks of Newfoundland, had pressed upon the helpless hull of the Star of the North, bearing her away whither they pleased.

So, unable to resist either the winds or the waves, these combined forces had driven her off her course at an oblique angle, thus converting the nor'-easterly, or easterly drift proper, of the Gulf Stream into a true sou'-westerly one, taking us from latitude 41° 30 minutes north and longitude 51° 40 minutes west, where we were on the previous Friday night, when we were forced to lie-to, to our present position on the chart.

To put the case more concisely, the Star of the North had been carried for the distance of four degrees and a half exactly of longitude backward on her outward track to New York and some two degrees or thereabouts to the southwards, placing us as nearly as possible in the position the skipper had already indicated, a direction of some five hundred miles more or less from our proper course and about midway between Bermuda and the Azores, or Western Islands.

While Captain Applegarth was explaining this, as much for my benefit and instruction, I believe, as anything, a thought occurred to me.

"Are we not now, sir, in the track of all the homeward-bound ships sailing on the great circle from the West Indies and South American ports?"

The skipper looked at me steadily, "smelling a rat" at once.

"I suppose, Haldane," he said somewhat sternly, "you want to get me back to that infernal ship again? Not if I know it, my lad. As you told Mr O'Neil just now, we've all had enough and to spare of that vessel and the wild-goose chase she has led us from first to last. I won't hear another word about her, by Jingo!"

Just then old Masters, who had gone up in the foretop to set something right which had struck his sailor eye as not being altogether as it should be aboard the Star of the North, raised his arm to attract the attention of those on deck below him.

"Hullo, there, bo'sun!" called out the skipper, seeing him, for he seldom kept his glasses away from the rigging of the ship and things aloft. "What's the row, eh?"

"I sees summit to win'ard, sir."

"By George!" exclaimed the skipper in a tone that made every one laugh who heard, all but Masters; the coincidence was so comical after what Captain Applegarth had said only a minute before. "Not another 'ghost-ship,' I hope!"

"No, sir," growled the boatswain rather savagely. "It bean't no ghost-ship this time, though she ain't far off, I knows, to my thinkin'!"

He added the last words as if speaking to himself, but I heard him, and his remark stopped my mirth instanter.

"What is it, bo'sun, that you do see, then?" cried the skipper impatiently; "that is, if you see anything at all beyond some vision of your own imagination!"

"I ain't dreaming," hailed back old Masters, not quite catching what he said. "I sees summit as plain as possible out to win'ard. Aye, it be a-driftin' down athawt our hawser, too, cap'en. Why, hullo! I'm blessed. Boat ahoy!"

IN THE NICK OF TIME

"A boat!" exclaimed Captain Applegarth, his jesting manner changing instantly to one of earnest attention. "Where away?"

"On our starboard beam, sir," sang out Masters from the foretop. "About two points off, I fancies, sir."

"I can't see her," said the skipper, looking in the direction the boatswain had indicated. "I thought she was close-to from your hailing her."

"She's further away now than I thought, sir!" shouted old Masters in reply to this, after having another squirm over the topsail yard. "I'm blessed, though, if I ain't lost her, with the ship's head bobbing all round the compass. No; there she be ag'in, sir. No—yes—yes. There she is, about a mile or so off, sir, I'm thinkin'."

"By George, Masters, you think too much, I think!" the skipper retorted angrily. "You don't seem to know what you're saying, and I believe you've gone off your chump since you saw that 'ghost-ship,' as you called it! Go aloft, Haldane, and see what you can make of this blessed boat he says he sighted!"

I was already in the weather shrouds before the skipper gave me this order, and in another minute I was on the top beside the boatswain, who pointed out silently to me a little black speck in the distance apparently dancing about amid the waves, which were beginning to curl before an approaching breeze that was evidently springing up from the westwards. Fortunately, I had a pair of binoculars in my jacket pocket, and I immediately levelled the glasses at the object in view.

"Well, Haldane!" at last sang out the skipper impatiently from the end of the bridge, where he still stood, looking up at me with his chin cocked in the air. "What do you make it out to be, eh, my lad?"

"It's a boat sure enough, sir," I shouted down to him, without taking my eyes off it. "She's a long way off, though, sir, and I think she's drifting further away, too."

"The deuce!" exclaimed Captain Applegarth. "Can you see any one in the boat?"

"No—no—not distinctly, sir," I replied after another searching look. "Stay; I do—I do think there's a figure at one end! and, yes—yes—I'm sure I noticed something that appeared like a movement, but it might have been caused by the rocking of the sea."

"But don't you see anybody, or can't you make anything else out?"

"Only the boat, sir, and that a breeze seems coming up from the westward. I see a white line on the water along the horizon. That's all I can see, sir!"

"Well, that's not much use to us," he growled below, beginning his customary "quarter-deck walk" up and down the bridge. "I wish some one would come up from the engine-room to say they had repaired the cylinder and that we could go ahead again!"

Almost as soon as he spoke thus I noticed Mr Stokes, who I thought was lying down in his cabin, coming towards the forepart of the ship where we were, from the direction of the engine-room hatchway.

"Hullo, Stokes," said the skipper, catching sight of him at once with his eagle eye that seemed to take in everything that went on, whether his back was turned or not. "I thought you were on the sick list still, and ill. You oughtn't to be bustling about so soon after your accident, my dear fellow!"

"No, but I feel better!" replied the old chief, who, although he was still pale and shaky, had a more cheerful look on his face than the day before, when he appeared decidedly ill. "I've been down below and I'm glad to say Stoddart and the other artificers, who I must say have worked well without me, you will be glad to know, have got the cylinder cover on again. They've made a splendid job of it!"

"Stoddart himself is a splendid fellow," said the skipper enthusiastically. "Aye, and the rest of your staff, too, my dear Stokes. By George, you've brought us good news!"

"But that isn't all, cap'en," cried the old fellow, beaming over with a broad smile of quiet enjoyment at the surprise the skipper showed. "They say below that they'll be able to start the engines as soon as there's a full head of steam on! Now what do you think of that, sir? Isn't that good news?"

The skipper looked ready to embrace our fat chief, and I believe only refrained from giving this expression of his joy by the sight of poor Mr Stokes' bandaged arm, which was still in a sling.

He contented himself, therefore, with patting him tenderly on the back and walking round him admiringly, like a cat purring round a saucer of cream.

"By George!" he cried. "I feel as pleased as if my grandmother had left me five thousand pounds!"

"I wish she had," laughed the old chief. "I would ask to go shares!"

"And so you should, my boy; so you should," repeated the skipper with much heartiness, and as if he really meant it. "How soon do you think we shall be able to start, eh?"

"Very soon, I think, sir. The after-boiler fires were lit early this morning and they've been getting up steam ever since."

"That's good!" cried the skipper, stopping in his excited walk up and down the bridge, which he had again resumed, being unable to keep still, when he looked up, caught sight of me and hailed me.

"I say, Haldane?"

"Aye, aye, sir?" I sang out from the top, where I had remained with the boatswain on the look-out, and hearing likewise all that transpired beneath. "What do you want, sir?"

"I hope you're keeping your eye on that boat, my lad. If she is there we may be able to overhaul her yet, if you don't lose sight of her!"

"No fear of that, sir," I shouted back, pointing with my finger in the distance. "There she is, still to win'ard, pretty nearly flush with the water."

"Then she really is there all right, my lad. Keep your eye on her."

The funnels had been emitting smoke for some time without our having paid much attention to the fact, the fires of the fore-boilers having been kept in and banked ever since our breakdown, in order to work the pumps and capstan gear when required; but now steam, I noticed, came out as well as smoke, and I could hear it plainly roaring up the waste pipe, besides making a fearful row.

Presently another sound greeted my ears and made me jump.

It was that of the electric bell in the wheel-house, giving warning that those below in the emporium wished to make some communication.

Mr Stokes went to the voice-tube that led down thither from the bridge.

"What's the matter?" he roared into the mouthpiece so loud that I heard every word he uttered, although a-top of the mast. "Anything wrong?"

I couldn't of course catch the reply that came up the pipe; and it certainly was not a satisfactory one, for Mr Stokes turned round at once to the skipper, who immediately stopped his quarter-deck walk to hear what the chief had to say.

"They've corrected the propeller, sir," he exclaimed with a chuckle that made his fat form shake all over; "and Stoddart says he's only waiting for your signal to close the stop valves and let the steam into the cylinder."

"By George, he shan't wait a minute longer!" cried Captain Applegarth, moving the engine-room telegraph. "Go ahead, my hearties, as soon as you please! Hullo, there, forrad, I want a hand here at the wheel. I suppose the steam steering gear is all right again now?"

"Oh, yes, sir," replied Mr Stokes to this. "Grummet fixed that up on Sunday afternoon, he told me. I am sure it was done. I remember he was doing it when that man-of-war came alongside and spoke you."

"Strange I didn't see him at the job; he must have been pretty smart over it!" replied the skipper. "But I'm very glad it is done, though."

In answer to the skipper's signal a sudden blast of steam rushed up the funnel abaft the wheel-house, and I could feel the ship tremble as the shaft began to revolve and the propeller blades splashed the water astern with the familiar "thump-thump, thump-thump."

All hands joined in a hearty cheer, to which Masters and I in the top lent what aid our lungs could give.

"Steady amidship, there," sang out the skipper as the old barquey forged ahead once more. "Steady, my man."

"Aye, aye, sir," answered the foremost hand, Parrell, who had come from the fo'c's'le to take the first "trick" at the steering wheel on the bridge. "Steady it is."

"How does the boat bear now, Haldane?"

"Two points off our starboard bow, sir," I replied to this hail of the skipper. "She's about three miles off, I think, sir."

"All right," he shouted back to me. "Port your helm, there!"

"Aye, aye, sir," repeated Parrell. "Port, sir, it is."

"We're rising her fast now, sir," I called out after a short interval. "There's a man in the boat; yes, a man, sir. I can see him quite plainly now, and I'm sure I'm not mistaken!"

"Are you quite sure, my lad?"

"Quite sure, sir. And he's alive, too, I'm certain. Yes, sir; he moved then distinctly. I could see him plainly. Why, the boat is so near now that you ought to see it from the deck."

"And so I can, by Jingo, Haldane!" replied the captain, peering out ahead himself with a telescope from the end of the bridge. "I fancy I can see a second figure, and it looks like another man, too, lying down in the bows of the boat, as well as the figure at the stern, who seems to me to be holding up an oar or something!"

"Yes, there is, sir," I called out, stopping on my way down the rigging to have another look. After a pause I exclaimed, "I can see both of them, and with my naked eye. I can see them now!"

"Well, then, you'd better come down from aloft. Tell your friend, the boatswain, to come down as well. He'll be wanted at the fo'c's'le when we presently come up to the boat, as I trust we shall!"

"Lucky Masters saw the boat, sir," said I when I reached the deck and up to the skipper's side again. "But even more fortunate it is for the poor fellows that our engines are working again, sir, for otherwise we could not have been able to get up to the boat and save them."

"It isn't luck, my boy," observed Mr Stokes, whom the death of poor Jackson and his own narrow escape from a like fate had led to think of other matters besides those connected with his mundane profession. "It's Providence!"

An Appeal For Aid

"Aye, that's the better way of looking at it," chimed in the skipper, raising his arm at the same time from his station at the end of the bridge, where he was conning the ship. He then called out sharply, to enforce the signal.

"Luff up, you lubber, luff!"

"Luff it is, sir," rejoined the helmsman, rapidly turning round the spokes of the little steam steering wheel. "It's hard over now, sir."

"Steady there," next sang out the captain. "Steady, my man!"

"Aye, aye, sir," repeated the parrot-like Tom Parrell, bringing the helm amidships again. "Steady it is!"

"By George, we're nearing the boat fast!" cried the skipper after another short pause, during which we had been going ahead full speed, with a quick "thump-thump, thump-thump" of the propeller and the water foaming past our bows. "Starboard, Parrell! Starboard a bit now!"

"Aye, aye, sir," came again the helmsman's answering cry from the wheel-house. "Starboard it is, sir!"

"Keep her so. A trifle more off. Steady!"

"Steady it is, sir!"

"Now down with it, Parrell!" sang out the skipper, bringing his hand instanter on the handle of the engine-room gong, which he sounded twice, directing those in charge below to reduce speed, while he hailed old Masters on the fo'c's'le. "Hi, bo'sun! Look-out there forrad with your rope's end to heave to the poor fellows! We're just coming alongside the boat."

"Aye, aye, sir!" replied Masters promptly, keeping one eye on the skipper on the bridge and the other directed to the little craft we were approaching, and now close to our port bow. "We're all ready forrad, sir. Mind you don't run her down, sir. She's nearly under our forefoot."

"All right, bo'sun," returned the skipper. "Port, Parrell!"

"Port it is, sir," repeated Tom Parrell. "Two points off."

"Steady, man, steady," continued the skipper, holding his hand up again. "Boat ahoy! Stand by. We're going to throw you a rope!"

At the same instant Captain Applegarth sounded the engine-room gong again, bringing the Star of the North to a dead stop as we steamed up to the boat slanting-wise, the steamer having just sufficient way on her when the screw shaft ceased revolving, to glide gently up to the very spot where the little floating waif was gently bobbing up and down on the wave right ahead of us, and barely half a dozen yards away, drifting, at the will of the wind, without any guidance from its occupants, who seemingly were unaware of our approach.

"Boat ahoy!" shouted the skipper once more, raising his voice to a louder key. "Look-out, there!"

The men in the bows of the boat still remained in the same attitude, as if unconscious or dead; but the other in the stern-sheets appeared to hear the skipper's hail, for he half-turned his head and uttered a feeble sort of noise and made a feeble motion with one of his hands.

"Now's your time, bo'sun!" cried Captain Applegarth. "Heave that line, sharp!"

"Aye, aye, sir," roared out Masters in his gruff tones. "Stand by, below there!"

With that the coil of half-inch rope which he held looped on his arm made a circling whirl through the air, the end falling right across the gunwales of the boat, close to the after thwart, where sat the second of the castaways, who eagerly stretched out his hand to clutch at it.

But, unfortunately, he failed to grasp it, and the exertion evidently being too much for him, for he tumbled forward on his face at the bottom of the boat, while the rope slipped over the side into the water, coming back home to us alongside the old barquey on the next send of the sea, the heavy roll of our ship when she brought up broadside-on, as well as the weight of the line saturated with water, fetching it in to us all the sooner.

"Poor fellows; they can't help themselves!" cried the skipper, who had watched the boatswain's throw and its unsatisfactory result with the deepest interest. "Bear a hand there, some one forrad, and have another try to reach them. The boat's drifting past, and we'll have to go astern to board her in another minute, if you don't look sharp!"

Having climbed into the fore-rigging, however, so as to have a good look at the boat and its occupants as we neared them, I was quite as quick as the skipper to notice what had happened, having, indeed, foreseen the contingency before it occurred.

So, ere Masters or any of the other men could stir a hand, having made up my mind what to do, I had seized hold of part of the slack of the line that remained inboard and, plunging into the sea, swam towards the boat.

A couple of strokes, combined with the forward impetus of my leap overboard, took me up to the little craft, and in a jiffey I had grasped the gunwale aft and clambered within her, securing the end of the line I had round one of the thwarts at once, amid the ringing cheers of the skipper and my shipmates in the old barquey, who proceeded to haul us up alongside without further delay, tugging away at the tar rope I had hitched on, yo-heave-hoing and hurrahing in one and the same breath right lustily!

So smart were they, so instantaneous had been the action of the moment during the episode, that we were close in to the ship's side and under her conning, immediately below the port end of the bridge, where the skipper stood leaning over the rail and surveying operations, before I had time actually to look round so as to have a nearer view of the unfortunate men whom we had so providentially rescued.

When I did though, one glance was enough.

I was horror stricken at the sight that met my eyes.

The man whom I had observed when we were yet some distance off to be lying huddled up in the bows motionless, as if dying or already dead, I now saw had received a horrible wound on the top of his head that had very nearly smashed in the skull, besides almost severing one of his ears which was hanging from the cheek bone, attached by a mere scrap of skin, the bottom boards of the boat near him being stained with blood that had flowed from the cut, and his hair likewise matted together with gore. Oh, it was horrible to see! He was not dead, however, as I had thought, but only in a state of stupor, breathing heavily and making a strange stertorous sound as if snoring.

His fellow-sufferer aft, who did not appear to have suffered so much as his comrade, had seemingly swooned from exhaustion or exposure; as, on my putting my arm round him and lifting up his bent head, the man opened his eyes and murmured something faintly in some foreign lingo—Spanish, I think it was; at any rate a language I did not understand.

But I was unable to notice anything beyond these details, which I grasped in that one hurried glance; for as I was in the act of raising up the poor chap in the stern-sheets, the skipper hailed me from the bridge above.

"Below there!" he sang out. "How are the poor fellows? Are they alive, Haldane?"

"They are in a bad way, sir," I replied. "They've got the life left in them and that's all, I'm afraid!"

"Neither dead, then?"

"No, sir."

"Bravo! 'whilst there's life there's hope,'" cried the skipper in a cheery tone. "Are they quite helpless, do you think, Haldane—I mean quite unable to climb up the side?"

"Quite unable, sir," I answered. "One's unconscious, and I don't think the other could move an inch if he tried!"

"Then we must haul 'em up," said Captain Applegarth, turning to Masters, who had popped his head over the bulwarks and was now looking down into the boat, like the rest of the hands on board. "I say, bo'sun, can't you rig up a chair or something that we can lower down for the poor fellows?"

"Aye, aye, sir," responded old Masters, drawing in his head from the bulwarks and disappearing from my view as I looked upwards from the stern-sheets, where I was still holding up the slowly-recovering man. "I'll rig up a whip from the foreyard and we can let down a hammock for 'em, tricing up one at a time."

"Stay, cap'en," cried Mr Fosset as the boatswain went bustling off, I suppose, though of course from my position I could not see him, to carry out this plan of his. "The davits here amidship are all right, as well as the tackle of our cutter that had got washed away in the gale. Wouldn't it be easier to let down the falls, sir, and run up the boat all standing with the poor fellows in her as they are?"

"By George, the very thing, Fosset!" exclaimed the skipper, accepting the suggestion with alacrity. "It will save the poor fellows a lot of jolting, and be all the easier for us, as you say. Besides, the little craft will come in handy for us, as we're rather short of boats just now!"

"Short of boats, sir!" repeated the first mate ironically as he set to work at once, with the help of a couple of the hands who jumped to his side to assist him the moment he spoke, casting off the lashings of the davits so as to rig them outwards, letting go at the same time the hooks of the fall blocks and overhauling the running gear. "Why, sir, we haven't even the dinghy left intact after that clean sweep we had from the wave that pooped us!"

"Oh, aye, I know that well enough," said the skipper drily. "But, look alive now, Fosset, with that tackle, and don't be a month of Sundays over the job! Send down two of the cutter's crew to overrun the falls and drop down into the boat. They can help Haldane in holding up that poor chap astern and also bear a hand in hoisting up."

"All right, sir; we're just ready," shouted back the first mate as he gave the word to let go. "Lower away there with the slack of those falls. Easy, my man, gently does it!"

In another instant down came the fall blocks, with one of the hands hanging on to each, the men alighting "gingerly" on the thwarts of the boat in the bow and stern of the little craft, which became immersed almost up to the gunwales with the additional weight.

This was only for a moment, for the next minute Mr Fosset gave the signal to "hoist away," the falls having been hooked on beneath the thwarts in a jiffey, and up we all went in mid air, "between the devil and the deep sea," as we say afloat sometimes!

"Bravo!" cried the skipper when we reached the level of the gangway and were all able to step out on to the deck. "That's very handsomely done, my lads! Now let us see about lifting the poor fellows out. That chap there in the bows seems in a very bad way! You'd better carry him into the cuddy at once and let Mr O'Neil look after him."

"Indade, I will, sor," said our doctor-mate, who was standing near by with a spirit flask in one hand and a medicine glass in the other, ready to give immediate succour to the rescued men. "Carry the poor beggar along an' I'll be afther ye in a minnit; for this other misfortunate gossoon here looks as if he wouldn't be the worst for a dhrop of good brandy, an' faith, I'll say to him fourst, avic!"

So saying the Irishman poured some of the contents of the spirit flask into the glass, which he held to the lips of the man. Mr Fosset and I were supporting him in our arms against the side of the boat, whence we had just removed him.

The poor fellow's strength returned to him almost as soon as he had sipped a drop or two of the brandy, and, starting away from the first mate and myself, as if no longer needing our aid, he stood erect on the deck.

"Mil gracias, amigos," he said, with a polite inclination of his head, in apology like for shaking himself free from us. "Estoy major!"

Captain Applegarth stepped up to him.

"I am sorry I can't speak Spanish, sir, though I understand you to say you're better. We're Englishmen all on board this ship, sir, and I'm glad we've been able to pick you up."

The eyes of the man glistened and a pleased expression stole over his face.

"What! You are English! he exclaimed excitedly. But—but I'm an American! Only I've been so long in Venezuela amongst Spaniards that I sometimes forget my own language."

Our skipper was equally delighted.

"By George!" he said. "I was sure you were no blessed foreigner, in spite of your lingo, sir! Welcome on board the Star of the North."

The stranger looked round and his manner changed at once, and he pointed towards our funnels anxiously and their escaping steam.

"A steam vessel, eh!"

"Yes, sir," said the skipper. "I command her, sir. Cap'en Applegarth, at your service!"

"The deuce! I was forgetting. We passed you last night, I remember now! and you're the captain?"

"Aye!" replied the skipper, not quite making out what the other was driving at. "I'm captain of this ship!"

"Merciful Heavens!" cried the rescued man, falling on his knees on the deck and bursting into a passion of sobs. "Thanks be to God! Yes, thanks be to God! You will save her, captain. You will save her?"

The skipper thought the evident suffering he had gone through had turned his brain.

"Save who?" he asked, adding in a kinder tone: "Of course, we'll do anything and everything we can for you, but I must know my bearings first, my friend."

The man was on his feet at once.

"I am not mad, captain, as you appear to think. I can see from your manner you think so," he said. "I want you to save my Elsie, my only child, my little daughter, whom those villains, those black devils, are carrying off!"

"Your only child, your daughter—black devils," echoed Captain Applegarth, astonished at the poor man's speech and at his wild and agonised look. "What do you mean, sir?"

"Heavens! We're losing time while those scoundrels are getting away with the ship!" exclaimed the other frantically and walking to and fro in a most excited state. "Fire up the engines, pile on the coals and steam like the devil! and go in chase of her, my good captain, you will? For Heaven's sake, captain, for the love of God, start at once in chase of her!"

"In chase of whom?" asked Captain Applegarth, still believing him to be out of his mind. "In chase of whom?"

The man uttered a heart-rending cry, in which anger, grief and piteous appeal were alike blended.

"In chase of a band of black miscreants who have committed murder and piracy on the high seas!" he ejaculated in broken accents. "The blood of a number of white men massacred by treacherous negroes calls for vengeance, the safety of a young girl and the lives of your brother sailors still on board the ship calls to you for help and rescue! Great Heaven! Will you stand idly by and not render the aid you can? Think, captain, a little girl like your own daughter—my Elsie, my little one! Yes, and white men, your brothers, and sailors, too, like yourselves, at the mercy of a gang of black ruffians! Sir, will you help them or not?"

We Start in Chase of the Ship

The effect of this appeal was electrical, not only on the skipper, but on all of us standing by.

"Great heavens, man!" cried the captain, staring at the other in wild astonishment. "What do you mean? I cannot understand you, sir. Your ship, you say—"

"My words are plain enough, captain," said the stranger, interrupting the skipper. "Our ship, the Saint Pierre, is in the possession of a gang of Haytian negroes who rose on us while we were on the high seas and murdered most of the officers and the crew. They then threw poor Captain Alphonse, who commanded her, overboard, after they had half killed him, and the rest of the unfortunate sailors and passengers, amongst them my little daughter, are now at the mercy of the black devils!"

"My God!" exclaimed the skipper, confounded by this lucid statement. "And you, sir?"

"I am an American!" said the other with a proud air, drawing himself up to his full height of six feet and more and with his eyes flashing, while a red flush mounted to his cheeks, which had formerly been deadly pale. "I'm a white man, captain, and it's not likely I would stand by and see people of my own colour butchered! Of course, sir, I went to the poor captain's assistance, but then the murderers served me almost as badly as they did him, chucking me overboard after him."

"I beg your pardon, sir, I'm sure, for appearing to doubt your story," cried the skipper, stretching forward his hand, which the other eagerly grasped. "The fact is, sir, I thought at first your sufferings had set your head wrong; but now I need hardly say I believe thoroughly every word you've told us, and you may rely on my aid and that of every man aboard here to help you and yours. There's my hand on it, sir, and my word you'll find as good as my bond, so sure as my name is Jack Applegarth!"

"And mine, captain, is Vereker, Colonel Vereker, at your service," returned the other, reciprocating the skipper's cordiality as he looked him straight in the face, holding his hand the while in a firm grip. He let go the skipper's fist, however, the next moment and a puzzled expression came into his eyes as he glanced round occasionally, apparently in search of some one or other. "Heavens! Where's my unfortunate comrade who was in the boat with me—poor Captain Alphonse? Alas, I had forgotten him!"

"We have not forgotten him, though, colonel," said the skipper smiling. "He has been carried below to the saloon on the maindeck, where my second mate, Mr O'Neil, who is a qualified surgeon, is now attending to his injuries. He has been terribly mauled, poor fellow; we could see that!"

"Aye, terribly!" repeated the other with a shudder, as if the recollection of all he and his fellow-sufferers had gone through suddenly came back to him at the moment. "But, great Heavens! captain, we're losing time and that accursed ship with those scoundrels and our remaining comrades, and with my darling child on board, is speeding away while we're talking here. You will, will you not, Señor Applegarth, go in pursuit of her, my friend?"

"By George I will, colonel; I will at once—immediately—if you'll tell me her bearings," cried the skipper excitedly. "When was it this terrible affair happened? When did you leave the ship, and where?"

"The revolt of the blacks, or mutiny, I should call it, captain, broke out four days ago, on last Friday, indeed, sir," said the American promptly in his deep musical voice, and whose foreign accent obliterated all trace of the unmelodious Yankee twang. "But we kept the rascals at bay until last night, soon after sundown, when they made an ugly rush and overpowered us. Captain Alphonse had just sighted your vessel in the distance and was burning a blue light over the stern to attract your attention, so as to get assistance at the time this happened."

"Was yours a large, full-rigged ship?"

"Yes, sir, the Saint Pierre is of good size and had all her sails set," replied the other to the skipper's question. "We were running before the wind with our helm lashed amidship, as it had been since the previous Friday, for we were all too busy defending our lives to think of attending to the ship."

"Steering about nor'-east, I suppose?"

"Confound it, captain!" said the colonel impatiently. "We were drifting, I tell you, sir, at the mercy of the elements, and heaven only knows how we were going! Fortunately, the weather was pretty fair, save the very day the mutiny broke out, when it blew heavily and our canvas got split to pieces as there was no one to go aloft and take it in. Otherwise we must have gone to the bottom!"

"By George!" exclaimed the skipper, turning round to old Masters and myself, who were still standing by with the hands who had come aft to haul up the boat. "Then my bo'sun here, and this young officer were right when they declared they saw a large full-rigged ship to the westward of us, though I only noticed the light of your flare-up. You were too far off for me to make you out."

"Ojala!" ejaculated the American, reverting again to the familiar Spanish tongue in his emotion. "Would to God, captain, you had seen us!"

"It would have been useless if I had, my friend," said the skipper soothingly. "We couldn't move to come to your assistance if every soul on board had seen you and known your peril, sir; for our engines were broken-down and we were not able to get up steam again until late this afternoon, when we ran down to pick you up!"

"But, sir," hastily whispered the colonel, suppressing a sob of emotion, "you can and will steam now?"

"Why ask?" replied the skipper. "The moment we know where to go in search of your ship, that very moment we'll start and try to overhaul her. You say you quitted her last night?"

"Quitted her? We were thrown overboard, sir, by the black devils!"

Captain Applegarth in reply said calmly, "Yes, yes, of course," accepting the correction and trying by his manner to soothe the infuriated man. "But what time was that?"

"I can't say the exact hour," replied the American, whose vexed tone showed that the captain's methodical mode of setting to work did not quite harmonise with the excited state of his feelings. "I think, however, it must have been nearly seven o'clock, as well, sir, as I can remember."

Then I chimed in. "Ah!" I exclaimed quickly, "that was just the very time that Masters and I heard the shooting in the distance to win'ard, and it was six bells in the second dog watch!"

"So it were, Master Haldane; so it were," agreed the old boatswain, looking from me to the skipper and then at Colonel Vereker. "Well, I'm blowed! and I'm glad, then, for that there ghost-ship wor a rael ship arter all said and done. Now who was right, I'd like to know?"

"Of course it was a real ship, you old dotard!" said the skipper gruffly and looking angrily at him. "Of course it was," he added, while our new acquaintance looked at us, unable, naturally, to understand the mystical allusion; but Captain Applegarth soon turned his roving thoughts into another direction by asking him a second question. "How long did you keep in sight of your vessel after leaving her, colonel, do you think?"

"She was in full view of us at sunrise this morning," replied the American. "The boat in which we were adrift kept near her all night as there was very little wind, if any. A slight breeze sprang up shortly after the sun rose and she then steadily increased her distance from us as the day wore on, finally disappearing from my gaze about noon, and taking with her my little darling, my pet, my Elsie."

The poor fellow broke down again at this point throwing up his hands passionately and burying his face in them, his whole frame convulsed with sobs, though not a man present thought his emotion a thing to be ashamed of, all of us being deeply interested in his narrative and as anxious as himself for the skipper to start off in pursuit of the black mutineers and pirates.

We were not long kept in suspense, the colonel's last words and violent burst of emotion apparently touching our "old man's" feelings deeply, and hastening his decision.

"Cheer up, sir, cheer up," said he to the other, whose shoulders still shook with his deep hysterical sobs. "And we'll find your little girl yet for you all right, and restore her to you, and we'll settle matters too, with those scoundrels, I promise. Now tell me how far off do you think the ship must have drifted from us by now, Mr Fosset."

"Between twenty and thirty miles, sir," replied the first mate. "She was lighter than us, and of course she had the advantage of what wind there has been, though, thank goodness, that has been little enough!"

"Away to the nor'-east, I suppose?"

"Aye, aye, sir," said Mr Fosset. "The breeze, what there was, has been from the sou'-east and the current trends in the same direction."

"Then if we steer east-nor'-east we ought to pick her up soon?"

"Not a doubt of it, sir. We have four good hours of daylight left yet!"

"Precisely my opinion," cried the skipper. "Mr Stokes, will the engines stand full speed now, do you think?"

"Oh, yes, sir," replied the old chief, who with the rest of us was all agog to be after the strange ship again, now that he had heard the colonel's explanation of her true character, "if you'll send some one below to tell Stoddart what you want. I would go myself, but I'm rather shaky in getting down the hatchway as yet. I twisted my arm just now when I went down."

"That's all right. Stoddart, I am sure, will excuse you," said the skipper kindly, and turning to me he added: "You, Haldane, run down and tell Stoddart we want all the steam we can get. He won't spare the engines, I know, when he knows the circumstances of the case, and you will explain matters!"

So saying, the skipper started off forwards in the direction of the bridge, while I dived down the engine-room hatchway, reaching the machinery-flat just as the "old man" sounded the gong to put on full speed ahead, the telegraph working quick as if he were in a great hurry!

Ere I could tell my story Stoddart sent an answering blast up the steam pipe to let the skipper know his signal was being attended to; and then, pulling back the lever of the throttle valve, the piston began to go up and down, the cylinder oscillated from side to side and the crank shaft revolved at first slowly, but presently faster and faster until we were now going to the utmost of our pace.

All this while I was yarning away, though I had to shout to the top of my voice in order to overcome the noise of the machinery, as I described all that had occurred.

I did not speak to unheeding ears.

"By Jove, Haldane!" cried Stoddart, who was a man of action if ever there was one. "The cylinder is all right again and will bear any pressure now, and I tell you what it is, the old barquey shall steam along in pursuit of those demons faster than she ever went in her life since she was launched and engined!"

"I am with you there, old fellow," said Grummet, our third engineer, hastening towards the stoke-hold. "I'll go down and see the firemen and stir them up and put some more oilers to work in the screw well, to lubricate the shaft so as to prevent the bearings from overheating."

"That's your sort, my hearty," said Stoddart. "So you can return on deck, Haldane, and tell the skipper and Mr Stokes that everything shall be done down here by us to overhaul your 'ghost-ship.'"

He laughed as he uttered this little piece of chaff at my expense, the story being now the common property of everybody on board, and I laughed, too, as I ran up the hatchway with my clothes nearly dry again, even drying in the short space of time I had been in the hot atmosphere below, although, goodness knows, they had been wet enough when I had gone down, having had no time or opportunity to shift them after my dip overboard when taking the line to the drifting boat.

On reaching the main deck I met Spokeshave.

He was coming out from the saloon, and from his puffy face and corpulent appearance generally, he looked as if he had been making a haul on the steward's pantry, although he had not long had his dinner and it was a good way off tea time.

"Hullo!" he cried out on seeing me. "I say, that chap O'Neil is having a fine go of it playing at doctoring. He has got a lot of ugly long knives and saws laid out on the cuddy table and I think he's going to cut off the chap's leg!"

"Which chap do you mean?" I asked; "not the colonel?"

"Aye," said he. "The chap with the moustache and long hair, like Hamlet, you know!"

"My good chap," said I, "you seem to know a good deal about other chaps, or think you do, but I never heard before of Hamlet having a moustache like a life-guardsman! Irving doesn't wear one when he takes the part, if I recollect right, my joker. You think yourself mighty knowing!"

"Quite so," replied Master Spokeshave, using his favourite phrase as usual. "But you don't call Irving Shakespeare, Haldane, do ye?"

"I don't know anything of the matter, old boy. I am not so well informed as you are concerning the dramatic world, Spokeshave. I know you're a regular authority or 'toffer,' if you like, on the subject. Don't you think, however, you're a bit hard on poor Irving, who, I've no doubt, would take a word of advice from you if you spoke kindly to him and without that cruel sarcasm which you're apt to use?"

The little beggar actually sniggered over this, being of the opinion that I was paying a just tribute to his histrionic acumen and judgement in things theatrical, on which he prided himself on account of his having appeared once behind the footlights in a theatre in Liverpool, as a "super," I believe, and in a part where he had nothing to say!

"Quite so, Haldane; quite so," chuckled Spokeshave, as pleased as Punch at the imaginary compliment. "I do believe I could teach Irving a thing or two if I had the mind to!"

"Yes, you donkey, if you had the mind to," said I witheringly, by giving an emphasis he did not mean to his own words. "'Very like a whale,' as our old friend Polonius says in the play, the real Hamlet, I mean, my boy, not your version of it. 'Very like a whale,' indeed!"

"I'm sure, Mr Haldane," he answered loftily, cocking his long nose in the air with a supercilious sniff, "I don't know what ye mean."

"And I've no time to waste telling you now," returned I.

At that moment we emerged on the open deck from under the back of the poop, where we had been losing our time and talking nonsense; and, looking towards the bridge forward, I saw Colonel Vereker, the very person about whom we had been speaking, standing by the side of the skipper.

"O, Lor', Spokeshave, what a crammer!" I cried. "You said not a moment ago that Garry O'Neil was about to cut off the colonel's leg, while there he is standing there, all right!"

"I didn't say he had cut it off yet," he retorted; "I said he was going to cut it off. O'Neil told me so himself."

"Then," said I, "instead of cutting off the poor colonel's leg, he was only 'pulling your leg,' my joker!"

The cross-grained little beggar, however, did not seem to quite understand the term I employed thus in joke, though it was used at sea to express the fact of "taking a rise" out of any one, and a common enough saying.

"I'm not the only fellow who tells crammers," he grimly muttered. "How about that yarn of yours of the blessed 'ghost-ship' you saw the other night, I'd like to know. I believe, too, that the colonel, as you call him, is only an impostor and that the skipper is going on just such a wild-goose chase after this ship of his, which he says was captured by pirates, as he did that Friday hunting your Flying Dutchman! wasting our time with your idiotic story. Pirates and niggers, indeed! Why, this chap, I'll bet, is a nigger himself, and more of a pirate than any one we'll come across if we steam from here to the North Pole. Put that in your pipe and smoke it, Dick Haldane; you and your confounded 'ghost-ship' together! Such utter humbug and nonsense, and thinking you take people in with such yarns in these days!"

Full Speed Ahead

I was so indignant at what the spiteful little brute said that I incontinently turned on my heel and left him without another word, going forwards towards the bridge to give the skipper Stoddart's message.

Here, the sight of Colonel Vereker's grand figure—one that would be remarkable anywhere, towering above the rail and almost herculean in its massive proportions, coupled with the sad look in his noble face, and which reminded me somehow or other of one of the pictures of the old Cavaliers of the Stuart days, made me resent the more the baseless imputation of his being an imposter.

The idea of such a thing being possible could only have occurred to an ignoble mind like that of Spokeshave; for one single glance at the distinguished-looking gentleman's speaking countenance, with its finely-chiselled features and lofty open brow, would have satisfied any unprejudiced person that his was a nature incompatible with deceit and meanness, even in the most remote degree.

"Well, young Haldane!" exclaimed old Mr Stokes, whom I found with Captain Applegarth and the colonel when I reached the wheel-house.

"What do those smart chaps of mine down below say, hey, my boy?"

His face beamed as he spoke and he looked as if he would have liked to have rubbed his hands together in his old way when he felt particularly jolly, but unfortunately his crippled arm, which was still in a sling, prevented that!

"Oh, that's all right, sir," I replied in an equally cheery tone, the old chief's genial address making me forget at once my anger at Spokeshave's contemptible nonsense. "Mr Stoddart directed me to tell the cap'en that he may go on ahead as usual, as he likes, for everything has been made taut and secure below and there need be no fear of another mishap. He says he intends driving the engines as they were never driven before, and he has put every fireman and oiler in the stoke-hold on the job."

"Bravo!" cried the skipper, sounding the gong again and yelling down the voice-tube that led below like one possessed. "Fire up, below there, and let her rip!"

"Dear, dear," panted Mr Stokes, whose fears for his engines, which he regarded with the affection which a young mother might bestow on her first baby, began to overcome his interest in the chase after the black pirates.

"I hope you and Stoddart, between you, won't be rash, cap'en. I hope—I do hope you won't!"

"Nonsense, Stokes, you old croker; just you shut up!" said the skipper. "Keep her steady, east-nor'-east, helmsman! Now, my dear colonel, at last we really are after those infernal rascals in earnest; and, sir, between you and me and the binnacle, we'll be up to them before long before nightfall, I'll wager!"

"I hope to heaven we will, Señor Applegarth," replied the other sadly, but eagerly. "But, alas! the ocean is wide, and we may miss the ship. I cannot bear to think of it!"

"Oh, but we won't miss her!" said the skipper confidently, and he was the last man to give up hope. "Take my davy for that, sir. She must be within a radius of from twenty to thirty miles of our present bearings on the chart, somewhere here away to the eastwards, sir; and if we make a long leg to leeward and then bear up to the north'ard and west'ard again, we'll overhaul her—I'm sure of it—yes, sure of it, in no time. Look, colonel, look how we're going now. By George, ain't that a bow wave for you, sir, and just see our wake astern!"

The old barquey was certainly steaming ahead at a great rate, the sea coming up before her in a high ridge that nearly topped the fo'c's'le, and welling under her counter on either hand in undulating furrows that spread out beneath her stern in the form of a broad arrow, widening their distance apart as she moved onward, while the space between was frosted as if with silver by the white foam churned up by the ever-whirling propeller blades, beating the water with their rhythmical iteration, thump-thump, thump-thump, thump-thump!

There was no "racing" of the screw now, for Neptune was in one of his quiet moods and there were no big rollers to surmount, or deep wave valleys to descend into; consequently the old barquey had no excuse for giving way to any gambolling propensities in the water of pitching and tossing, steaming away on an even keel and using every inch of power of her engines, with not an ounce to waste in the way of mis-spent force!

And so on we went, tearing through the water, a blue sky overhead unflecked by a single cloud, a blue sea around that sparkled in sunshine and reflected harmonies of azure and gold, save where the bright fresh western breeze rippled its surface with laughing wavelets that chuckled as they splashed the spray into each other's faces, or where we passed a stray scrap of gulf-weed with its long yellow filaments spread out like fingers vainly clutching at the wavelets as if imploring them to be still, or where again the dense black smoke from our funnels made a canopy in the sky athwart our track, obscuring the shimmering surface of the deep with a grim path of shadow that checked the mirth of the lisping young wavelets and even awed the sunshine when it came in closer contact anon, as the wind waved it this way and that at its will.

"Hi, bo'sun!" shouted out the skipper presently, after carrying on like this for a goodish spell, the deck working beneath our feet and the Star of the North seeming to be flying through water and air alike by a series of leaps and bounds, quivering down to her very kelson with the sustained motion and the ever-driving impulse of her masterful engines spurring her onward. "How is she going now, eh?"

Old Masters was away aft on the poop hauling in the patent log, which had been hove over the side on our beginning the run, and the next minute, as soon as he was able to look at the index of the instrument, he answered the skipper's question.

"Sixteen knots, sir!" he sang out, and then we could hear the old sea dog add his customary comment, whether of approval or discontent, "Well, I'm blowed!"

"By George, colonel!" cried Captain Applegarth to our melancholy-looking guest at his side. "We're going sixteen knots, sir; just think of that! I didn't believe the dear old barquey had it in her!"

"It is a good, wonderful speed, captain," replied the other, who, I noticed, was looking even more exhausted now than when we removed him from the boat. "Remember, though, sir, the Saint Pierre is sailing on all this time before the wind, as she was this morning and must be miles ahead of us!"

"Aye, I know she's going; or at least, I suppose so, and I've made every allowance for that in my calculation of her whereabouts," returned our skipper, in nowise daunted by the colonel's argument. "But if she had every rag set that she could carry, she couldn't go more than three or four knots at the most, in this light breeze; and for every foot she covers we're going five!"

"That is true," said the American, with a very weary and absent look on his face. "But—but I'm afraid we may be too late after all! I—I'm—God protect—my—my—"

"The fact is, my dear sir," cried the skipper abruptly, interrupting him as the other hesitated in his speech, turning a deadly white and clutching at the bridge rail in front of him, as if to save himself from falling or fainting. "You're completely worn out and your nerves shaken! Why, you can't have had much, if any, sleep the last three or four days—not since that rumpus broke out aboard your ship, eh?"

"Heavens!" ejaculated the other. "I don't think I have closed my eyes, señor, since Friday, excepting when I was drifting in the boat, part of which time I must have been senseless; for though I recollect seeing your vessel and trying to signal her by holding up a piece of the bottom planking of the boat, as we hadn't oar or sail in her, I have no remembrance of seeing your vessel steaming up to help us, or of this brave young gentleman here jumping into the water and swimming to our assistance, as you tell me, captain, that he gallantly did. Believe me, sir, I shall never forget you, and I shall be ever and eternally grateful to you for that noble act of yours!"

He half-turned and bowed to me politely as he said this, but I was too much confused by his exaggerated estimate of what I had done to say anything at the moment in reply. And, after all, it was only a very simple thing to do, to swim with a line to a boat; any other fellow could have done the same, and would have done it under the same circumstances.

The skipper, however, spoke for me.

"Come, come, sir," he said. "Haldane only did his duty, like the brave lad he is; and I'm sure you only make him uncomfortable by your thanks. I want you, colonel, to go below and have a little rest and some refreshment. Besides, I promised Mr O'Neil to send you down to have your wounded leg dressed and seen to more than half an hour ago, when he came up on deck after attending to that other poor chap, and yet here you are still, talking and exciting yourself. How is your leg now, colonel? Easier?"

"Confound it! No, no!" replied the other, with a writhe of torture as he changed his position so as to relieve the strain on the wounded limb, which I had quite forgotten about, the brave follow having stoically repressed all indication of pain while urging on the pursuit of the black mutineers. "It's hurting me like the devil! But, sir, I cannot rest or leave the deck till we come up to that accursed ship and save my poor child, my little darling—if we be not too late, too late!"

"This is nonsense, sir," said the skipper bluntly, and rather angrily, I thought, and he continued:

"The ship, we know, must be a goodish bit ahead of us still, and we can't possibly overhaul her for an hour or more at the earliest. So come, cheer up, and come along with me and have your leg attended to at once. I insist, colonel; come."

"But," persisted Colonel Vereker, evidently trying to make out the time in arguing, and loth to leave the scene of action, though apparently ready to drop now from sheer pain and exhaustion combined, "Who will—who will—"

"My first officer here, Mr Fosset, will remain on the bridge during our absence below," interposed Captain Applegarth, anticipating his last, unuttered objection. "He's quite competent to take charge, and I'm sure will let us know the moment the ship comes in sight, if she appears before we return on deck."

"Aye, that I will, sir," cried out Mr Fosset. "I'll keep a sharp look-out, and I'll hail you, sir, sharp enough, as soon as she heaves in sight on the horizon."

"There!" exclaimed the skipper in an exultant tone, taking hold of the colonel's reluctant arm and placing it within his own, so as to lead him away and to give him the benefit of his support down the bridge-ladder. "Won't that satisfy you now, sir, and you see you'll lose nothing by going below for a spell? Come, come, my good friend, have the leg seen to and eat something, for you must require it. Why, colonel, unless you keep up your strength and spur yourself up a bit you won't be able to tackle those black scoundrels when we get up to the ship and catch them and it comes to a fight, as I expect it will. So come along, my hearty; rouse yourself and come!"

This concluding remark of the old skipper affected more than all his previous persuasion, the colonel at once allowing himself to be helped down the laddering without further demur, and so along the gangway on the upper deck, towards the lower entrance to the saloon under the beak of the poop, I lending the aid of my shoulder for the crippled man to lean on as he limped painfully onward, having to pause at almost every step, his wounded leg dragging now so much, now that excitement no longer sustained his flagging frame; the skipper gave aid too, his arm propping him up on the other side.

Doctor and Patient

"Faith, it's moighty glad I am, sor, to say you at last!" cried Garry O'Neil, starting up from his seat at the cuddy table, on our ultimately reaching the saloon, where the Irish mate was having a rather late lunch with Mr Stokes, who had preceded us below. "I was jist comin' after ye ag'in, colonel, whin I had snatched a bit mouthful to kape the divvil out of me stomach, sure. I want to inspict that game leg o' yours, sor, now that I've sittled your poor f'ind's h'id. Begorrah, colonel, somebody gave him a tidy rap on the skull whin they were about it!"

"It was done with a hand-spike," explained the other, groaning with pain as we assisted him to a seat at the further end of the table, where the skipper's armchair was drawn out for him to fix him up more comfortably. "One of those treacherous niggers came behind his back and dealt him a terrific blow that landed on the side of his head partly, nearly cutting his ear off!"

"Aye, I saw that, sor, of course," put in Garry, pouring out some brandy into a tumbler which he proceeded to fill up with water—"aqua pura," he called it. "I've shtrapped it on ag'in now, and it looks as nate as ninepins. But jist dhrink this, colonel, dear. It'll warrm the cockles of your heart, sure, an' put frish loife into you!"

The American took a sip first at the glass proffered him, and then drained off the contents with a deep sigh of satisfaction.

"Ah!" he exclaimed, "I feel a little better. But how is poor Captain Alphonse now?"

"Bedad, he's gitting on illegantly," replied Garry, sniffing at a soup plate containing some steaming compound which Weston, the steward, had just brought in, and directing that worthy to place it in front of our poor invalid guest. "There was a nasty paice of bone sphlinter sticking in the crayture's brainpan; but, first, I trepanned him an' raymoved the impiddimint, an' the poor chap's now slayping as swately as a babby, slayping in the cap'en's cot over yonder! But come, colonel, I want ye to take some of this pay soup here afore I set to work carving ye about. Begorrah, it's foine stuff, an'll set ye up a bit to roights!"

"Thank you a thousand times," returned he, taking a mouthful or two of the soup which Weston had placed before him, eating very sparingly at first like one who had been deprived of food for some time. "I'm not afraid of your handling me, sir. I have undergone too many operations for that!"

"Faith, colonel," cried the Irishman, laughing in his usual good-tempered racy manner, "you'd best spake well of the craft or I'll be afther payin' you out, sure, alannah, whin I get your leg in me grip! Jist you stow some more o' that illigint soup inside your belt, sor, before I start on the job, an' while ye're aitin' I'll tell you how I once sarved out an old woman whom I was called in to docther, whin I was at ould Trinity, larnin' the profession, in faith!"

"That's right, O'Neil," said the skipper, seeing his motive in trying to set our sad guest at his ease and to try and distract his thoughts from the awful anxiety and grief under which he was labouring. "Have I heard the yarn before, eh?"

"Faith, not that I know of, cap'en," returned the doctor pro tem in his free and easy manner. "Begorrah, the joke's too much ag'inst meself, sor, for me to be afther tillin' the story too often!"

"Never mind that; it will make it all the more interesting to us," said the skipper with a knowing wink to Mr Stokes, both of them knowing Garry's old stories only too well, but at such a time as this they would have listened to anything if it would only serve to distract the poor colonel's thoughts for a few minutes, and they chuckled in recollection of the many jokes against himself that Garry had perpetrated. "Fire away with your yarn."

"Bedad, then, here goes," began O'Neil with a grin. "Ye must know, colonel, if you will have it, that I was only a 'sucking sawbones,' so to spake, at the toime. Faith, I was a medical studint in my first year, having barely mastered the bones."

"The bones!" interrupted the skipper. "What the deuce do you mean, man?"

"Sure, the inthroductory study of anatomy, sor," explained Garry rather grandiloquently, going on with his yarn. "Well, one foine day whin I an' another fellow who'd kept the same terms as mesilf were walking the hospital, wonderin' whin we'd be able to pass the college, sure the hall porter comes into the ward we were in an' axes if we knew where Professor Lancett, the house surgeon, was to be found, as he was wanted at once.

"'Faix,' says Terence Mahony, my chum, the other medical studint who was with me. 'He's gone to say the Lord Lieutenant, who's been struck down with the maysles, an' the divvle only knows whin he'll get back from the castle, sure! What's the matter, O'Dowd? Who wants ould Lancett at this outlandish toime of day?'

"The hall porter took Mahony's chaff, faith, in all sober sayriousness. 'It's moighty sorry I am,' says he; 'Master Lancett's gone to the castle, though proud I am for ould Trinity's sake, sayin' as how the Lord Lieutenant has for to send to us, sure, bekase them murtheren' 'sassa docthers that he brought from over the say with him from Inkland ain't a patch on our chaps! But, faix, sor, a poor woman as the professor knows is took moighty bad in her inside, some of her neighbours says, an' wants help at onst!'

"'Who is it, O'Dowd?' I asks. 'Do you know where she lives?'

"'Mistress Flannagan's her name,' says the porter. 'She's Mistress Lancett's ould la'ndress, sor; a cantankerous ould woman, too, an' wid the divvle of a temper! She lives jist out of Dame Strate, sure, in Abbey Lane. Any one'll till ye the place, sure!'

"'What say you to goin' to say the poor crayture?' says I to Terence Mahony. 'We'll lave word where we're gone, an' I'm sure Mr Lancett will be plaised to hear we're looking afther the ould lady!'

"'Begorrah, that he will, sor,' agreed O'Dowd, the porter. 'It's moighty kind of you two young gintlemen going for to say her, an' I'll make a p'int of lettin' the docther know whin he comes back from the Lord Liftinnint!'

"'All right, O'Dowd,' says I. 'Mind you till the professor, an' he can thin follow us up on his return to the college—that is, if he loikes!'

"With that off the two of us wint on our errind of mercy, though it was lucky I lift that message with O'Dowd, as ye'll larn prisintly!

"It didn't take us long to find the house where the sick woman was, for as we turned into the strate, a dirty ould hag, smoking a short pipe, came up to us with a smirk on her ugly phiz.

"'God save Ireland!' says she, addressing Terence. 'Be yez the docther jintlemen from the hospital, avic?'

"'Faix, we're that,' says my companion; 'the pair of us!'

"'Thin come along,' says she. 'Mistress Flannagan is dyin' to say you, sure. The soight of yez is good for sore eyes!'

"'Begorrah!' says Terence, 'I wouldn't have come at all at all if she hadn't been dyin', the poor crayture! Where is she?'

"'In the corner there,' returns the old hag, removing her dirty little black dhudeen of a pipe for a minnit from between her teeth, in order to spake the bether. 'She's a-sottin' in that cheir there, as she hav' been since the mornin', widout sayin' a worrd to mortial saol afther she tould us to sind for the docther. May the divvle fly away with me, but Peggy Flannagan can be obstinate in foith, whin she likes!'

"Terence Mahony and I then poked our noses into the corner of the room, the old hag stirrin' the turf fire on the hearth to give us a bit of loight; an' then we saw the ould crayture, who looked as broad as she was long, sittin' in a big armchere, an' starin' at us with large, open eyes. But though she was breythin' hard loike a grampus, she didn't spake nothin'!

"'What's the mather, my good woman?' says Mahony, going up to her an' spaking kindly to the poor crayture. 'Let me feel your pulse.'

"He caught hold of her hand, which hung down the side of the chere and fumbled at the wrist for some toime, the ould woman starin' an' sayin' nothin' at all at all!

"'Faith, Garry O'Neil, I can't foind any pulse on her at all at all. She must be di'd, worse luck!'

"'Och, you omahdaun; can't ye say her eyes open?' says I. 'Git out o' the way an' let me thry!'

"Begorrah, though, I couldn't fale any pulse at all aythar.

"'She's in a faint, I think,' says Terence, pretendin' for to know all about it. 'We had jist sich a case in hospital t'other day. It's oine of suspended animation.'

"'Blatheration, Terence,' I cried at hearing this. 'You'll be a case of suspended animation yoursilf by-and-bye.'

"'Faith, how's that?' says he. 'What do you mean?'

"'Why, whin you're hung, me bhoy! for your ignorance of your profession. Sure, one can say with half an eye the poor crayture is sufferin' from lumbago or peritonitas on the craynium, faith!'

"As we were arguin' the p'int, the ould hag who had introduced us brought our discussion to an end jist as Terence made up his mind that the case was cholera or elephantiasis or something else equally ridiculous!

"'Bad cess to the obstinate cantankerous ould crayture,' cried she, catching the poor sick woman by the scruff of the neck an' shakin' her violently backwards an' forrads, afther which she banged the poor thing violently on the sate of the chere. 'Will ye now spake to their honours, or will ye not? Won't ye now? She be that stubborn!' said she, turnin' to us; 'did ye ivver see anythin' loike it afore?'

"Mahony then tould her to put out her tongue, but the divvle a bit of her tongue saw we! Nor would she say a worrd as to her ailment, to give us a clue, though I believe on me oath, colonel, we mintioned ivery complaint known in the Pharmacopaia, Terence even axin' civilly if she had chilblames in the throat, for it was the depth of winter at the toime, to prevent her talkin'!

"But our coaxin' was all in vain, loike the ould hag's shaking!

"Faith, not a worrd moved our patient. She was that in all conscience, sure.

"'Begorrah, I'll sind a bucket of could wather over her an' say if that'll tach her manners!' said the ould hag, who tould us her own name was Biddy Flynne, on our giving her an odd sixthpence for a dhrop of drink. 'It's a shame to bring yez honours out for nothin'!'

"She was jist going to do what she had threatened, sure enough whin, providentially, in walked the professor from the college.

"He'd been listenin' outside the door, I believe, all the toime Terence an' mesilf were talkin' an' arguin' about the ould dame's complaint, puzzlin' our brains to find out what was the mather with her, for the baste of a man had a broad grin on his face, loike that you say on a mealy petaty whin the jacket pales off of it, whin he toorned round to us afther examinin' poor Mistress Flannagan, now all a heap on her chere.

"'Faith, I must complimint you, jintlemin, on the profound skill an' knowledge you have shown in your profession,' says he. 'I don't think I ivver heard a more ignorant or illeterate diagnosis of a case since I've been professor at Trinity College!'

"He was a moighty polite man was Professor Lancett. Terence an' I both agrayed on his sayin' this, an' thought our fortunes were made an' we'd git our diplomas at once, without any examination, sure!

"But his nixt remark purty soon took the consate out of both of us.

"'It's lucky for you two dunder-headed ignoramases!' he went on to say in a nasty sneerin' way the baste had with him whin he was angry and was any way put out. 'Preshous lucky for you, Misther Terence Mahony, an' you, too, Garry O'Neil, that I chanced to come afther you, thinkin' ye'd be up to some mischief, or else ye'd have put your foot in it with a vengeance an' murthered between you this poor, harmless ould woman lying here. I am ashamed and disgusted with you!'

"He thin prosayded to till what the poor crayture was sufferin' from, an' what d'ye think her complaint was, colonel? Jist give a guess, now, jist to oblige me, sure."

"Great Scot!" cried the American, smiling at O'Neil's naïve manner and the happy and roguish expression on his face, our guest's appearance having been much improved by the food of which he had partaken as well as the stimulant, which had put some little colour into his pale cheeks. "I'm sure I can't guess. But what was it, sir, for you have excited my curiosity?"

A Black Business

"Be jabers, sor!" exclaimed the Irishman in his very broadest brogue and with a comical grin on his face that certainly must have eclipsed that of which he complained in the professor of his college who had caught him and his fellow-student trespassing on his medical preserves. "To till the truth an' shame the divvle, colonel, the poor ould crayture, whose complaint we couldn't underconstumble at all at all, sure, was sufferin' from a fit of apoplexy—a thing aisy enough to recognise by any docther of experience, though, faith, it moight have been Grake to us!"

We were all very much amused and had a good laugh at this naïve confession, even Colonel Vereker sharing in the general mirth, in spite of his profound melancholy and the pain he felt from his wounded leg, which made him wince every now and again, I noticed, during the narration of the story Garry O'Neil had thus told, with the utmost good humour, it must be confessed, at his own expense, as, indeed, he had made us understand beforehand that it would be.

"By George!" cried the skipper, after having his laugh out, "you'll be the death of me some day with your queer yarns if you can't manage to do for me with your professional skill or by the aid of your drugs and lotions, poisons, most of 'em, and all your murderous-looking instruments, besides!"

"No fear of that, cap'en; you're too tough a customer," rejoined the doctor with a knowing look in the direction of Mr Stokes, who had made himself purple in the face and was panting and puffing on his seat, trying to recover his breath. "Faith, though, sor, talkin' of medical skill, the sooner I say afther that leg of our fri'nd here, the better, I'm thinkin'."

"With the best of wills," assented the colonel, who had finished his luncheon by this time and certainly presented a much improved appearance to that he had worn when entering the saloon. "I am quite at your service, doctor, and promise to be as quiet as that first patient of yours of whom you've just told us!"

"Belay that, colonel; none o' your chaff about the ould leddy, if you love me, sure!" growled Garry, pretending to be indignant as he knelt down on the cabin floor and slit up the leg of the colonel's trousers so as to inspect the wound. His nonsensical, quizzing manner changed instantly, however, on seeing the serious state of the injured limb, and he ejaculated in a subdued tone of voice, "Holy Moses!"

"Why, sir," said the patient quietly, "what's the matter now?"

"Ah, an' ye are axin' what's the mather?" cried Garry in a still more astonished tone. "Faith, it's wantin' to know I am how the divvle you've iver been able to move about at all, at all, colonel, with that thing there. Look at it now, an' till me what ye think of it yoursilf, me darlint. May the saints presairve us, but did any one iver say such a leg?"

It was, in truth, a fearful-looking object, being swollen to the most abnormal proportions from the ankle joint to the thigh, while the skin was of a dark hue, save where some extravasated blood clustered about a small punctured orifice just above the knee.

Colonel Vereker laughed and shrugged his shoulders.

"The fortune of war," he explained. "One of those brutes shot me where that mark is, but I think the bullet travelled all round my thigh and lodged somewhere in the groin, I fancy, for I feel a lump there."

"Sure, I wonder you can fale anythin'!" cried Garry, who was probing for the missile all the time. "A man that can walk about, faith, loike an opera dancer, with a blue-mouldy leg loike that, can't have much faling at all, at all, I'm thinkin'!"

"Ah!" groaned his patient at last, on his touching the obnoxious bullet near the spot the colonel had indicated. "Whew! that hurts at any rate, doctor!"

"Just be aisy a minnit, me darlint," said the other soothingly, exchanging his probe for a pair of forceps and proceeding deftly to extract the leaden messenger. "An' if ye can't be aisy, faith, try an' be as aisy as ye can!"

In another second he had it out with a triumphant and gleeful shout.

"Ah!" ejaculated the colonel, the excessive pain causing him to clench his teeth with an audible snap.

"Faith, you may say 'ah' now as much as you please," said Garry, as he held out the villainous-looking bullet gripped in his forceps. "For there's the baste that did you all the damage, an' we'll soon pull you up, alannah, with that ugly paice of mischief out of the way, sure!"

"Oh! dear me!" the poor colonel exclaimed as the doctor went on dressing the wound and afterwards set-to to bandage the whole leg, swathing it round like a mummy with lint, and then saturating it with some liniment to allay the swelling. "Would to God all the mischief could be as easily made good! Oh, my little Elsie, my darling little girl!"

"Cheer up, colonel, cheer up," whispered the skipper, coming in from the state room on the starboard side of the saloon, whither he had gone to hunt up some special cigars while Garry O'Neil was accomplishing his surgical operation. "We're going ahead as fast as steam and a good ship can carry us, and we'll rescue your child, I'll wager, before nightfall. Have a smoke now, my friend; and while you're trying one of the Havanah's, which never paid duty and are none the worse for that, you can tell us how it all happened from the beginning to the end. I should like to hear the account of your voyage right through, colonel, and how those blacks came to board you."

"Certainly!" said Colonel Vereker, leaning back in his easy chair when Garry O'Neil had made an end of bandaging his leg, and accepting one of the choice cigars the skipper offered him. "I will tell you willingly, captain, and you, gentlemen, turning round and bowing to us, the sad story of our thrice ill-fated voyage."

"Thrice ill-fated?" repeated Mr Stokes inquiringly, the chief being rather argumentative by nature and possessing what he called a strictly logical turn of mind. "But how's that, sir?"

The colonel had his answer quite ready.

"I said 'thrice ill-fated' advisedly, sir," he replied, removing his cigar from his lips to emit a cloud of perfumed smoke, and then restoring the fragrant roll of tobacco to the mouth again. "In the first place, sir, from my having been unlucky enough ever to start upon the voyage at all. Secondly, from the fact of a calm delaying us when passing between Puerto Rico and San Domingo, thereby enabling those treacherous negro scoundrels to see our ship in time to put out for us from the shore; and thirdly, because Captain Alphonse would not take my advice and use strong measures when the mutiny originally broke out, which might have prevented the terrible events that afterwards occurred! But, sir, if you will allow me, I shall get along better by telling you what happened just in my own way!"

"Certainly, sir," immediately replied Mr Stokes, profuse in his apologies. "Pray pardon my interruption!"

The colonel bowed in token of his forgiveness and then resumed his yarn.

"Our ship, the Saint Pierre, of Marseilles, Jacques Alphonse master and part owner, sailed from La Guayra on October 25, barely a fortnight ago!" said he. "In addition to her captain, of course, she carried two mates and a crew of twenty-five hands all told, and she was bound for Liverpool, with a general cargo of cocoa, coffee and hides, besides a mixed assortment of indigo, orris root, sarsaparilla and other raw drugs for the English market."

"Were you and your little daughter the only passengers?"

"No, Señor Applegarth," replied the other. "There were also on board Monsieur and Madame Boisson, from Caracas, returning home to Europe after a lengthened residence in the Venezuelan capital, where they had carried on a large millinery business, supplying the dusky señoritas of the hybrid Spanish and native republic with the latest Parisian modes; Don Miguel, the proprietor of an extensive estancia in the interior; and little Mr Johnson, a Britisher, of not much account in your country, I guess, not a gentleman—at all events, in my humble opinion. He was travelling for some mercantile house in London connected with the manufactory of chocolates or sweets, or something of that sort. I cannot say I cared much for the lot, as they were not people of my class, so I did not allow my Elsie, my darling, my pet, to associate with them more than could be helped, save with Madame Boisson, who was a kind, good-natured sort of woman, though decidedly vulgar. Oh dear me! It was a thousand pities we ever started on that disastrous voyage. It was unlucky from the very first!"

"Faith!" interposed Garry O'Neil. "But how was that, sor?"

"We were too late in reaching La Guayra in the first instance," replied Colonel Vereker. "I had planned, my friend, to take the French steamer for Brest, but on arriving at the port I found she had already left, and while deliberating about what I should do under the circumstances—for there would not be another mail boat for a fortnight at least—I met Captain Alphonse. He was an old friend of mine, a friend of long standing, so, on his telling me that his vessel was going to sail on the following day and would probably convey me to Brest, where he said he would have to report himself prior to proceeding to Liverpool with his cargo, quite as soon as I should arrive if I waited for the next steamer, I made up my mind to accompany him."

"But, colonel," suggested Captain Applegarth, "you might have gone direct to England by one of the West India mail steamers which touch at La Guayra on their route homeward from Colon."

"I know that, my friend," said the other. "I could have caught one of them the following week. This would not have suited my purpose, however, sir. I wished to proceed direct to Brest, for I could get easily on to Paris, where I intended placing my little Elsie at school in the convent of L'enfant Jesu, at Neuilly, under the guardianship of some good nuns, by whom her poor mother was educated and brought up. It was a promise, my friend, to the dead."

"I see, colonel," rejoined the skipper apologetically, lighting his cigar again, having allowed it to go out while listening to the other; "I see, sir. Go on; I'm all attention."

"Well, then," continued the colonel, "these preliminaries being all arranged, Elsie and I went aboard the Saint Pierre, a full-rigged sailing ship of some eight hundred tons, the morning of the twenty-eighth of last month; and on the evening of the same day, as I have already told you, we made sail and quitted the anchorage where the ship had been loading—abreast of San Miguel, a port that guards the roadstead to the eastward, where it is open to the sea."

"Aye, I know La Guayra well, colonel," put in the skipper at this point, showing that he was following every detail. "I was in the Royal Mail Line when I was a nipper, before joining my present company."

"I recollect the night we sailed," resumed the other, paying no attention to Captain Applegarth's remark, but speaking with his eyes fixed, as if in a dream and seeing mentally before him the scenes he described. "The moon was shining brightly when we got under way, lighting up the Trinchera bastion and making the mountains in the background seem higher than they were from the deep shadows they cast over the town lying below. This latter lay embosomed amid a mass of tall cocoanut trees and gorgeous palms, with other tropical foliage, and had a shining beach of white sand immediately in its front, stretching round the curling bay, on which the surf broke in the moonlight, with a phosphorescent glow and a hollow sound as if beating over a grave. Heavens! It was the grave of all my dearest hopes and plans, for that, sir, was one of the few last peaceful nights I have of late known, and very probably ever shall know again!"

"Faith, don't say that now, sir," cried out Garry at this. "You'll have a peaceful one to-night, sure, or I'm no prophet. Begorrah, though, I niver was, so far as that goes!"

The skipper grinned at this sympathetic interpolation, and the colonel's sombre face lighted up a bit as he turned his pathetic eyes on the speaker, as if wishing to share his hopefulness.

"Ah, doctor, you do not know what grief and anguish are like!" he said mournfully. "But to go on with my story. I may tell you that, had our voyage progressed like our start, I should have nothing to deplore, for, the land breeze filling our sails, we bore away buoyantly from the Venezuelan coast, the ship shaping a course north by west towards the Mona passage, as the channel way is called, from a rock in its centre, lying between Hayti and Puerto Rico. This route is held to be the best, I believe, for passing out into the open Atlantic from the labyrinthine groups of islands and innumerable islets that gem the blue waters of the Caribbean Sea. It is a course, too, which by its directness and the northerly current and westerly wind there to be met, saves a lot of useless tacking about and beating to windward, as you, no doubt, captain, very well know."

The skipper nodded his head.

"You're quite a sailor, colonel," he said approvingly. "Where did you manage to pick up your knowledge of navigation and sea-faring matters, if I may ask the question, sir?"

"In the many voyages I have made during a somewhat adventurous life," replied the other. "I have invariably kept my ears and eyes open, captain. There are many things thus to be learnt, I have found out from experience, which, although seemingly unimportant in themselves, frequently turn out afterwards to be of very great use to us, sometimes, indeed, almost unexpectedly so!"

"Aye, aye, colonel. My opinion, sir, right down to the ground," said the skipper, looking towards me. "Just you put that in your pipe, Dick Haldane, and smoke it!"

"Yes, young sir," added Colonel Vereker, emphasising this piece of advice. "That rule of life has stood me in good stead on more than one occasion, both on land and on shipboard. Had I not learnt something of the ways of your sailors, for instance, I might not have thought of lashing the Saint Pierre's helm amidships on the breaking out of the mutiny, and so prevented all our going to the bottom subsequently, when it came on to blow; for all of us were then fighting for our lives and no one had time to attend to the ship, save in the way of letting go what ropes were handiest."

"Aye, that may be well enough, colonel," observed the skipper in his dry fashion. "But your argument cuts both ways. If your helm hadn't been lashed down, remember, the ship would have been yawing about and drifting in this direction and that, and we should probably have come across her long ago, like that boat from which we picked you up, instead of her bearing away right before the wind and our having to go in chase of her, sir, as we are now doing."

"It is true! I did not think of that!" returned the colonel impulsively, half-starting from his seat in his excitement. "We must be near her now, captain, though, surely. We must find them, and I must see my little girl again!"

"Kape aisy, me darlint; kape aisy," here interposed Garry O'Neil, before Captain Applegarth could answer the question. "Sure, Mr Fosset promised to give us the worrd whin she hove in sight, an' you're only distarbin' yoursilf for nothing, colonel! More's the pity, too, mabruchal, whin your leg is progressin' so illigantly an' the swillin' goin' down as swately as possible. Now kape aisy, if only to oblige me. Faith, colonel, me profissional reputation's at shtake!"

The Irishman all the time he was talking was carefully attending to the injured limb, loosening a bandage here, tightening another there, and keeping the lint dressing moist the while with a lotion which he applied gently to the surface by means of a sponge. So, impressed alike by his tender solicitude thus practically shown on his behalf as much as by his opportune admonition, the colonel was forced to remain quiet.

"I wish he'd be quick about it!" he muttered to himself. "Well, doctor, as you will not let me move, I suppose you will let me go on with my tale; that is, if it interests you!"

"Aye, aye; I want to hear everything," said the skipper. "And fire away, colonel; there's plenty of time for you to reel off your yarn before we overhaul the chase."

"All right,—then, I will proceed," replied the other. "All went well with us on the voyage until the afternoon of the third day after sailing from La Guayra, when, unfortunately, the weather changed and the westerly wind, which had favoured us so far, suddenly failed us after wafting us through the Mona Passage, and we became becalmed off Cap San Engaño, to the northward of Hayti."

"Hayti!" exclaimed old Mr Stokes, waking up from a short nap he had been having on the sly, and pretending to be keenly alive to the conversation. "That's the famous black republic, ain't it?"

"Famous black pandemonium, you mean!" retorted the colonel fiercely, his eyes flashing at once with fire. "Excuse me, sir, but I have seen so much of these negro brutes, who ape the airs of civilisation and yet after a century of freedom are more uncivilised in their habits and mode of life than the African slaves, their forefathers whom Toussaint-L'Overture, as he styled himself, their leader, freed from the yoke of their French masters a hundred years ago, that I feel the glorious name 'republic' to be dishonoured when associated with such vile wretches, wretches a thousand times worse than the Fantees of the West Coast from whom they originally sprang!"

"My dear sir," said Mr Stokes, aghast at the tempest he had raised by his innocent remark, "you surprise me!"

"Heavens! you would be surprised, sir, if you knew these Haytians as I know them to be," continued the colonel, his indignation still struggling for the mastery—"a race of devil worshippers and cannibals, who confound liberty with license, and have added all the vices of civilisation to the inherent savagery of their innate animal nature. Ah, sir, I should like to tell you a great deal more, but have not the time now. I am afraid I am forgetting myself. Where was I?"

"Becalmed off Cape San Engaño," promptly replied the skipper, sailor fashion—"at least, so you said, colonel; but I fancy you must have had a little rougher weather in that latitude than you mentioned at first!"

"We had," said Colonel Vereker meaningly. "Towards nightfall we drifted with the current more inshore, Captain Alphonse not dropping our anchor, as we expected the land breeze would spring up at sunset. This did not come for an hour later, however, for already darkness had begun to surround us and we could see the fireflies illuminating the brush beyond the beach. But this wasn't all observed, sir. Just as our sails filled again and the ship slowly drew out into the offing, we heard the splash of oars in the water astern. It was a boat coming after us, propelled by a dozen oars at least, pulling as hard as those handling them knew how, a shot or two from the shore and the sound of musket balls ripping the water explaining, in some way, the reason for their anxiety to get beyond the range of the firing, on which account they sought the shelter of the Saint Pierre, of course—at least, so we thought!

"'Who goes there?' shouted out Captain Alphonse, who was standing alone with me, close to the taffrail. 'Poor devils! there is probably another insurrection at Port au Prince, and President Salomon up or down again. He is always one or the other every year or so, and these poor fellows may be flying to save their miserable necks. Who goes there? Who goes there?' But, whether wanting all their energy for their oars or for some other reason known to themselves, those in the boat made no reply to our hail, and the next moment, ere the ship gathered way sufficient to gain on them, they were alongside, their long unwieldy craft grating against the ship's timbers beneath her counter.

"'Look-out there, forrads!' cried Captain Alphonse, seeing the boat making apparently for our bows, but before a hand could be raised to prevent them, without asking permission in any way or offering the slightest apology or excuse in advance for their conduct, a number of negroes jumped out of her and began climbing aboard the Saint Pierre.

"Heavens! gentlemen, clad in little beyond Nature's own covering, as the majority of the intruders were, and looking in the dim light as black as the ace of spades, they seemed like so many demons, come to take possession of our unfortunate ship—as indeed they were. Oh dear me!"

THE MARQUIS DE POMME-ROSE

"A pretty kettle of fish that!" exclaimed the skipper, pitching the butt-end of his cigar through one of the stern ports as he got up from his seat and began to pace up and down the saloon in his usual quarter-deck fashion. "You must have been mad, colonel, to let them come aboard so quietly and in such a manner, too!"

"Stay, you have not heard all," said the other. "As the black rascals tumbled over the side, one of them called out something in the French tongue. This, sir, at once disarmed Captain Alphonse, who had prevented me from teaching them good manners, which I otherwise should have done, for I had my six-shooter ready, with the barrels all loaded, being always prepared for any such little unpleasantness by my experiences in Venezuela, where a man often carries his life in his own hands!

"But Captain Alphonse would not let me fire, though, by heavens! I would have accounted for half a dozen of them, I know, before they had advanced beyond the precincts of the ship!

"'No, no, be quiet!' cried he, knocking my arm up to prevent my taking aim at the leader of the gang, whom I had spotted dead in the eye. 'These are my countrymen!'

"It was no use my talking after that, sir. The sound of the French tongue, which these blacks of Hayti speak with a better accent than the gamins of Paris, gained over Captain Alphonse; while Madame Boisson declared the whole episode truly charming, her fat husband, who was entirely under her thumb, shrugging his shoulders and giving them both encouragement and a welcome.

"These charming compatriots of theirs, therefore, being allowed to take us by storm without let or hindrance, now advanced aft, when their ringleader, a plausible scoundrel who described himself as the 'Marquis de Pomme-Rose,' or some other similar shoddy title belonging to the black peerage of Hayti, to which I did not give heed at the time, beyond in my own mind thinking it ridiculous and that it was probably a name made up for the occasion, this man came up to Captain Alphonse with a smile on his black face and told a wonderful story which he had calculated would excite our pity while allaying our fears.

"There had been another revolution at Port au Prince, he said, as Captain Alphonse had surmised. A band of patriots, of whom he, the speaker, had the honour to be the chief, had attempted to depose the reigning despot Salomon from his post of president, but that that astute gentleman got wind of the conspiracy in time, and as he had a very efficacious mode of quickly dealing with those opposed to him in political matters, the nigger marquis and his fellow-plotters thought it best to seek refuge in flight.

"Salomon, of course, at once despatched his myrmidons after them, but having a few hours' start of the pursuers the runaway revolutionists contrived to clear off from Port au Prince, concealing themselves in the mountain fastnesses at the eastern end of the island.

"Here, while in hiding, they saw the Saint Pierre rounding Cape San Engaño. Subsequently observing that she was becalmed, they waited for nightfall, when they stole a boat that lay on the shore and pulled out towards our ship, just avoiding capture in the nick of time; the regiment of black soldiers Salomon had sent after them having hit upon their trail and being so close up behind that they were able to open fire on them ere the boat got into deep water, two of the fugitive patriots being struck by the bullets that came whistling in their rear.

"The 'marquis' was of the belief that we were bound for Cuba, so he declared at all events at the moment, and he asked Captain Alphonse with the utmost indifference to give him and his companions a passage thither, assuring him that he would be handsomely rewarded for so doing by some of their friends belonging to the Haytian revolutionary party, who had established their headquarters at Havana.

"In reply to this request Captain Alphonse declared he was 'desolated,' but that, unfortunately, the Saint Pierre was bound for Europe and not to the greater Antilles; but, strange to say, for I was watching him keenly the while, our friend the 'marquis' did not appear either surprised or dismayed at his supposition as to our destination turning out to be so erroneous, as he would have been, so I thought, had he been speaking the truth in his original narrative and acting in good faith towards us!

"From that moment, sir, something in my mind seemed to warn me against the black villain, though I had been previously rather prepossessed in his favour by his manner and bearing, in spite of a strong antipathy to republicans of his complexion!"

"Ah, colonel," whispered the skipper. "I suppose it comes from living amongst them too much, but I see you don't like negroes."

"No; you mistake my meaning greatly if you think that, Señor Applegarth. Black, white or yellow, the colour makes no difference to me, providing the individual I may have to deal with be a man in the true sense of the word! In the old days, before our war, I had a good deal to do with niggers, for my father and his father before him owned a large plantation in Louisiana, and long before President Lincoln issued his proclamation of emancipation every hand on our estate was a free man; so, you see, sir, I do not advocate slavery at all events. But between slavery and unbridled liberty there is, Señor Applegarth, a wide margin; and though I do not look upon a nigger in the abstract as either a brute beast or a human chattel, still I do not consider him quite fit to govern himself, nor do I regard him in the light of my brother, sir, nor even as my equal in any way!"

The skipper laughed.

"'What's bred in the bone,' colonel—you know the rest!" said he. "Your old experience in the Southern States prejudices you against the race."

"Pardon me," rejoined Colonel Vereker warmly, "I don't dislike them at all. On the contrary, I have found some negroes more faithful than any white man of my acquaintance, being true to the death; and I know that if I came across, to-morrow, any of the old hands on our Louisianian plantation whom my father made free, I should be as glad to see them as they would be to meet me. But, sir, at the same time, allowing all this, I cannot admit the negro to be on an equality with the white races. They are inferior, I am certain, alike in intelligence, disposition and nature, and I hold him as little qualified for self-government on the European system as a child is fit to be entrusted with a case of razors for playthings. Hayti is an illustration of this, sir!"

"All right, my dear sir," said the skipper good-humouredly, glad to see the colonel taken out of himself and forgetting his grief about his little daughter for the moment in the discussion. "Carry on; we're listening to you!"

His enthusiasm, however, did not last very long.

"Heavens! Señor Applegarth, and you, too, gentlemen," he went on in a changed tone. "I have cause to love those Haytian scoundrels well, I tell you! Well, sirs, to proceed with my story, the terrible end of which I have nearly reached, this dog of a black rascal, the so-called marquis, seemed quite content, much to my surprise, when Captain Alphonse told him we were not bound for Cuba, but for Liverpool.

"It was all the same to him, he said, and as they were going the longer voyage, perhaps Captain Alphonse would allow him and his companions to work out their passage by assisting the crew in the navigation of the ship.

"Captain Alphonse was delighted at this, for we had only half a dozen good seamen on board, the rest of the hands being a lot of half-bred mulattoes and niggers—some of the scourings of South America whom he had picked up at La Guayra, most of whom knew how to handle a cutlass better than a rope—so the proposed addition to the strength of our ship's company was a very acceptable one, particularly as the 'Marquis' pointed out two of his companions as being expert sailors and qualified pilots and navigators."

"Ha! You kept your eye on those gentry, colonel, I bet you did?"

"Yes, sir. They were the first I spotted when the row began; but I'm anticipating matters."

"The divvle a bit, sor," interposed Garry O'Neil. "Let me jist change the dressin' of your leg, an' ye can polish off the rist of the rascals as soon as ye plaize."

"A thousand thanks," returned the other, shifting his position to allow his leg to be attended to. "They did not disclose their purpose, though, or 'show their hand,' as they say at the game of monte, all at once; for, moved by their voluntary offer to help work the ship, Captain Alphonse promised the 'marquis,' who when making this offer had urged a request to that effect, calculating on the captain's generosity to put in and leave the lot at Bermuda, should they make a fair passage up to the parallel of that island, but in the event of their being delayed by foul winds or the voyage appearing as if it must be a long one, the Haytians must be contented to cross the ocean.

"The bargain was struck at once, this proviso being accepted with alacrity as it just suited their purpose, and never saw I men work as those Haytians worked in the way of tumbling up at all hours and pulling and hauling, shaking out reefs and setting fresh sail, the next day or two when the weather was contrary, and we had to tack about a good deal to windward in getting out into the open Atlantic.

"Heavens! How they exerted themselves; so much so that I quite shared Captain Alphonse's admiration for them, but, unlike him, I watched them and I noticed that they and the coloured men of our crew who had been picked up at La Guayra seemed on a more friendly footing than was altogether warranted by the short time they had been on board. Captain Alphonse and the other passengers, however, would not see this.

"But, sir, I had an old negro servant on board with me, who had followed my fortunes from the States to Venezuela after the war, Louisiana then being no longer a fit place for a white man to live in. Poor old Cato; he was the most faithful soul the Almighty ever put breath into!

"Him I acquainted with my suspicions, and sent amongst the blacks, to gather what information he could of their designs, for I was confident, sirs, they had not boarded us for nothing, and were hatching some deep plot with a view, very probably, of getting possession of our ship in order the better to further the interests of the revolutionary party to which they belonged that was opposed to Salomon, the president in power.

"Whatever their object might be, however, I distrusted them in every way, believing them, indeed, actuated by other motives than such as might be prompted by their political aspirations, my suspicions being confirmed by the looks and bearing of the gang, who seemed capable of any atrocity, judging them by their villainous faces and generally hang-dog appearance, besides which they were continually whispering together amongst themselves and consorting and confabbing with the mulattoes and other coloured men belonging to the crew.

"In addition to that, Señor Applegarth, and you too, gentlemen, I noticed that our friend 'the marquis,' although he gave himself great airs on account of the aristocratic blood and descent to which he lay claim, pretending to think himself much superior in position to both Captain Alphonse and myself, and regarding poor Cato, my servant, as mere dirt under his feet, albeit the faithful negro was of a like colour to himself—did not esteem it beneath his high dignity to associate with the scum of the forecastle and bandy ribald obscenities, when he believed himself unobserved, with his fellow scoundrels.

"Aye, I watched my gentleman carefully, and so, too, did my poor faithful Cato!"

The Seventh of November

"My faithful negro, however," continued the colonel, pausing at this point to puff out another cloud of smoke from his fragrant cigar,—"well, he was unable to learn anything of the Haytians, though he tried to make friends of them, for they always stopped their talk amongst themselves on his approach, and would only reply to his overtures in monosyllables expressive of distrust, accompanied by contemptuous gestures that angered poor Cato greatly, for as he considered that he belonged to me he felt the insult to be directed not only at himself but at the whole family.

"'Golly, massa!' he said to me after a couple or so of attempts that proved fruitless to ingratiate himself into the confidence of the gang, 'you just wait; I catch dem black raskils nappin' by-an'-bye, you see, massa. You see, "speshly dat tarn markiss!"'

"He managed this sooner than he thought, and pretty smartly too, for the very next day he caught the noble scoundrel, who was his particular aversion, walking off with a pair of pistols from Captain Alphonse's cabin. On Cato coming up and stopping him in the very act, the 'marquis' put down the pistols quickly, saying in his off-hand manner that he was merely examining the locks, remarking how well they were made. 'But,' said Cato, 'guess he no bamboozle dis chile!'

"The following day, sirs, was the seventh of November, last Friday, that awful, that terrible day!

"Cato, who had been away forward early in the morning to see about our breakfast, came back aft with a terrified face.

"'Yay, massa,' said he, 'guess dose tam niggars up to sumfin'! I'se hear um say dey smell de lan' an' de time was 'rive to settle de white trash, dat what dey say, an' take ship. One ob de tam raskel see me come out of gully, an' say cut um tongue out if I'se tell youse, massa!'

"Of course on hearing this I put Captain Alphonse immediately on his guard, and we locked up all the spare arms and ammunition until we should require the same, excepting our own revolvers and three other pistols, which we served out to the two mates and the boatswain, all of whom were good men and brave Frenchmen. Monsieur Boisson, when he was asked if he would have one, shrugged his shoulders and said he was a simple passenger, he did not understand fighting—it was not his affair; while little

Mr Johnson said he was an Englishman and preferred using his fists. Don Miguel had a pistol of his own.

"Jingo! The emergency we dreaded came soon enough, sir; indeed, sooner than we expected, and it was fortunate we had been forewarned!

"It was just after the noontide hour, I recollect that well, for Captain Alphonse had just taken the altitude of the sun to ascertain our position, when, as he came up from his cabin where he had gone to consult his chronometers and work out 'the reckoning,' as you sailors call it, that that black devil the 'marquis' mounted the poop with a simpering and fawning air.

"'Ah well, captain,' said he, with a very polite bow, 'where do you make us out to be, monsieur? Near the Bermudas yet?'

"'My word, yes,' replied Captain Alphonse. 'We are some ten leagues or so the westward of the islands, but we're bearing up now, as you see, to reach them.'

"'And what time, monsieur,' said the 'marquis,' speaking louder so that some of the other niggers who were on the deck below could hear what he said. 'Do you think it will be possible for us to land? My companions and myself, monsieur, as you can well imagine, are most anxious to get ashore as soon as possible, so that we may procure a ship to take us on to Havana.'

"'But, yes, your anxiety is natural enough,' responded poor Captain Alphonse, suspecting nothing from this. 'I hope to approach near enough to Port Saint George to put you ashore some time in the afternoon.'

"'Ohe, below there!' cried out the Haytian in reply to this, addressing his companions in the waist, who, I noticed, were gradually edging themselves more and more aft. 'Do you hear that, my brave boys? We are going to land at last. Get the boat ready!'

"This was evidently a signal, for he shouted out the last words in a still higher key than that in which he had been speaking.

"'You need not hurry, my friend!' said the captain, surprised at this order and smiling at the Haytian's impulsiveness, as he thought it. 'There will be plenty of time for lowering the boat when we come in sight of land.'

"'I think differently, monsieur,' rejoined the other, scowling and assuming an arrogant tone for the first time. 'I say the time is Now!'

"This he yelled out at the top of his voice.

"Instantly the gang of blacks made a rush at the poop on both sides at once, and Captain Alphonse clutched at his revolver, which he had in his pocket, but was unable to get it out in time.

"Mine, however, was in my hand and ready cocked."

"Houly Moses!" ejaculated Garry O'Neil, his Irish blood making him all attention now at the mere mention of fighting. "I hope ye let 'em have it hot, sor!

"Guess I did!" replied Colonel Vereker grimly, dropping unconsciously into his native vernacular, which up to now he had almost seemed to have forgotten from his long residence amongst a Spanish-speaking race. "You may bet your bottom dollar on that, sir! I aimed at that scoundrel the 'marquis,' but he jumped backward in his fright and his foot catching in one of the ringbolts, he tumbled right over the poop-rail on to the deck below; the shot I had intended for him dropping the black pilot, his constant companion, and who was invariably behind him. He dropped down as dead as a herring!

"Don Miguel, who luckily had just come up from the saloon, being handy with his revolver from the rough times he had experienced, like myself, in Venezuela, settled another darkie; while little Johnson, the Englishman, caught up a long hand-spike, bigger than himself, and with it knocked down two of the Haytians to his own cheek.

"Madame Boisson, meanwhile, was screaming for her husband, her brave Hercules, to come to the rescue; but the 'brave Hercules' had locked himself in his cabin, as my little Elsie told me afterwards; for fortunately the poor child was not feeling well and I had desired her to remain below during the hot noontide heat of the sun; and, she also said, she could hear him crying and sobbing and calling down imprecations on everybody, including 'my wife' and himself for both being in such a position, Madame Boisson hammering at the door all the time, and, after finding he would not reopen to her appeal for help, apostrophising him as a coward! a pig!

"During this time we were pretty busy on deck, the second mate, Basseterre, and another French seaman, who was with him in the crossjack yard, having come down from aloft to our assistance. Captain Alphonse got his revolver out, when he and Don Miguel and I giving them a volley altogether, and the others supporting us with what weapons they had, we rushed the rascals off the poop quicker than they came up, the lot returning to the forecastle along with the 'marquis,' who, I was very glad to see, had cut his face considerably by his tumble.

"Captain Alphonse thereupon, seeing the coast clear, sang out for Housi, his second officer, and the boatswain, who he thought were away forward, to come up aft and join us, so that we might all be together, but instead of these men, Cato, my own black servant ran up the poop-ladder and told us in much trepidation that Monsieur Housi, with the boatswain Rigault and one of the French sailors, were imprisoned in the forepeak, while the two white sailors and the steward were hard and fast in the main hold, whither they had descended to get some provisions, the mutineers slipping on the hatchway cover over them, on the 'marquis,' that devil, giving the signal!"

"Ah, my poor fellows!" cried Captain Alphonse. "That, then, means there are only ourselves left. Good heavens! What shall we do?"

"Why, hoist a signal of distress," I suggested at once. "We are near Bermuda, on the cruising ground of the English men-of-war; and as these scoundrels have no friends or assistance, I daresay we'll be able to hold out here until some vessel bears up to our aid!"

"'Good, my friend,' replied Captain Alphonse, who with Basseterre, the second mate, and Don Miguel, remained to keep guard with their revolvers, both seated on top of the skylight hatchway, which commanded the approaches to the poop by way of the ladders, while I, with the last of the white sailors, ran aft. Then I called out, 'Hoist the French flag!'

"I knew that the locker with the flags was in the wheel-house, close to the taffrail, and there being no one to interfere with us, the negro who had been attending the helm having bolted the moment I pulled out my revolver at the first alarm, the traitor flying to join the other mutineers, my sailor and I soon ferretted out an old ensign, the Tricolour; when, binding it on to the signal halliards, we hoisted it about half-way up the peak of our spanker, whence it could best be seen by a passing ship."

"Did you know what that signal meant, colonel?" said Captain Applegarth in an inquiring tone, "that you had a death aboard, eh?"

"Si, señor. Oh yes, of course," repeated the colonel, correcting himself almost as soon as he spoke for his lapse again into the Spanish tongue. "There were half a dozen dead Haytians there, whom, by the way, Captain Alphonse and I presently pitched over the side! But, beyond that, sir, I believe all sailors regard a flag hoisted in that way, 'half-mast high,' as it is termed, to be a signal of distress!

"Without doubt, sir," answered the skipper. "I was only testing your nautical experience, that's all!"

"I am glad then, I did not make a blunder about it, as I thought I had done from your question," returned Colonel Vereker, quite seriously, not noticing that the skipper was only poking fun at him in his way and did not mean anything beyond a bit of chaff. "Well, sir, after hoisting the flag the French sailor and I seized the opportunity to lash the helm amidships so as to keep the Saint Pierre on her course, for we could not spare him to do the steering, and Captain Alphonse and Don Miguel, with the plucky little

Englishman and myself, had all our work to do watching the mutineers with our revolvers!

"After a time, as the rascals kept pretty quiet in their part of the ship, and as my poor little daughter Elsie had been a long time now shut up below, I thought she might come up on the poop to get a breath of fresh air while it was still light; there being no fear of the blacks assailing us again so long as they knew we could see to shoot straight and had our weapons handy!

"So I sent Cato down to fetch her on deck, and she came up the next moment, all full of curiosity and alarm, as you may imagine, the little one wanting to know what had occurred; for the reports of my revolver and the subsequent stillness had occasioned her great fright, Madame Boisson and her husband, the 'brave Hercules,' being but poor comforters.

"All at once, while I was explaining to her about the flag, telling her that we had hoisted it in order to summon any passing ship to our assistance, she suddenly went to the side and looked over the bulwarks towards the north.

"The next moment she gave vent to a cry of joy.

"'Oh, my father,' she suddenly exclaimed. 'You have only just hoisted the flag in time. There's a big steamer! Look, look! there it is, and coming up to help us!'

"'Where? where? Where is it? I cannot see it. Nonsense, Elsie; you are dreaming, my child!' I said, looking out eagerly to where she pointed, but could see nothing. 'There's no ship there, little one!' and I felt angry at the false alarm.

"'But, my father, you are wrong,' still insisted the child, as positive as you please. 'I can see the vessel there in the distance quite plainly. See how the black smoke comes puffing out of the chimneys.'

"I laughed at this.

"'Little darling,' said I, 'there was no ship, and there are no "chimneys" on board ships at sea. Sailors call them funnels, my dearest one.'

"She pretended to pout on my thus catching her tripping in her talk.

"'Well, my father,' said she, with a shrug of her shoulders, as is her habit sometimes, 'I may be wrong about the chimneys, but I am not wrong about seeing a ship. Why, my father, there she is now, coming closer and closer, and quite near; so near that I can see—yes, I can see—I am quite sure—a big boy there. Look, look, father, dear! There he is in front of the smoke. He has quite a pleasant face.'

"Elsie turned in my direction as she spoke, and, though I was still gazing all the while, I could see nothing, and I was vexed, very vexed with my little girl for her persistency in the matter.

"'Why, it has gone—quite disappeared!' she cried out the instant after, on rushing to the side and looking over. 'What does it mean? Why did she not come and help if she saw the flag?'

"'You have dreamt it, little one,' I replied shortly, as I had done before. 'It's a freak of the imagination, and you fancied it, you funny little woman.'

"But it was a curious incident, though, sir, was it not, at such a time, with our hearts all full of expectancy and hope?"

Captain Applegarth was greatly excited by the narrative, and so, it may readily be believed, was I.

He asked abruptly, "When did this happen? Tell me, colonel, at once. It is strange—very so!"

The other looked up with surprise, while Mr Stokes stared at him with wonder, and the Irishman opened his big blue eyes wide to the full.

"I have already told you, sir," replied Colonel Vereker very quickly. "As I told you before, it was the seventh of November—last Friday."

"Yes; but I mean what time of the day, sir?"

"Oh, I should think about five o'clock in the afternoon. Perhaps a little later, as the sun was going down, I recollect, at the time."

I could not restrain my astonishment at this.

"It must be the very ship I saw!" I thought to myself.

"Is the young lady slight in figure, and has she long golden-coloured hair hanging loose about her head, sir?" I eagerly asked, almost breathless in my excitement. "And, tell me too, did she have a large black Newfoundland or retriever dog by her side that same evening, sir?"

Colonel Vereker seemed even more astonished by this question of mine than I had been by his reply to Captain Applegarth the moment before.

"My brave young sir," said he, using this somewhat grandiloquent form of addressing me, I suppose, in remembrance of the slight service I had done him by swimming with the line to the drifting boat when we picked up him and his companion. "My little Elsie is tall and slight for her age, and her hair is assuredly of a golden hue, ah, yes! like liquid sunshine; though, how you, my good young gentleman, who, to my knowledge, can never have seen her face to face in this life, can know the colour of her hair or what she is like, I must confess that passes my comprehension!"

"But the dog, sir?"

"That is stranger still," remarked Colonel Vereker. "I had forgotten to mention that I brought with me on board the Saint Pierre from my old home at Caracas a splendid Russian wolf-hound, as faithful a creature as my poor negro servant Cato. His name is Ivan, and he is now, I sincerely hope and trust, guarding my little darling girl, as I would have done if I had remained with her, for not a living soul would dare to touch her with him there. Ivan would tear them limb from limb first. He is a large greyish-black dog, with a rough shaggy coat, and in reply to your enquiry, I must tell you he was on the poop of the ship, by the side of my child, at the very time that she declared she saw that steamer, which I, myself, could not see anywhere!"

For the moment I was unable to speak. I was so overcome at this unexpected confirmation of the sight I had seen on that eventful Friday night, though I had afterwards been inclined to disbelieve the evidence of my own senses, as everybody else had done, even the skipper at last joining in with the opinion of Mr Fosset and all the rest, save the boatswain, old Masters. Yes, yes; every one them imagined that I had dreamt of "the ghost-ship" as they called my vision, and that I had not seen it at all!

But this statement from the colonel absolutely staggered the skipper, and he looked from me to the American and back again at me in the most bewildering manner possible; the old chief, Mr Stokes, and Garry O'Neil staring at the pair of us with equal amazement.

"By George, the girl and the dog, the girl and the dog. Why, it's the very same ship, as you say, Haldane; it must be so, and, by George, my boy, you were right after all! By George, you were!" at length exclaimed the skipper in a voice, the genuineness of whose astonishment could not be doubted. "Colonel Vereker, I would not have credited this had any one told it me and sworn to the truth of it on oath, but the proof is so strong that I cannot possibly disbelieve it, sir, though it is to my mind a downright impossibility according to every argument of common sense. It is certainly the most wonderful thing that has ever happened to me, and the most wonderful thing that I have ever heard of since I have been at sea!"

"Heavens!" cried the other. "But why? You surprise me, sir."

"Aye, colonel," rejoined the skipper. "But I am going to surprise you more. Now don't laugh at me, and don't think me an idiot and gone off my head, sir, when I tell you that this lad, Dick Haldane, here, whether by reason of some mirage or other I cannot tell, for it's beyond my understanding altogether, distinctly saw your ship with her signal of distress, and says he saw your little daughter with the dog by her side, aboard her, last Friday night at sunset. More than that, sir, he described to me at the time, exactly as you have done now, colonel, everything he saw, even to the very hue of the young girl's hair and the colour and texture of the dog's coat! It is altogether marvellous and, indeed, incredible!"

"Well, but—" said Colonel Vereker slowly, and pausing between every word as if trying to comprehend it all. "Why, how is that, sir?"

"Your ship, colonel, must have been more than five hundred miles away from ours at the time—that is all!"

Butchered

"Dios!" exclaimed Colonel Vereker. "Are you—certain of this, sir?"

Captain Applegarth shrugged his shoulders.

"Ask Mr Stokes here and your doctor there, Mr O'Neil, whether they did not hear Haldane's yarn about your ship five days ago, sir, before we ever clapped eyes on you," said he in a slightly aggrieved tone, as if he thought his word was being doubted. "Why, colonel, this poor lad was becoming the butt for everybody's chaff on board on account of it!"

"Gracious!" cried the other. "This is indeed really wonderful!"

"Aye, colonel, and more than that! But for the lad seeing this mirage, or whatever else it was, and telling me about it, we would not have gone off our course in search of you to render what assistance we could—yours being the 'ship in distress' Haldane reported having sighted to the southward. This divergence from our track, sir, took us into the very teeth of the gale which we encountered later on, that same evening, and conduced to our breaking down."

"Faith," put in Garry O'Neil, "that's thrue for sure, sor!"

"This breakdown of ours, colonel, led to our drifting to the southward into the trail of the Gulf Stream," continued the skipper, following up the strange sequence of events as they occurred, one by one. "Your ship—the real ship, I mean—was drifting north and east meanwhile, carried along by the same current, and then it came about that, although apparently going in opposite directions and acted on by different causes, our tracks crossed each other on the chart last night—at least, that is my opinion."

"I see, I see," cried Colonel Vereker quickly, interrupting him, and in a state of great excitement. "Thank God! But for that you would never have sighted our drifting boat and picked up myself and poor Captain Alphonse! Thank God, Señor Haldane saw us in that mysterious way. It seems to have been an interposition of heaven to warn you of our peril and bring you to our aid!"

"Just so, colonel; that's what I think myself now," said the skipper impressively, taking off his cap and looking upward with a grave reflective air. "Aye, and I thank God, too, for putting us in the way of helping you, with all my heart, sir!"

"Ah!" observed old Mr Stokes, who had remained silent the while. "The ways of Providence are as wonderful as they are mysterious!"

There was a pause after this in our conversation which no one seemed anxious to break till Garry O'Neil spoke.

"Faith, sor, you haven't tould us yit how ye come by this wound in your leg, an' about that poor chap in yander," he said to the colonel, nodding his head in the direction of Captain Applegarth's inner state cabin, where the French captain was lying in his cot. "Sure, we're dyin' to hear the end of your scrimmage with those black divvles!"

Colonel Vereker heaved a sigh.

"Well, I ought not to doubt that the good God is watching over my little, darling daughter after what I have just learnt, my friends," said he in a more hopeful tone than his depressed manner indicated, looking round at us with his large, melancholy, dark eyes. "I ought not to despair!"

"Certainly not, sir; I dare say we'll soon overhaul the ship now, for we're more than an hour and a half in chase of her at full speed," remarked the skipper, recovering himself from his fit of abstraction and looking at his watch to see the time. "Go on, colonel; go on, please, and tell us the end of your story."

"There is little more for you to hear, sir," replied the other, settling himself back in his seat again, after Mr O'Neil had once more dressed the wound in his leg. "Before it was dark that terrible night I sent Elsie below, while Captain Alphonse with myself stayed up on the poop for the first watch, each of us with a loaded revolver, besides having a box of cartridges handy on the skylight near by, should we want to replenish our ammunition. But the Haytians, sir, had evidently had enough of us for that evening, making no further attempts to attack us as the hours wore on.

"They were as watchful as ourselves, though, for as Cato, anon, trying to creep forwards so as to release the French sailors confined under the main hatchway, had a narrow escape of his life, a heavy spar being suddenly let down by the run almost on top of his head when he ventured out on the exposed deck. This was at midnight, when the second mate, Basseterre, and Don Miguel, with the French sailor Duval, relieved Captain Alphonse and me, taking the middle watch.

"Next morning, however, soon after Captain Alphonse and I, with the little Englishman, had resumed charge of the poop and the others were resting—alas, my friends, without my knowledge or sanction, poor Cato made another attempt to reach the hatchway, which, unfortunately resulted in his death!

"Hearing Ivan growl and my little daughter cry out as if something had frightened her, I had gone down to the cabin shortly after daylight to see what was the matter, cautioning Captain Alphonse, who hardly needed my caution, not to leave his post for a moment, and not thinking of Cato, who had disappeared from the top of the companion-way and had gone below to Elsie—heard her cry, I thought, and gone to her even before myself.

"He was not in the cabin, however; nor did I find anything much the matter with my child, who had evidently unconsciously cried out in some dream she had, Ivan, of course, gushing in sympathy and waking her up. So, telling Elsie to compose herself and go off to sleep again, as everything was going on all right and there was nothing to be alarmed about, beyond the snoring of Monsieur and Madame Boisson at the further end of the cabin, I, feeling greatly relieved, returned on deck.

"I looked round for Cato at once, naturally, for our forces were not so strong that one would not be missed, especially such a one as he!

"But my faithful negro was nowhere in sight! Captain Alphonse said, too, he had not seen him during my absence below, nor indeed, for some time prior to my going down to the cabin.

"I then searched the wheel-house aft without discovering him.

"'Cato!' I called out, 'where are you? Come here immediately!'

"My poor servant did not answer, but that black fiend, the pseudo 'marquis' advanced from the forepart of the deck, sheltering himself, you may be sure, from my aim in the rear of the windlass bitts, which were in a line between us.

"'You will have to call louder,' he cried with a mocking laugh like that of a hyena, and full of devilish glee. 'I assure you, much louder, my friend, before that spy slave of yours will ever be able to answer you again!'

"Heavens! I feared the worst then. Poor Cato! They had caught him reconnoitring.

"'What have you done with him, you son of Satan?' I yelled out, full of rage and anger, and with a terrible foreboding. 'If you have hurt a hair of his head I will make you pay dearly for it, I can tell you, you fiend!'

"The malicious, murdering wretch only replied to my threat with another mocking laugh, which his companions echoed, as if enjoying a joke, while I noticed them dragging at a shapeless mass from the forecastle forwards.

"'Kick the carrion aft!' I heard the inhuman brute say to his followers. 'Let the "white trash" see the dog's carcass! He will then believe what I have said, Name of God! and know what is in store for himself!'

"My God! Señor Applegarth and you, gentlemen, I can hardly tell you what followed. It is all too horrible.

"The sight of what I saw will haunt me to my grave!

"For the shapeless mass I had observed slowly raised itself up from the deck, and I saw that it was my poor Cato. The savages had hacked the unfortunate man to pieces with their knives!

"He recognised me, poor creature, and appeared to try to speak, but only made an inarticulate noise between a sob and a groan that rings in my ears now, while the blood gushed from his mouth as he fell forwards, facing me, dead, huddled up in a heap again upon the deck!

"Those devils incarnate, besides mutilating his limbs, had, would you believe it, cut out his tongue as they had before threatened, for warning us of their treachery!"

"God in heaven!" exclaimed Captain Applegarth, stopping in his quick walk up and down the saloon and bringing his fist down on the table with a bang that made the glasses in the swinging tray above jump and rattle, two of them indeed falling over and smashing into fragments on the floor. "The infernal demons! Can such things be? It is dreadful!"

All of us were equally horror stricken and indignant at the colonel's terrible recital, even old Mr Stokes waking up and stretching out his hand to the skipper as if pledging himself to what he wished to urge before he spoke.

"Horrible, horrible, sir!" he panted out, his anger taking away his breath and affecting his voice. "But we'll avenge the poor fellow and kill the rascals when we come up with them, won't we, sir? There's my hand on it, anyway!"

I did not and could not say anything; no, I couldn't; but you can pretty well imagine the oath I mentally registered.

Not so Garry O'Neil, though.

The Irishman's face flamed with rage and anger. "Kill them, sor!" cried he, springing to his feet from the chair in which he had been seated alongside the colonel, whose injured limb he had been carefully attending to again all the while, his reddish beard and moustache bristling, and his steel-blue eyes flashing out veritable sparks, it seemed of fire. "Faith, killin's too good for 'em, sure, the haythen miscreants! I'd boil 'em alive, sor, or roast 'em in the stoke-hold, begorrah, if I had me own way with 'em. I would, sor, so hilp me Moses, if all the howly saints, whose names be praised, an' the blessed ould Pope, too, prayed me to spare 'em. Och, the murtherin' bastes, the daymans, the divvles!"

He was almost beside himself in his rage and passionate invective. So much so, indeed, that Mr Stokes, despite his own hearty sympathy with the like cause, looked at the infuriated Irishman in great trepidation, for his face was flushed, and his hair seemed actually to stand on end, while his words tumbled out of his mouth pell-mell, jostling each other in their eagerness to find utterance.

The chief really fancied, I believe, that he had suddenly gone mad, as he literally fumed with fury.

After a few moments, however, Garry cooled down a bit, restraining himself by a violent effort, and he turned to his whilom patient with an apologetic air.

"Faith, sor, I fancied I had that divvle, your fri'nd, the markiss, sure, be the throat," said he, with a feeble attempt at a grin and biting his lips to keep in his feelings while he dropped his arms, which he had been whirling round his head like a maniac only just before. "By the powers, wouldn't I throttle the baste swately, if I had hould of him once in these two hands of mine!"

Colonel Vereker stretched out both his impulsively, and gripped those of Garry O'Neil.

"Heavens!" he cried, with tears in his eyes. "You are a white man, sir. I can't say more than that, and I am proud to know you!"

"Och, niver moind that, colonel," said the Irishman, putting aside the compliment, the highest the colonel thought he could give. "Till us what you did, sure, afther the poor maimed crayture was murthered by that Haytian divvle. Faith, I loathe the baste. I hate him like pizen, though I haven't sane him yit, more's the pity; but it'll be a bad job for him when I do clap my peepers on him!"

"I could not do much," said the other, proceeding with his account of the struggle with the mutineers on board the Saint Pierre, "but Captain Alphonse and myself emptied our revolvers at the scoundrels and floored three of them before they retreated back into the forecastle; but the 'marquis,' the greatest scoundrel of the whole lot, escaped scot free, though I fired four shots at him point blank as he dodged behind the mainmast and windlass bits, keeping well under cover, and mocking my efforts to get a straight aim. The villain, I think, bears a charmed life!"

"Niver you fear, sor," put in Garry, in answer to this remark. "His father, ould Nick, is keepin' him for somethin' warm whin I git hould of him. Faith, sor, you can bet your boots on that, sure!"

Colonel Vereker smiled sadly at the impulsive Irishman's remark. He could see that he had moved every fibre of his feeling heart and warm nature and that he was following every incident of his terrible story of atrocities and sufferings with an all-engrossing interest.

"I rushed to the poop-ladder to make for the mocking brute, intending to grip him by the neck, as you have suggested, sir," said he, "when, by heavens, I would have choked the life out of his vile carcass!

"But Captain Alphonse prevented me.

"'My God! dear friend,' he cried, catching hold of me round the body in his powerful arms, so that I could not move a step. 'Remember the little one, your little daughter, who would have no one to protect her should these rabble kill you. Besides, my friend, the good Cato is dead now, and the useless sacrifice of your life, of both our lives probably, if you go forwards, and perhaps too the life of the little one, who cannot even help herself, will never bring back the breath to the brave lad's body! No, no, colonel, I promise you,' said he, at the same time kissing the tips of his fingers and elevating his shoulders, in his French fashion, 'We will do something better than that. Only wait; be patient. We will avenge him, you will see, but I pray you do nothing rash, for the sake of the little one.'"

ALL ADRIFT

"Aye, colonel," sang out the skipper, as if in response to these words of the French captain, "to avenge him; that's what all of us here have sworn to do, I know, for I can answer for them as if I were speaking for myself. Yes, and so we will, too. We'll avenge him—the poor fellow whom they butchered. We will, by George!"

"Begorrah!" exclaimed Garry O'Neil. "You can count on me for one on that job, as I tould ye before, and I don't care how soon we begin it, cap'en!"

"And me too," put in old Mr Stokes, again becoming very enthusiastic. "The whole lot must be punished, sir, when we catch them!"

"I thought so," said the skipper, looking round at us and then turning to the colonel with a proud air. "You see, sir, we're all unanimous; for I can answer for this lad Haldane, here, though the poor chap's too bashful to speak for himself!"

"I know what the gallant youth can do already," said the other, looking at me kindly as I held up my head like the rest, but with a very red face. "Thank you, gentlemen all, for your promises. Well, then, on my friend Captain Alphonse putting the matter in the way he did, to make an end of my story, I held back, and all that day—it was last Saturday—we remained on the defensive, we five holding the after part of the ship, and the Haytians and mutineers of our crew the forecastle. All of us, though, kept on the watch; they looking out for land, we for help in response to our signal flag half-mast high.

"But neither party saw what they looked out and longed for; no corner of land on the horizon gratified the desire of their eyes, no ship hove in sight to bless ours with the promise of relief!

"The next morning, Sunday, it came on to blow, and our vessel was taken aback and nearly foundered. Fortunately, though, the mutineers not interfering, most of them being seasick forwards, Captain Alphonse and Basseterre started down into the waist to cast off all the sheets and halliards they could reach, letting everything fly; whereupon we drove before the wind and so escaped any mishap from this source, at all events!

"Probably on account of their prostration from the effects of sea-sickness, our enemies did not molest us in any way throughout the day; but towards the morning my little Elsie came up the companion-way in a state of great terror, saying she heard a sort of scratching in the hold below, and that Ivan, her dog, was growling as if he smelt somebody trying to get in, though we could not hear the dog on deck from the noise of the wind and sea, and a lot of loose ropes and swinging spars which were making a terrible row aloft.

"I went down at once with her, and without even taking the trouble to listen I could clearly distinguish the sound of tapping beneath the cabin deck, despite the confused jabbering of Monsieur Boisson, and the shrill tones of his wife.

"I knelt down then and put my ear to the planking, Monsieur Boisson watching me with his bottle-brush sort of hair standing straight up on end with fright, and Madame, who I thought had more courage than he, though such, evidently, I now saw was not the case—well, she was rolling on one of the saloon settees in a fit of hysterics, screaming and yelling at the top of her voice.

"'Who's there?' I called out in French. 'Are you one of those Haytians, or a friend and one of us? Answer! I will know who it is when you speak!'

"'I am a friend!' came back instantly in Spanish. 'Let me out, sir; I am nearly stifled down here. The three of us who were locked in the main hatch have worked through the cargo and broken the after bulkhead, making our way here, but we can't get out of this, for the trap is fastened down, sir!'

"It was Pedro Gomez, the steward, who had gone down into the hold with two of the white sailors just before the outbreak of the mutiny to obtain some salt pork and other food for the use of the very scoundrels who had imprisoned them, and who, probably, believed they had all three died by this time, like poor Cato, only through suffocation, instead of being murdered as he was!

"Needless to say, I immediately drew back the bolts of the hatchway cover leading down into the after-hold, which was just under the flooring of little Elsie's cabin, and released the three, overjoyed not only at finding alive those whom we had thought dead, but doubly so at having such a welcome addition to our small force of five—I couldn't rely upon that coward Boisson—opposed as we were to the thirty, whom the enemy still mustered, after deducting those we shot.

"Why, with this adventitious aid, we could now attack the cursed wretches in their stronghold, instead of our merely remaining on the defensive, waiting for them to assail us, as we had been forced to do all along!

"I thought it best, however, not to let the Haytian scoundrels know of this increase to our strength until the morrow, believing that if we waited till daylight we might be able to take them more completely then by surprise and ensure a victory; for in the dark we might get mixed up and, firing at random, hit our friends as well as our foes. So I went up above and spoke to Captain Alphonse, who agreed with me about it, and we planned a pleasant little fête for the morning.

"This broke auspiciously enough, the sun rising on a tolerably calm sea, while the strong wind of the previous evening had graduated down to a gentle breeze from the south-west.

"But hardly had we made all our arrangements as to the distribution of arms and settling our form of attack, when our plans were upset by the villainous 'marquis' advancing aft with a pistol in his hand, supported by another of the scoundrels, a negro like himself from Port au Prince, and black as a coal, but a regular giant in size, and who likewise held a revolver.

"Heavens! They had previously been without firearms, wherein lay our superiority in spite of numbers; but these weapons now put us almost on level terms, notwithstanding the reinforcement we had received.

"'Where could they have got 'em, sir?' said little Mr Johnson to me, he and Captain Alphonse and myself being in counsel together at the time, it being the watch below of Don Miguel and Basseterre and the sailor Duval, all three of whom were asleep in the wheel-house, recruiting for their night duty. 'They didn't have no firearms yesterday, colonel, I'll swear. Do you think they've murdered the mate and bo'sun forrads, and robbed 'em?'

"As a similar idea flashed through my mind, that devil, the 'marquis,' answered the little Englishman's question as I, too, had feared!

"'Oh! my friend,' he called out, as I covered him with my revolver from my rampart behind the poop-rail on the top of the ladder, where a roll of tarpaulin served us for shelter. 'Don't be too handy with your pistol. We have got firearms too, now. Stop a minute. I have got something to say to you.'

"'You had better make haste with your speech, then,' said I. 'My finger is itching to pull the trigger, and you know, to your cost, I'm a dead shot!'

"'You will not do much good by killing me,' he retorted with that mocking hyena laugh of his, which always exasperated me so much. 'I want to tell you that we know you have got three more men with you now than you had yesterday, for we searched the hold this morning and found the nest empty and the birds flown. But recollect, my friend, we can get to you aft through the cargo, in the same way as those white-livered wretches have done!'

"'Bah! I'm not afraid of your threats, you black devil,' I replied, although my heart went down to my boots at the thought of my darling child being caught unawares and being left to the mercy of such demons. 'We have scuttled the after part of the ship, and at the least noise being heard in the hold we will let in the water and drown you all like rats in a hole, and see how you like that!'

"This idea, which occurred to me on the spur of the instant, evidently impressed the scoundrel, for I could see a change come over his ugly face.

"'Let us make a compromise,' he suggested after a pause, during which he whispered to his companion, the giant negro, both keeping much behind the mainmast. 'You can take that boat you have there at the stern, the lot of you, if you like, and leave us the ship.'

"'My word, that's a very good proposal, marquis,' said Captain Alphonse, coming to my side. 'You won't interfere with us, I suppose, if we go away and give you absolute power to do what you please with the Saint Pierre, eh?'

"'Assuredly not, my friend; we promise that,' eagerly replied the scoundrel, deceived by the manner of my poor friend. 'You can take anything you like of your personal effects too; you and the other whites.'

"'Ah, but my friend, you are too good!' said Captain Alphonse, firing quickly as he spoke at the 'marquis,' who had incautiously exposed himself, thinking we had been gulled by his proposal and were ready to fall into the trap he had cunningly prepared for us. 'Take that, you pig, for my answer!'

"His revolver gave out a sharp crack, and simultaneously with the report, the other's pistol fell from his hand, the scoundrel's elbow being shattered by the shot.

"Ere I could send a shot in the same direction to finish him off, the big negro, who had accompanied him to the front, instantly dragged back the 'marquis,' howling with rage and pain, behind the shelter of the mainmast; and then, picking up his revolver for him, the two of them blazed amongst us pretty securely from that retreat, without, however, doing any damage to our side. A bullet of mine, though, flattened the big negro's nose a little more than Nature had already done for him, and which did not improve his beauty, as you can well believe.

"We kept on popping away at them whenever we saw we had a shot, the whole of this day; well, that was only yesterday, but appears ages ago to me, sirs! We kept on firing without materially diminishing their strength, but they only replied feebly to our fire, with an occasional shot fired at intervals, making up by their shouting and demoniacal yells for their failure to harm us more effectively.

"From this we became convinced that they were obliged to husband their ammunition, having no more cartridges beyond those still remaining in the chambers of the revolvers they were using, which had been loaded when served out to Monsieur Henri and the boatswain, to whom the weapons originally belonged. There was, likewise, little doubt but that the mutineers had robbed those poor fellows, after murdering them like poor Cato, in the forecastle, as the little Englishman had surmised.

"Towards sunset, later on in the afternoon—last night that was—Señor Applegarth, remember, we sighted your vessel in the distance.

"Heavens! She looked to us in our desperate strait as an angel of mercy might appear to the spirits of the damned in hell; and, at once, the thought of abandoning our accursed ship, which that fiend of a black 'marquis' unwillingly suggested, rapidly matured itself into a resolve.

"But our intentions in carrying out this determination were very different to his, for we believed that with your help we should the sooner be able to overcome the rascally gang, and re-conquer the vessel we might be compelled ere long to surrender, all of us now being pretty well worn out with the struggle!

"'This is grand! this is magnificent!' cried Captain Alphonse, when I unfolded this scheme to him; for, sirs, I may say with pardonable pride, it was my plan entirely. 'It is good tactique to beat the retreat sometimes in war. They retreat that they may the more easily advance!'

"Don Miguel was also of a like opinion, and so was the little Englishman, Mr Johnson, whose snobbishness had by this time been completely put in the shade by his manly pluck and straightforwardness; while, as for Basseterre, the mate, and the French sailors, they implicitly believed all that Captain Alphonse approved of must infallibly be right!

"Our first idea was to attract your attention without letting the Haytians see what we were up to, as, to the best of our belief, they had no inkling of your proximity; so we were puzzling our brains how to let you learn our need in some quiet way, when little Mr Johnson suggested our burning a devil, composed of wet gunpowder piled up in the form of a cone. This was accordingly done, and the 'devil,' when lit, placed on the top of the wheel-house, all the rest of those around discharging their revolvers in rapid succession at the rascals on the forecastle to take off their attention while the firework fizzed and flared up.

"This signal, however, sirs, did not appear to be observed by your vessel."

"It was, though," interposed the skipper. "We thought you were burning a blue light to let us read your name astern, but you were too far off for that!"

"Ah! we did not know that, and the failure discouraged us," replied the colonel. "Still, whether we were observed or not, we noticed your steamer was lying-to, and we made up our minds to try and reach her if possible, should we be able to get out of the Saint Pierre before those rascally blacks got wind of our scheme and tried to prevent our leaving.

"So we set about our preparations forthwith.

"The four French sailors were ordered to prepare the boat which hung from the stern davits and to get it ready for lowering, it being now dark enough to conceal their movements, while Captain Alphonse and Basseterre kept guard over the approach to the poop on our side, and Don Miguel and the Englishman defended the other ladder leading up from the lower deck.

"Leaving these at their respective stations, I went down into the saloon, accompanied by Pedro Gomez, the steward, to procure some tinned meats and biscuits, with some barricoes of water and other things to provision the boat, intending also to warn Monsieur and Madame Boisson of our contemplated departure; not forgetting also, you may be sure, to make every arrangement for the safety of my child, who, with the dog, her constant companion, had remained below with the ex-milliner and her husband, though these two had retired to their cabin, whence I could not get them to stir, either by threat of being left behind or any entreaty. No, they were both as obstinate as mules in their cowardice and foolish fears!

"Madame declared they had been 'betrayed,' and asserted they could 'die but once'; while monsieur, 'le brave Hercule,' on his part, said he 'washed his hands of all responsibility.' It was not his affair, he considered himself perfectly satisfied, and gave me to understand he would not interfere on either side, except, I expect, the victorious one!

"Finding all remonstrances in vain, I was just going to force them away against their will, when suddenly there came a loud shout from the deck above, and the hasty tramp of feet overhead, which was at once responded to by Madame Boisson with a shriek at the top of her voice, while monsieur cursed everybody in a whining voice.

"Telling Elsie to stop where she was until I returned for her, I rushed up the companion-way, followed by Pedro Gomez, only to find everything all but lost!

"The French sailors, it seems, so Mr Johnson told me afterwards in a few hurried words of explanation, had 'got into a fog' over the falls of the boat they had been sent to lower, and seeing the clumsy way they were setting to work at the job, both Basseterre and Captain Alphonse thoughtlessly left their post to show the men the proper way to do the task ordered. Alas! though, in a second, while the whole lot of them all had their backs turned to the Haytians, these demons, grasping the opportunity in a moment, rushed up on the poop by the port-ladder way, now unguarded!

"Captain Alphonse, hearing the noise of their approach, faced about, fronting his foes like a tiger at bay, and drew his revolver from his belt.

"But, sir, he was too late!

"Ere he could put up his hand to guard himself, for I could see it all in an instant, as I emerged from the companion-hatchway, the giant negro, who had abandoned his pistol for a hand-spike, brought down this fearful weapon with a tremendous thwack on the side of my poor friend's head with the result you have seen."

"Aye, faith," said Garry O'Neil. "It must have been a terrible blow, sure, sor!"

"It was," replied the colonel grimly. "It knocked him down like a bullock, and then, before I could interfere, the big brute took up Captain Alphonse, all bleeding and senseless as he was, but still breathing, and chucked him into the sea.

"That was the negro's last act, however; for as he broke into a huge guffaw of triumph over the ghastly deed I fired my revolver, the barrel of which I shoved almost into his mouth and blew his brains out!"

"Hooray!" exclaimed the impulsive Garry O'Neil on hearing this. "Faith, I ounly wish, colonel, I had been there with ye. Begorrah, I'd have made 'em hop at it, sure, I bet, sor!

"After that," continued the narrator, we had some stiff work for five minutes or so, but by keeping the skylight between us, the continuous fire of our four revolvers at such short range proved too much for them, and we succeeded in driving the blacks off the poop. The whole lot of them retreated back to the forecastle, leaving five of their number dead about the decks, besides half a dozen or so of the others badly wounded; all of us, fortunately, escaping with only a few slight bruises from blows from the Haytian's clubs and hand-spikes—the only weapons they used.

"All save poor Captain Alphonse, that is; for it was only when the coast was clear of the scoundrels and the poop safe again that I had time to think of him.

"Pedro Gomez, remaining with Basseterre and one of the sailors, to guard the port-ladder way with their six-shooters loaded and levelled in front, commanding all approach aft, in the same way as the mate and poor Captain Alphonse had done in the first instance, I went off with all haste to the stern gallery to see what had become of my unfortunate friend, taking the other three sailors with me, for though taking part in the general scrimmage when the blacks invaded the poop so unexpectedly, Don Miguel and Johnson had stuck valiantly to their post by the starboard rail, and so I had no fear of another surprise on now proceeding aft.

"It was still light enough to distinguish objects near, and as I looked over the side, what was my astonishment to see his body yet afloat, not far from the ship. Aye, sir, there he was; and, stranger still, as my eye caught sight of him, the poor fellow, unconsciously, no doubt, raised one hand out of the dark water with a quick, convulsive action, just as though he were beckoning to me and imploring me to save him!

"On noticing this—a fact, of course, which showed plainly enough that he was still alive—without thinking of what I was doing, I jumped on a projecting bollard and dived from the deck of the ship into the sea.

"I soon rose to the surface, when, swimming up to the almost lifeless body in a few strokes, I caught hold of a portion of the poor fellow's clothing and commenced turning it towards the stern of the vessel just underneath the davits, whence the boat we had been preparing for our flight was suspended all ready for lowering, and with the French sailors standing by above.

"'Look sharp!' I sang out to them from the water. 'Look sharp, there! Lower away!'

"In their haste and flurry, however, the men mistook my order, and thinking I had said 'cut away,' instead of 'lower away,' one of the fools, who held a cutlass he had caught up to defend himself with when those infernal niggers rushed at us, the confounded idiot made a sweeping cut at the falls from which the boat hung, severing them at one blow!

"Down came the little craft at once with a splash, almost on the top of me; and though she managed to ship some water through her sudden immersion, she quickly righted herself on an even keel, right side up."

"By George, I'd have keel-hauled 'em wrong side down!" cried the skipper, out of all patience at hearing of this piece of gross stupidity. "The damned awkward lubbers!"

"Yes, sir; French sailors are not like English ones, nor do they resemble our American shellbacks, who do know a thing or two!" replied the colonel. "Well, gentlemen, to make an end of my story, I may tell you that I had some difficulty in lifting the body of poor Captain Alphonse into the boat when I had clutched hold of the gunwale; but after a time I succeeded in getting him into the bows, rolling him over the side anyhow.

"Then I tried to get in myself by the stern, and had just flung one of my legs over when that villain the black 'marquis,' catching sight of me from the forecastle, ahead of which the boat somehow or other had drifted by this time, fired at me with probably the last cartridge he had left in his pistol, and which the devil no doubt had reserved for me."

"Be jabers!" exclaimed Garry O'Neil, unable to keep silent any longer. "The baste! An', sure, that's how you came by that wound in the groin, faith?"

"Yes, sir, doctor. The shot struck me when I was all of a heap, and where it went heaven only knows, till you probed the wound and extracted the bullet.

"I must have tumbled into the boat while in a state of insensibility, like poor Captain Alphonse, for I do not recollect anything that occurred immediately after I felt the sting of the shot as I was hit, and when I came to myself again I was horrified to find I was far away from the ship, which I could only dimly discern in the distance.

"But this did not daunt me at first, for I thought I should be able to row alongside again and get taken aboard through one of the stern ports; but, will you believe it, when I came to search the boat for the oars, which Basseterre had expressly told those clumsy sailors in my hearing to be sure to put into the boat the very first thing of all, can you credit it? lo and behold, not a scull nor oar was in her; not a stick of any sort or kind whatever!"

"The lubbers!" said Captain Applegarth, indignant again as he paced backwards and forwards impatiently, casting an occasional hurried glance at the "tell-tale" suspended from the deck above the saloon table, the shifting dial of which showed we were now changing course to the westward. "The damned lubbers; the damn—"

The colonel here broke in with— "This discovery, I think, broke my heart," cried he, heaving a heavy sigh. "It took the last flickering gleam of hope away from me, and I sank back again to the bottom of the boat, appalled and terrified in my mind by the reflections and thoughts of what might happen to my darling child and those others whom I had left on board the Saint Pierre, deprived at one fell blow of both Captain Alphonse and myself.

"When daylight dawned after a night that seemed a century long, so full of pain and awful thought it was to me, I saw the Saint Pierre low down on the horizon to the westward of where I and my poor friend, Captain Alphonse, were drifting on the desert sea. The sight of the ship again, even in the distance, and the warmth of the sun's bright beams, which made the stagnant blood circulate in my veins once more, gave me hope and renewed courage, for I recollected and thought that after all, there were eight white men still left on board the ill-fated vessel to keep possession of her and defend my little one—eight good men and true, not counting that dastardly coward Boisson, who was skulking below!

"But, sir, the wind and tide wafted the Saint Pierre away beyond my vision; and—and—sirs, the—the end of it all you all know better than I can tell you!"

"Aye," put in the skipper, "we saw your boat adrift—at least, old Masters did—I'll give him the credit for that. Then we picked you up, and here you are!"

Hardly had the skipper uttered these words, completing the colonel's story, when Mr Fosset suddenly poked his head through the skylight over the after end of the saloon, the hatch of which opened out on the deck of the poop above.

Nor was the first mate merely satisfied with the abrupt intrusion of his figurehead into our midst, for he rattled the glass of the skylight in no very gentle fashion at the same time, the better, I suppose, to attract our attention, though we were all staring open-mouthed at him already, all startled by his unexpected appearance on the scene.

But he rattled the glass all the same as he looked down upon us, none the less; aye, all the more, rattled it with a will, frightening us all!

"Hi! Cap'en, Cap'en Applegarth!" he sang out at the very top of his voice, as excited as you please. "That ship's in sight! the ship's in sight, at last, sir. She's hull down to leeward about seven miles off! But we're overhauling her fast now, sir, hand over hand!"

Within Hail

"By George! is that so?" ejaculated the skipper, starting off with a mad clutch at his cap, which he had thrown off on to a locker close by in the heat of his excitement during the colonel's yarn. "I'll be on the bridge in a jiffey! Thank God for that news!"

"Hooray!" shouted Garry O'Neil, as we all immediately jumped from our seats on hearing this joyful intelligence, long though it had been in coming, even the poor colonel, sliding his bandaged leg off its supporting chair and standing on his feet, prepared to follow the skipper on deck without a moment's delay. "Be the powers! I knew we'd overhaul them divvles before sundown! Faith, an' I tould ye so, colonel; I tould ye so, you know I did!"

But just then an unexpected interruption arrested us as we all moved towards the companion-way to regain the deck above.

"Look here, colonel," cried a voice from the skipper's state room aft, where the commander of the Saint Pierre was supposed to be reposing in an almost insensible condition. "Get out of here! you are not worth being angry with."

"Begorrah, it's your poor fri'nd in there!" said Garry O'Neil to the colonel. "What's the poor crayture parleyvooing about, instid of slaypin' loike a Christian whin he's got the chance? Sure, I'll have to stop his jaundering there, or he'll niver git betther!"

"Stay a moment; he's beginning again, poor fellow," remarked the colonel, holding up his hand.

"Listen!"

"You villains! take that!" called out the Frenchman in a louder key and in a tone of anger, as if battling with the blacks on board the Saint Pierre over again; and then, after a pause we heard a piteous cry. "My God! they are going to shoot me! Look! Look! To the rescue, colonel, quickly, quickly, to the rescue."

"Bedad, he's in a bad way entoirely!" said Garry, as he and the colonel, with myself at their heels, entered the after cabin, where we saw Captain Alphonse sitting up in the skipper's cot and gesticulating frantically. "What can he be after sayin' now, sor?"

"He is going over the boat scene on the poop of our unfortunate vessel, when the Haytian blacks, as I told you, made at him and the other sailor before I rushed up from below, too late to save him, poor fellow!" explained the colonel. "He's calling out for help, as I suppose he did then, though I didn't hear him!"

"It sounds moighty queer, anyhow," continued the Irishman. "Whisht! There, he's at it again! What does that extraordinary lingo mean now? I can't make h'id nor tale of it, sor!"

"Hoist the flag immediately! Close furl the main topsail!" exclaimed the poor wounded man in short jerky sentences, as he sat up there in the swinging cot, with his hands tearing at the bandage that was bound round his head, looking as if he had just risen from the dead, and reminding me of a picture I once saw depicting the raising of Lazarus. His eyes were rolling, too, in wild delirium, and after gazing at us fixedly for a second or two without a sign of recognition on his pallid face, he fell back prostrate again on the mattress, crying out in a pitiful wail, "Alas, for the ship! Too late, too late, too late."

"Heavens!" said the colonel, turning to Garry. "Can't you do anything for him?"

"I'll put somethin' coolin' on the dressin', an' that'll make the poor chap's h'id aisier," replied the other, suiting the action to the word. "Ice, sure, 'ud be betther; but, faith, there isn't a morsel aboard!"

Whatever he did apply, however, had a quieting influence, and presently, after tossing from side to side convulsively, Captain Alphonse closed his great staring eyes and began to snore stertorously.

"Heaven be praised!" cried Colonel Vereker. "He's sleeping again, now!"

"Faith, an' a good job, too, for him, poor crayture," said Garry. "He's in a bad way, I till you, sor! an' he'd betther die aisy whin he's about it, sure, than kickin' up a row that won't help him."

"What!" returned the colonel. "Do you think he's going to die?"

"Begorrah, all the docthers in the worrld wouldn't save him!"

"My poor friend, my poor friend!" cried the colonel. "I will stay with him then, to the end, so as to soothe his last moments!"

There was evidently a struggle going on in Colonel Vereker's mind between his desire to do his duty, as he thought, to the dying man, and his natural anxiety to be on deck participating in all the excitement of the chase after the runaway ship and the coming fight with the Haytians, when the black rascals would be called to a final account for all the misery and bloodshed they had caused.

Garry O'Neil saw this, and pooh-poohed the idea of the colonel remaining below.

"Faith, there ain't the laste bit of good, sor, in yer stoppin' down here at all, at all," said he in his brisk, energetic way. "The poor chap won't be afther stirrin' ag'in for the next two hours or more; an' if he does, bedad, he won't ricognise ye, or any one ilse for that matther!"

"But, sir doctor—"

"Houly Moses! I till you, colonel, there ain't no use in your stoppin' another minnit!" impatiently cried the good-natured Irishman, interrupting his half-hearted expostulator. "Jist you clear out of this at once, an' go on deck an' say the foightin' with those murtherin' bleyguards. I'll moind my paychant now till that old thaife Weston's finished all the schraps lift in the plates an' bottles from lunch; an' thin, faith, he shall take charge of him an' I'll come up too, to say the foon. Now, be off wid ye, colonel, dear; you'll say the poor chap ag'in afther the rumpus is over. Dick Haldane, me darlint, hind the colonel the loan of yer arrum, alannah. There, now off ye both go. Away wid ye!"

So saying, he fairly pushed us out of the cabin; and, the colonel limping by my side and using my shoulder as a crutch, as he had previously done, we both went up the companion-ladder, and gained the poop.

The scene here presented a striking contrast to that we had just left, the fresh air, bright sun, and sparkling sea all speaking of life and movement, in exchange for the stuffy atmosphere of the darkened saloon and its association of illness and approaching death.

A stiff breeze was blowing now from the southward, and running, as we were, to the northward, right before it, the skipper had ordered all our square sails forward to be set so as to take every advantage of the wind, in addition to our steam-power, the old barquey prancing away full speed ahead, with her topsails and fore canvas bellied out to their utmost extent, their leech lifting occasionally with a flicker as she outran the breeze and the clew-gallant blocks rattling as the sheets slackened and grew taut again, while the wind hummed through the canvas aloft like a thousand bees buzzing about the rigging.

The black smoke, too, was rushing up the funnel and whirling in the air overhead, uncertain which direction to take, from the speed of the vessel inclining it to trail away aft, while the stiff southerly breeze blew it forwards; so we carried it all along with us, hung up above our dog vane like an awning as we careered onwards, raising a deep furrow of swelling water on either side as we cut through the dancing sunlit waves, and leaving a long white wake astern that shone through the blue, far away behind in the distance, to where sea and sky melted into one, far away on the horizon line.

Old Masters, the boatswain, was on the poop when the colonel and I came up from below, in the very act of hauling in the patent log to ascertain our speed.

"Well," said I, as he looked at the index of the ungainly thing, which is something of a cross between a shark hook and a miniature screw propeller. "What's she doing, bo'sun?"

"Doing? Wot she's a-doing on, sir?" he replied, repeating my own words and mouthing them over with much gusto. "Why, sir, she's going sixteen knots still, and the bloomin' old grampus has been keeping it up since four bells. She carries the wind with her, too; for jist as we bore up north awhile ago, astern the chase, I'm blessed if the breeze didn't shift round likewise to the south'ard, keepin' astern of us as before!"

"Where is the chase?" I asked, not being able to see forwards on account of the swelling foresail and other intervening objects. "I suppose she's right ahead, eh?"

"No, sir. Jist come here alongside o' me at the taffrail," said he. "Now foller my finger, sir. Look, there she is, two points off our starboard bow. She was hull down jist now, but we're rising her fast, sir. See, there she be right under the foreyard there!"

I looked in the direction he indicated, and could very faintly in the distance see something white like a sail, almost out of sight on the ocean ahead.

"But, Masters," said I, having no glass with me to bring her nearer, and seeing she was too far off for me to distinguish her with the naked eye, "are you certain she's the same craft?"

"As sartin, Master Haldane," he answered solemnly, "aye, as sartin as that when we goes aboard her, as go aboard her we must, we shall both be a-goin' to our death! That's the 'ghost-ship,' Master Haldane, as you and I've seed three times afore. May I die this minute if she ain't!"

"Die! don't talk such nonsense, Masters."

"It ain't no nonsense, Master Haldane," he retorted, and looking the picture of misery and unhappiness. "That there ship means no good to you nor me, nor to none of them as seed her afore, I knows. It's her, sure enuff. No mortal ship could sail on like that continually since Friday, right afore the wind, and still allers be a-crossin' our hawser, though her canvas be tore to ribbings and never a man aboard, as we've seed. It ain't nat'ral, nohow. Aye, she be the 'ghost-ship' and no mistake,—and God help us all!"

I noticed at the moment a telescope lying on the top of the saloon skylight, which Mr Fosset must have left behind him in his haste, when he came from the bridge to hail the skipper and then hurried back to his post; so, quickly catching up the glass, I scanned the distant sail, which grew more perceptible every minute.

Yes, there was no doubt about it.

She was a full-rigged ship running before the wind, but going a bit every now and then off her course as if under no proper guidance or management, while all her sails were torn and hanging anyhow, and her spars and rigging apparently at sixes and sevens, as though she had been terribly mauled by the weather.

"For Heaven's sake, tell me!" cried the colonel, who had approached me unobserved while I was looking through the telescope. "Tell me, is she there? Can you see her?"

"Yes, sir," said I. "I can see her, and it's the same ship I saw the other night. It is the Saint Pierre!"

"Ha!" he exclaimed, his black eyes flashing into a passion that made him forget his lameness, as he strode to the side of the vessel, where, resting one hand on the rail, he shook the other menacingly at the ill-fated craft, now with her hull well above the horizon. "Ah, you black devils, we'll settle you at last!"

Meanwhile, the skipper, who had gone up to join Mr Fosset on the bridge after leaving us below so suddenly, was making his way aft again; and on the colonel turning round from the rail he found him at his back, looking over his shoulder at the ship we were approaching.

The skipper was all agog with excitement.

"By George!" he exclaimed. "We're closing on her fast now, colonel!"

"How soon, Señor Applegarth, do you think we'll be before we're alongside her?"

"In about half an hour at the outside, sir, unless something gives way. We would have been up to her before if she had been lying-to; but she's going ahead too, like ourselves, and not making bad way either, considering the state she's in aloft, and her yawing this way and that. It is wonderful how she keeps on!"

"Oh dear! oh dear! she's possessed, as your companion here said just now to the young Señor Haldane."

"Oh, you mustn't mind what the bo'sun says," observed the skipper. "He's chock full of the old superstitions of the sea, and makes mountains out of molehills."

"The deuce! he's not far wrong about the Saint Pierre, though, for if ever a ship had the devil aboard, I'm sure she has, in the shape of that villainous black 'marquis'!"

"Then the sooner the better for us to see about 'Scotching' your de'il," cried the skipper with a laugh that meant business, I knew. "I'm now going to call the hands aft and prepare for the fight, and they shall have it hot, I can tell you," said he.

"Have you got arms enough for them, sir? Those rascals will make a stubborn resistance, and there's a big lot of them still left in the ship, remember!"

The skipper laughed outright at this.

"Lord bless you, colonel!" said he, "the steamers of our line are fitted out in their way very like men-of-war; and I have enough rifles and cutlasses in the arm chest below to rig out more than twice the number of the crew we carry, besides revolvers for all the officers. This, however, will be short and sharp work, as we're going to run your black devils by the beard; so I shall only serve out cutlasses."

"But you'll spare me a revolver, Señor Applegarth? I left mine, as you are aware, behind me," said he with a smile, "and I should like to have another shot or two at my friend, the 'marquis'!"

"Aye, aye, colonel, you shall have one, and a good one too, and so shall all those who know how to use a pistol properly; but, for close hand-to-hand fighting, I prefer cold steel myself."

Colonel Vereker joined in the skipper's grim chuckle, which suited his mood well.

"Yes, sir, that's true," he rejoined; "but a revolver isn't to be sneezed at, all the same!"

"No colonel, your leg'll bear witness to that," said the skipper as he turned to me. "Run down quickly, Haldane, to the arm chest in my state room—here are the keys—and pick out a dozen or so cutlasses and boarding-pikes, with a revolver apiece for all on the quarter-deck, and half a dozen rounds of ammunition. You can get Weston to help you to bring the lot up here. Look smart; I want to serve them out at once, as we're now coming up with the chase, and there's no time to lose."

Down I scuttled into the saloon with the skipper's bunch of keys; and, calling the steward to help me, went into the after cabin, where Garry O'Neil still remained, wetting the bandage round the head of the French captain, and doing it too with greater delicacy of touch than the most experienced and flippant of hospital nurses.

Garry was delighted when I told him what I came about.

"Houly Moses!" he ejaculated; "why that's the virry job for me, sure. Here, Weston, you ugly thaife of a son of a gun, come here! There's going to be some rare foightin' on deck prisintly; an' as I know ye don't loike to be afther spoilin' that beautiful mug o' yours, you jist sit down there, alannah, an' moind this poor chap here till I come below ag'in, whilst I help Musther Haldane, too, with thim murtherin' arms that give one a could chill, faith, to look at, bad cess to 'em."

He gave me a sly wink as he said this, which was unperceived by Weston, who accepted the proposed change of duty with an alacrity that showed he had no stomach for warfare procedure, and Garry and I very speedily took up a bundle of weapons each on to the poop, laying them down close beside the skipper, who stood against the rail.

"Ah, doctor," said the colonel, who was sitting down near by on the skylight hatchway, resting himself before the battle should begin, on seeing Garry come up the companion, "how's my poor friend now?"

"Faith, he's still unconshus," replied he, handing him a big revolver with a cartridge belt attached; "ah, sure, I 'spect he'll remain so, too, colonel, till you've had toime to polish off the rest of thim schoindrels we're afther. Indade, it's going off loike that the poor crayture will be, I'm afeard, whin it comes to the ind. I don't think he'll ayther spake or move ag'in in this loife."

But Garry was mistaken in this diagnosis of his, as events turned out; but, ere he could say another word, just then as the colonel was going to make a reply to him, the skipper hammered on the deck with a marling-spike to attract attention and give a hail at the very top of his voice that made us all jump, it was so loud and unexpected.

"Ahoy there, forrad!" he shouted in stentorian tones that rang fore and aft like a trumpet. "Bo'sun, send the hands aft."

"Say, cap'en," sang out Mr Fosset from the bridge, "shall I call up the fellows down below in the stoke-hold, sir?"

"Aye. Ring the engine-room gong. I want every man-jack on deck that Mr Stokes can spare; tell him so."

While old Masters was sounding his boatswain's pipe and while busy feet were tramping aft, the men were beginning to cluster in the waist immediately below the back of the poop. And here Captain Applegarth stood stern and erect like an old lion, his cap off and his wavy grey hair fluffed out over his head by the wind. While this was happening we could hear the distant sound of the engine-room bell, and then there came a hail from Mr Fosset.

"Mr Stokes is sending up every one from below, sir," yelled out the first mate. "He says he can manage by himself now that we're nearly up to the chase, with the help of a couple of the other firemen; and the engineers and stokers, the whole lot of them in a batch, have volunteered to come on deck and join the boarding party."

"That's your sort, my hearty," cried the skipper enthusiastically, looking down at the sea of excited faces below gazing up expectantly at his, awaiting the stirring words they knew to be coming, all having got wind of the approaching fray. "Now, men, I have summoned the lot of you aft because—well, because I've got something to say to you."

"Bully for you, old man," exclaimed one of the men, amidst a grand roar, while I could distinguish, distinctly above the other voices of the crew, Accra Prout, the mulatto cook's laugh as he called out approvingly, "Golly, dat so, sonny!"

"Heavens!" ejaculated Colonel Vereker, seemingly, like myself, to recognise the voice at once, "who's that?" said he sharply.

Accra Prout, who stood a head taller than any other of the men clustered round him, caught sight of the colonel as the latter cast his eyes downwards, rising from his seat and coming to the side of the skipper; and the mulatto's eyes grew as large as saucers, while his eyeballs rolled in delight and his wide mouth extended itself from ear to ear.

"Bress de Lor'!" he cried out, with all a darkey's emphatic enthusiasm, breaking into a huge guffaw that was almost hysterical—"bress de Lor'! it's de massa; it's Mass' Vereker from de plantation, for surh!"

"Yes, it's me, myself, sure enough, Prout; and I'm right glad to see you," said the colonel, equally delighted. "There, Señor Applegarth, didn't I tell you any of my old Louisianian hands would like to see me again, in spite of what I said about those infernal niggers who seized our ship?"

"Aye, you did, colonel, you did," replied the skipper, waving his hand in the air; "but never mind that now—I'm going to speak to the crew."

"Now, me bhoys, altogether," cried Garry O'Neil, looking over the top of the booby-hatch over the companion-way, "three cheers for the cap'en, horray!"

"Horray!" roared the lot below with a kindred enthusiasm, "Horray! Horray!"

"We're almost within hail now of the chase, sir," sang out Mr Fosset from the bridge when the echo of the last deafening cheer had died away; "I'm going to slow down, so that we can sheer up alongside."

"That's just what I was waiting for," said the skipper in answer to this. "Now, men, you see that ship ahead of us?"

"Aye," called out the foremost hand, who had before spoken—the usual leader, and the wit of the fo'c's'le—"the ghost-ship, cap'en."

"Well, ghost-ship, devil-ship, or whatever she may be, my lads, we're going to board her and rescue a young lady, a child in age, the daughter of my friend, Colonel Vereker here, and a lot of white men like yourselves, who are now at the mercy of a gang of black demons who have murdered the rest of the passengers and crew and taken possession of the vessel. Are you going to stand by me, lads?"

His answer was another deafening cheer, heartier and louder even than the first.

"Ah, I thought I could reckon on your help," cried the skipper in a tone of proud satisfaction, glancing round at the colonel. "I have got your tools handy for you, too, my lads; and if you will come up to the poop in single file by the port-ladder, going down again by the starboard gangway, each shall be supplied in turn. Mr O'Neil, please serve out the cutlasses and boarding-pikes. Now, my men, way aloft there! Single file, and no crushing, mind, and we'll get the job done all the quicker!"

Ere he had finished speaking the arming of the men had already begun, and within a very few minutes the cutlasses and long boarding-pikes had all been distributed, every man having some weapon.

"Now, bo'sun, pipe the men to their stations," sang out the skipper, who appeared to have already matured his plan of action. "Starboard watch forrad, port watch aft, and all the stokers and firemen amidships, under the bridge. Have a couple of hands, too, in the forechains, with a hawser and grapnel, ready to make fast to the ship when we come alongside her."

"Aye, aye, sir," hailed back Masters. "Starboard watch ahoy! Away forrads with you along o' me!"

Our engines had already slackened speed; and, the helm being put down, we came up to the wind, to leeward of the ship and not a half cable's length away from her, broadside-on.

"Stand by there, forrad," shouted the skipper. "Ship ahoy there! Surrender, or we'll run you aboard."

A wild savage yell came back in reply from a number of half-naked negroes who were mustered on the after part of the vessel, as well as on the forecastle, not a single white man being visible, while her Tricolour flag—so conspicuous before, and which I fancied having seen but half an hour or so previously when looking at her through the telescope—was now no longer to be seen.

Could our worst fears have been realised?

Another savage yell almost confirmed the thought. "Heavens!" exclaimed Colonel Vereker, rendered almost frantic with grief and excitement, and noticing the appalling evidences of the Haytians' triumph, while we stared aghast at each other. "My poor darling child, and those brave fellows I left behind, where are they all; where are they? For God's sake find them! Alas! alas! those black devils have murdered them all."

A Free Fight

But hardly had the colonel given vent to his despairing exclamation, expressive alike of his own dismay and ours also, when the bitter feeling of disappointment at being too late, that had for the moment weighed down upon us, crushing our enthusiasm, was suddenly banished and the hearts of all filled with renewed hope and fierce determination.

We were not too late after all!

No.

For as we gazed in blank surprise at the howling mob of Haytians, who appeared to have gained complete possession of the Saint Pierre, and were dancing about and gesticulating in their wild, devilish fashion, calling out to us with wild derisive cries, as if mocking at our efforts to save those whom they had already butchered, a bright flame of fire flashed out from the skylight hatch of the doomed ship, followed by the sharp crack of a revolver; and at the same instant one of the half-naked devils massed on the poop leaped into the air and then fell on his face flat on the deck, uttering a yell of agony as he writhed his limbs in the throes of death.

An exulting cheer broke from all of us in the Star of the North on seeing this, every man gripping his weapon tightly, and setting his teeth hard, ready for action, as the two vessels sidled up nearer and nearer.

Then if word were wanted to spur us on, the skipper gave that word with a vengeance!

"By George! my lads, we're in time yet to save the child and our other white comrades!" he cried out loudly, at the same time jumping into the mizzen rigging, where he hung on the shrouds with one hand, while in the other he held a cutlass which he had hastily clutched up, whirling it round his lionlike old grey head. "See, men, they've retreated to the cabin below, where they're fighting for their lives to the last. Tumble up, my lads, and save them, like the British sailors that you are! Boarders, away!"

As he said this, Mr Fosset, who was still on the bridge conning the old barquey, having at once ported our helm, on the skipper holding up his cutlass, taking this for a signal, we came broadside-on, slap against the hull of the other ship with a jolt that shook her down to her very kelson, rolling a lot of the darkies, who were grouped aft, off their legs like so many ninepins. At the same moment, before the two craft had time to glide apart, both having way upon them, old Masters forward, and Parrell, the quartermaster, who was stationed in the waist of our vessel, just under the break of the poop, hooked on grapnels, with hawsers attached, to the weather rigging of the Saint Pierre; and ere the skipper's rallying cry and our answering cheer had died away, drowned by the voice of our escaping steam rushing up the funnels on the engines coming to a stop, now that their duty for the nonce was done, there we were moored hard and fast together, alongside the whilom dreaded "ghost-ship!"

Then with another wild hurrah that made the ringbolts in the deck jingle, and swamped the sound of the rushing steam and everything, the men, closing up behind the skipper, who led us so gallantly over the side, far in advance, brave-hearted old sea dog that he was, bounded across the intervening bulwarks, and were the next instant engaged in all the maddening excitement of a hand-to-hand tussle with the black villains, pistol shot, sword cut and pike thrust coming in turn into play, amid a babel of hoarse shouts of rage and cheers and savage yells—mingled with the swish of blows from capstan bars, the loud reports of revolvers fired off at close range and the heavy thud of falling bodies as they tumbled headlong on the deck ever and anon, accompanied by some cry of agony or groan of pain too deep for utterance.

Aye, it was a discord of devilry that must have appeared a veritable pandemonium to the spirits of the air, were any such looking down on the wrathful, sanguinary scene from the clear blue heavens above, all radiant now with a golden glow that came from the west, where the declining sun was just beginning to sink below the horizon!

"Fuaghaballah, may the divvle take the hindmost!" cried Garry O'Neil, leaping after the skipper on to the poop of the Saint Pierre, a revolver in his right fist and a cutlass in his left, laying about him with a will amongst the mass of infuriated negroes who tried to resist his rush, clutching at his legs and arms in vain, for he seemed bewitched. "Come on wid ye, me darlints, an' let us make mincemate of 'em, faith!"

I followed in his wake, but a crowd of our men, some of whom had served in the navy and were accustomed to the work, pushed me on one side, going into the thick of the fight themselves, and all was such a jumble of confusion that I hardly knew where I was until "a pretty tidy tap on the top of my head," as Garry would have said, brought back my recollection in a very effective manner, when I found myself right in front of an extremely ugly-looking negro, whose appearance was not improved by a slice having been taken off the side of his face, and from which blood was streaming down all over his black body, and that destitute of clothing.

I noticed that this gentleman had a long piece of wood like a boat stretcher in his hands, with which he had evidently given me the gentle reminder I have mentioned, being brought to this conclusion by the fact that the rascal had it raised ready to deal another blow.

Putting up my arm instinctively to ward off the impending stroke that I saw coming, I cocked and levelled my revolver at him in an instant.

Before I could fire, however, some one behind me shoved me aside again, and crash came a heavy capstan bar down upon the negro's skull, which I heard crack like a walnut shell as he dropped dead on his face.

"Golly, Mass' Hald'n," exclaimed Accra Prout, our stalwart mulatto cook, whose sinuous arm had thus incontinently settled the dispute between my sable opponent and myself. "I'se guess dis chile gib dat black debble goss, noh ow!"

But ere I could say a word to him for his timely aid, Accra Prout had bounded onward in front, and I then saw he was following Colonel Vereker, who had managed somehow or other, in spite of his lameness, to gain the deck of his old ship along with the rest of us.

Crack, crack, crack, went his revolver with venomous iteration from the other side of the vessel, where he was standing by the bulwarks, close to the hatchway of the companion-ladder leading to the cabin below, which he was apparently endeavouring to reach, while a crowd of Haytians barred his further progress towards those imprisoned in the cabin, whom they thus prevented his releasing, a fresh foe starting up for every one he disposed of, and a rough and terrible fight going on all round him all the time.

"'Top a minnit, Mass' V'reker!" shouted Accra Prout, darting into the middle of the throng, clearing a pathway for himself with the capstan bar. "I'se here; I'se come help you soon!"

"A thousand devils!" hissed a tall black near by—a man with a large, crinkly, ink-black moustache, and certainly with the most satanic visage I had ever beheld before. "A thousand devils!" repeated he, giving him a thrust with a large knife that pierced poor Accra's arm, and making him drop the capstan bar. "Take care of yourself—beast!"

A cry from the colonel told me who this was.

"Ah, villain, villain!" he sang out, looking him full in the face and grinding his teeth and trying with all his might, but vainly, to get at him through the press of struggling figures by whom he was surrounded. "I've been looking for you, Marquis des Coupgorges!"

The black scoundrel gave out a shrill laugh like that of a hyena, as Colonel Vereker had described it to us when telling his yarn.

"Pardon me, sir, I am here," he yelled out mockingly. "I am here. I do not run away like your white trash! Why don't you come and fight me? Bah! I spit on you, my fine plantation colonel. When I get at you I will serve you just as I did your sly slave the other day, whom you sent to betray us, though you, yourself, were too great a coward to come amongst us, yes, to come amongst us yourself. Aha! colonel."

He said this in plain English, which language he spoke as fluently as he did French, the native language of Hayti, uttering his abusive threats loud enough for us to hear every syllable; but though I aimed at him while he was speaking twice point blank, and my revolver spoke out quite as loudly as he, while the colonel likewise shot at him and the skipper made a slash in his direction with his cutlass, the miscreant escaped all our attacks without a single wound, dodging away from us amongst his dusky compatriots, who were now pretty thickly mixed up with our men in a fierce mêlée, at the further end of the poop, overlooking the waist below.

In the midst of this awful scrimmage there came a wild rush aft of all the remaining blacks who had been engaged with some of the hands amidships, pursued by our second boarding party, led by Mr Fosset and Stoddart, who had made their way over the bows and cleared the fo'c's'le, fighting onward step by step along the upper deck; and hemmed in fast thus, between two fires, the black desperadoes made a last stand, refusing to surrender, or throw down their arms in spite of all promises of quarter on our part.

All of them could see for themselves how completely overmatched they were, and must have known the utter uselessness of attempting any further resistance to us; but the mutineers of the negro portion of the Saint Pierre's crew, who were now in the majority, feared to give in owing to the fact of their believing they would be ultimately hanged if taken alive after the atrocities they had committed; so being of the opinion they were bound to be killed in any case, they determined apparently, if die they must, they would die fighting.

Whatever might be their motive or conviction, I will give them the credit of being plucky, and must say that they fought bravely, though with a ferocity that was more than savage, to the bitter end, their last rally on the break of the poop being the fiercest episode of the fray, several hand-to-hand combats going on at one and the same time with hand pikes and capstan bars whirling about over the heads of those engaged, where cutlass cuts were met with knife-thrusts from the formidable long-bladed weapons the negroes carried in their hands only to sheathe them in the bodies of their white antagonists.

My brain got dizzy as I watched the mad turmoil and my blood was at fever heat, taking part in the fight too, you may be sure, whenever I saw an opening, and dealing a blow here or parrying one there, as chance arose, with the best of them, young though I was, and totally inexperienced in such matters!

It was coming near to the finish, being too warm work to continue much longer, and I think all of us had had pretty well enough of it, when, looking round for Colonel Vereker, whom I suddenly missed from among the combatants, I saw him struggling with one of the blacks in a regular rough and tumble tussle on the deck.

The two were rolling about close to the after skylight from whence we had observed the flash of the pistol shot as we approached the ship, and which the colonel had been trying to get near to ever since he boarded her, but had been prevented from reaching by one obstacle or another until now, when this negro clutched hold of him and forced him back again.

He and the Haytian were tightly locked in a deadly embrace, the negro gripping him with both arms round the body, and the colonel endeavouring to release his revolver hand, the two rolling over and over on the deck towards the rail forward.

"Ha!" muttered the colonel, who was hard pressed, through his set teeth. "Only let me get free."

Strangely enough, the glass of the skylight above the spot where the pair were struggling was instantly shattered from within, as if in response to his muttered cry; and with a loud bark that could have been heard a mile off, a big dog burst forth from the opening, making straight for the colonel and his relentless foe.

Then there came a startled yell from the negro, who, releasing his late antagonist, staggered to his feet.

"Holy name of—" he screamed out in wild affright, but he had not time to reach the concluding word of his sentence—the name of his patron saint, no doubt—"the devil!"

For before he could get so far, giving a fierce growl, the dog at once sprang up at him, his fangs meeting in the Haytian's throat, whereupon the latter, toppling backwards over the poop-rail, fell into the waist below, with the dog hanging on to him; and I noticed presently that both were dead, the brave animal who had come so opportunely to the rescue of the colonel, his master, being stabbed to the heart by a knife which the negro still held in his lifeless hand, while his own neck had been torn to pieces by the dog whom death could not force to relinquish his grip!

Immediately running up to the colonel, who was feebly trying to rise, his wrestle with the black having crippled his wounded leg and arm, I helped him to his feet as quickly as I could, while others clustered round to shelter us.

"Poor Ivan, true as steel in death as in life!" he faintly muttered, glancing from the break of the poop on the two bodies huddled together below, the blood of the faithful dog flowing with that of his ruthless foe into a crimson pool that was gradually extending its borders from the middle of the deck to the lee scuppers. "He has defended my little Elsie, I am sure, to the last, likewise, even as he defended me. I hope and trust my child is still safe in the cabin. Help me aft, my lad, to see; quick, quick!"

Of course I assisted him as well as I could under the circumstances, but as he limped along towards the companion-hatchway, the leader of the desperadoes, that villainous "marquis," who I thought had met with his just deserts long since, not having seen him for some little time among the other fighters, most unexpectedly jumped from the rigging in front of the colonel and aimed a vindictive blow at him with a marline-spike.

This must have settled the colonel if it had fallen on his uncovered head. Fortunately though, dropping quickly the colonel's arm, I fended off the blow with the revolver I held in my hand, while at the same time I gave the scoundrel a drive in the face that must have astonished his black lordship a good deal, for my clenched fist met him square on the mouth and shook his teeth, making them rattle, as well as disarranging the twist of his crinkly moustache!

He came at me with a snarl like an angry tiger, and then, hugging me tight, with his hideous black face thrust close against mine, and his muscular arms pressed tightly around my ribs, he squeezed every ounce of breath out of my body.

I thought my last hour had come.

But help came to my aid from a most unlooked-for quarter.

"Ah! you blackguard," cried a voice that sounded dimly in my ears, my head at the time seeming to be whirling round like the arms of a windmill from the sense of suffocation and the rush of blood to the brain. "Coward! miscreant! you are here again."

Breathless though I was, I was so surprised, and indeed frightened at the voice and accent of the speaker, which I immediately recognised, that I at once came to myself and opened wide my half-closed eyes.

Good heavens! Shall I ever forget the sight? Yes; it was Captain Alphonse, whom I had last seen only half an hour or so previously in the skipper's cot on board the Star of the North, when Garry O'Neil said he would probably never wake to consciousness again in this life, or move out of the skipper's state room!

Here he was though, all the same, looking like an apparition from the dead, wild, ghastly, awful, but quite sufficiently in his senses to recognise his terrible enemy, the pseudo "marquis."

It is a scene I shall never forget, as I remarked before.

Like poor Ivan, and with equal ferocity, the Frenchman sprang at the ugly villain's throat, the whole lot of us tumbling headlong on the deck together, which caused the wretch to release me in order to protect himself from Captain Alphonse, who, kneeling on the top of him, hammered him against the bulwarks as though trying to beat the life out of him.

Making a last desperate effort, the Haytian "marquis" gripped his antagonist round the waist as he previously gripped me, dragging him down beside him again; and then, as the two came with all their might against the side of the ship where the port flap was loose, the whole of the planking gave way, and poor Captain Alphonse, with that scoundrel the black "marquis," crashed through the splintering wood together, falling with a heavy splash overboard into the sea beneath, going to the bottom locked in each other's arms—a terrible ending to the terrible episode of this, their last meeting.

For the minute the colonel seemed overwhelmed with grief at this awful and sudden termination of poor Captain Alphonse's life, and we would all sooner have seen him die unconsciously if not quietly, in his bed; but such are the ways of Providence, and we cannot control them!

But this day certainly witnessed a series of surprises, so it seemed to me, the most wonderful things happening every moment.

Colonel Vereker had dragged himself as well as he could up to where I lay on the deck, after being set free from the bearlike hug of the negro, helping me up on my legs in the same Good Samaritan way in the which I had saved him shortly before; and we were both looking over the side, talking excitedly of the dreadful catastrophe that had just happened, and wondering whether the poor captain's body would rise to the surface again, when all of a sudden, something bright crossing the deck caught my eye like a flash of light, and I heard the sound of light and hurried footsteps.

Wheeling round hastily I was amazed at the beautiful object that met my gaze, for I saw standing there, only a pace or two off, a lovely young girl, with a profusion of long silky hair of a bright golden hue, that streamed in a tangled mass over her shoulders, and reaching down almost to her feet.

"My father, my dear father!" she exclaimed in broken and ecstatic tones, her voice sounding to me like the soft cooing of a dove, as she flew and nestled herself into the outstretched arms of the colonel, who had also turned round at her approach, some sympathetic feeling having warned him of her coming, telling him who it was even before he saw her.

"Oh, my father! my father! At last, at last!"

And then, unable to control herself longer, she burst into a passion of tears and sobs.

Colonel Vereker, on his part, was equally overcome.

"God be thanked!" cried he, raising his face to heaven, clasping her at the same time fondly to his heart and kissing her trembling lips again and again. "My darling one, my own little daughter, whom I thought I had lost for ever, but whom the good God has preserved to be the delight of my eyes again, my little one, my precious!"

For a few minutes I too had a lump in my throat, but turned aside, and then, not wishing to appear to be observing them, I left them alone and went off to another part of the ship.

Hors de Combat

A grand hurrah just then burst forth from the deck below us, where the skipper and most of the men were massed, telling as plainly as triumphant cheer could tell, that the fight was ended and that victory had crowned our arms with success. I rushed back to tell the colonel.

On hearing my footsteps, however, little Elsie turned round and caught sight of me.

"Oh, my father!" said she, untwining herself from the colonel's embrace, though she still nestled up close to him, as she stared at me shyly, with a puzzled look on her mignonne face. "Why, who is this young sir, my father? I seem to know him, and yet I do not remember having ever seen him before!"

"Look at him again, darling one," said her father, petting her caressingly, while another hearty cheer went up from the hands in the waist. "He is Señor Dick Haldane, a gallant young gentleman whom you must thank, my little daughter, for having saved my life."

At this the graceful young girl advanced a step or two towards me, and catching hold of my hand, before I could prevent her, kissed it, greatly to my confusion; as albeit it was an act expressive amongst the Spanish with whom she had been brought up, of deferential courtesy and gratitude, but it made me blush up to my eyes and feel hot all over.

"A thousand thanks, sir," she began; but as she raised her eyes to my face in thus giving utterance to her thanks for having, as the colonel had told her, saved her father's life, a flood of recollection seemed to come upon her, and she exclaimed:

"Ah, I remember now! My father, yes, he is like the gentleman whom I saw on the deck of the steamer that awful night when the negroes rose up against us—last Friday, was it not? But it seems so long ago to me! You, you naughty papa, would not believe that your little girl had seen anything at all, not even a ship, but that I only fancied it in my foolishness. However, there is the same steamer that I saw (pointing with her finger to the Star of the North), and here is the same, for I am sure he is the same, the very same young officer. Am I not right?" And looking up at her father, she exclaimed, "Your little girl told the truth after all."

"And you, young lady," said I, smiling at her recognition of me, strange coincidence as it was, corroborating my own experience of the same eventful night, "yes; you are the same little girl I saw on board the 'ghost-ship,' as all the men here called your vessel, not believing, likewise, my story that I had seen her or you either. Yes, I would have known you anywhere. You are the girl whom I saw with the dog!"

The next moment I could have bitten my tongue out, though, for my thoughtlessness in alluding to the poor dog; for at the bare mention of him Elsie's face, which had a sort of absent, wandering look about it still, at once lighted up, and she glanced round in all directions.

"Ah, I declare I had quite forgotten Ivan in the joy and happiness of seeing you again, my father," she exclaimed excitedly. "Where is he, the brave fellow? Ivan, Ivan, you dear old dog. Come here; come here, sir, directly!"

She looked round again, with a half smile playing about the corners of her pretty rosebud of a mouth and a joyous light in her eyes, expecting her faithful friend and companion would come bounding up to her side; but she now waited and watched and listened in vain, there being no response to her summons either by bark or bound or wag of poor Ivan's bushy tail.

Nor would there be any more, for his ringing bark was hushed, his body and tail alike stiff and cold, while his noble heart which only throbbed with affection for those whom he loved when living, had stopped beating for aye.

"My dear child, poor Ivan is dead!" said Colonel Vereker tenderly after a short pause, drawing the young girl up to him so that she might not see the gruesome sight on the deck below. "The brave dog sacrificed his life for mine, and but for his help, little one, I should not now be by your side."

This account of the poor animal's heroic end, however, did not comfort little Elsie, who gave a startled glance at her father's face; where, seeing something there that made her comprehend her loss, she buried her golden head on his breast, sobbing as though her heart would break.

"Poor, poor, dear Ivan; he never left me once, never, my father, since you—you went out of the cabin that last night and told him to watch me!" she exclaimed presently, in halting accents between her convulsive sobs, neither the colonel or myself dry-eyed as we listened to her tale, you may be sure. "But—but all at once, after all the noise and that dreadful firing that seems now to go through my ears, I—I heard your voice quite distinctly on the deck; and so, too, did poor Ivan, for I saw him instantly put up his ears, while he whined and looked beseechingly at us."

"Well, after that, my child," said the colonel, on her stopping for the moment, overcome with emotion, "what happened next?"

"He made a dash at the cabin table and jumped up on it, and then the poor fellow growled savagely at some one outside. Then—then before I could hold him back he made a most desperate spring and sprung right up through the glass roof on the top of the sky—skylight, and he must have cut himself very very much. Poor, poor doggie! And now you say my poor Ivan is dead, and that I shall never see the dear good faithful creature again. Oh, my father!"

At this point the young girl again broke down.

Nor were her tears a mere passing tribute of grief. For, though dead, Ivan is not forgotten, like some people, the remembrance of whom is as evanescent as the scent of the flowers that hypocritical mourners may ostentatiously scatter upon their graves; his little mistress, little no longer, preserving his memory yet green in her heart of hearts, close to which she wears always a small locket containing likenesses of her father and mother, together with a miniature of Ivan—her father's preserver—with a tiny lock added from the brave dog's curly black coat.

Some ultra-sanctimonious persons may feel inclined to cavil with this association on Elsie's part of "immortal beings," as they would style her parents, and the recollection she cherishes of a "dead brute," because, forsooth, they hold that her four-footed favourite had no soul; but were these gentry to broach the subject before her, being a somewhat outspoken young lady from her foreign bringing up, which puts her beyond the pale of boarding-school punctiliousness, she would probably urge that she estimated poor Ivan's sagacious instinct combined with his courage and noble self-sacrifice, at a far higher level than the paltry apology for a soul that passes current for the genuine article with matter-of-fact religionists of the stamp of her questioner.

But Elsie was "little Elsie" still, at the time of which I am speaking, and too young, perhaps, for such thoughts to occur to her mind, which at the moment was too full of her loss.

The cheering that had followed the last tussle of our men with the black mutineers had now ceased, and all these things happening, you must understand, much more rapidly than I can talk or attempt to chronicle them, the skipper, with Mr Fosset and Garry O'Neil, came hurriedly up on the poop.

Both expressed their unbounded delight at seeing the child was safe and in the care of her father.

Sure, an' what's the little colleen cryin' for? eagerly inquired Garry, his smoke-begrimed face, which bore ample evidence of the desperate struggle in which he had been so gallantly engaged, wearing a look of deep commiseration as he gazed from her father to me, and then again at her. "Faith, I hope she's not been hurt or frightened?"

"No, thank God!" replied the colonel huskily. "Grieving for her poor dog Ivan, who—"

"Och yes, I saw the noble baste," interrupted Garry in his quick, enthusiastic way. "Begorrah, colonel, he fought betther than any two-legged Christian amongst us, an' I can't say more than that for him, sure, paice to his name!"

Before he could say anything further, and you know he was a rare one to talk when once he commenced, the skipper advanced again, holding out his hand to the colonel exclaiming— "Yes, thank God you are all right and that your little child is safe, and escaped any harm from those scoundrels, except her nerves probably being much shaken, but that she will soon recover at her age—and I told you she should be restored to you, you know. By George! Though, we've paid them out at last for demon's work aboard here!"

"The devils!" ejaculated Colonel Vereker savagely, his mood changing as he recollected all he had seen and suffered at their hands. "Have you killed them all?"

"All but half a dozen of the rascals, whom we had a rare hunt after through the hold and fo'c's'le before we could collar them. They are fast bound now, though, lashed head and feet to the mainmast bitts; and it will puzzle them to wriggle themselves loose from old Masters' double hitches, I know. Besides which, two of our men are guarding there, with boarding-pikes in their hands and orders to run 'em through the gizzard if they offer to stir."

"Faith," observed Garry O'Neil reflectively, "It was as purty a bit of foighting as I ivver took a hand in, whilst it lasted!"

"But let us go and see what has become of all those chaps below—all those you mentioned as belonging to the French crew, whom you left on board with your daughter," went on the skipper. "We saw the flash of a pistol, you remember, when we came up alongside, and somebody must have prevented those villains from getting into the cabin, or else—"

He stopped here and looked meaningly at Elsie.

"Heavens!" exclaimed the colonel, attempting to rise, but falling back on the hen-coop along the side of the bulwarks he had been using for a temporary seat, he seemed so utterly exhausted. "Ah, those brave fellows, I was almost forgetting them; but I can't move, Señor Applegarth, or I should have gone down before this to see what had become of my old comrades; but I'm helpless, as you see."

Elsie now lifted her head, looked up and turned towards the skipper.

"They are all wounded," said she, clasping her hands together and with a look of fright on her face. "Two of the men—the French sailors, I mean—and the English gentleman."

"That's the little Britisher I told you about, who was so plucky," explained the colonel—"Mr Johnson."

"Well, my father," continued the young girl, "these three rushed down the stairs into the cabin, shortly before the steamer thumped against the side of our ship, when I thought we were all going down to the bottom of the sea."

"Yes, my child," said the colonel encouragingly, "go on and tell us what happened next."

"The English gentleman spoke to me and said that the terrible negroes had conquered them all on deck, but that he and the two Frenchmen had escaped from them in time, and were going to barricade the doorway leading down from above to prevent the black men from coming below and murdering us all.

"He told me, though, did the kind English gentleman, that I must not be frightened and all would come right in the end, for that they had seen a very large steamer approaching, coming quite close to us, and that they would be able, he thought, to hold out until we were all rescued. They then piled up heaps and heaps of things against the door at the foot of the stairs where the sailors remained; then the Englishman stood on the table, under the skylight, to keep the negroes from getting through there. It was the Englishman who fired at them through the glass, for he was the only one who had a pistol, and he made a hole and then through that we heard all the shrieks and the noise of the pistols; and your voice, my father, Ivan heard, and then he jumped up through the hole, making a much bigger one, and ran to your rescue, my dear, dear father."

"But what has become of Monsieur Boisson, and Madame all this time; where were they?" asked the colonel, on Elsie thus concluding the account of what had occurred under her immediate notice, a little sob escaping her involuntarily at the mention of her poor dog's name, and at the recollection of what she had just witnessed. "Did they do anything, my dear child to help themselves, or you?"

"No, my father," she replied, apparently surprised at the question. "They are still in the big cabin at the end of the saloon where you left them when you went away, and, I'm afraid they are very ill indeed, for all the time the firing was going on overhead Madame was screeching and screaming, and I am sure I heard Monsieur groaning a good deal. He was doing so again just now, before I found my way upstairs to you, to find you, and to see what had happened, everything had become so suddenly still after all the noise, and—and—those—awful horrible yells of the negroes—oh! I—I—can hear them still!"

She turned quite pale when uttering the last words, words spoken with visible effort, shuddering all over and hiding her face again on her father's shoulder.

"Faith, sor, don't ask her any more questions," cried Garry, "but we'd bether be sayin' afther those poor fellows ourselves, an' at once, too!"

"Do quickly, sir doctor," said the colonel, "and I only wish I could come with you! but—"

"Now jist you shtop where ye are, me friend," rejoined Garry, putting out his hand to prevent his stirring from his seat. "Sure the cap'en an' me, with Dick Haldane here, will be enough to look afther 'em all."

With this he made for the companion-way and descended the "stairs," as Elsie, ignorant of nautical nomenclature, called the ladder, the skipper following close behind him.

On getting to the bottom we found the panels of the door smashed in, though of hard oak, strengthened with cross battens of the same stout wood, which showed to what fierce assault it had been subjected, the furniture piled up against it from within having duly prevented the negroes from finally forcing an entrance, as well, no doubt, as our appearance on the scene.

This barricade had, however, been now partly removed, probably to allow of little Elsie's exit, and, quickly pitching the remaining obstacles aside, the three of us managed to squeeze ourselves inside the cabin, which was in such a state of confusion, with the long table overturned to serve as a breastwork for the gallant defenders and the settees and lockers turned away from the deck, as well as the glass of the skylight all smashed, that it looked like a veritable "Hurrah's vest" as we sailors say.

On a pile of cushions belonging to the lounge aft—the only piece of furniture that was left intact in the place, I believe—lay the brave men who had stubbornly held the ship to the last against the mutineers.

All were covered with blood and blackened by powder and so utterly worn out from fatigue in battling throughout the night and day that had almost elapsed since the colonel had left them, besides being crippled by the injuries they had received in the fray, that they hardly moved on our entrance, though one—a little chap whom I judged to be the Englishman spoken of by the colonel and Elsie—brightened up as we bent over him, a look of satisfaction and content stealing over his drawn and haggard face, as we cauld see from the rays of the setting sun streaming down through the broken skylight, exposing the utter desolation around.

He was the first to speak.

"I'm afeard you've come too late for us, sirs," said he slowly, with a deep groan of pain. "Those damned niggers have done for me, one of them giving me a dig of his knife in the ribs—did it through the doorway just now, when the fight were nearly over. You might do summat, though, for my companions here, who stood up to the darkies like Britons, in spite of them being only Frenchmen, though that ain't their fault. But how's the little girl? I hope she's all right. Tell her father, if he's alive—and I feel almost sure I heard his voice awhile ago up on deck—tell him that I kept my word, sirs, and fought for her to the last. I think I'm dying now, and—I—must—leave—off. But listen while I've a little breath, for I want to say something. My name is Robert Johnson, and my old mother, God bless her, lives at Camberwell, near London. You'll find all my papers in my pocket and a letter with the address, and if any of you chances to be going back to England as I were, worse luck, you'd be doing a favour by seein' her and letting her know why I didn't turn up home this Christmas as I promised her. I know you will. I'm going now, I'm so tired. Good-night to you all—good-night—good—"

As he said this he gradually fell back on the cushion he was resting against, and his eyes closed.

Captain Applegarth and I both thought him dead.

Not so, however, Garry O'Neil.

"Sure, he's ounly fainted," exclaimed the Irishman; "run, Dick, me bhoy, an' say if there's sich a thing as a stooard's pantry knockin' about anywheres in those latituodes, wid a dhrop of water convenient. That an' a taste of this aqua vitae here, which, the saints be praised, I took the precawshin to put in me pocket afore we shtarted on this blissid and excoitin' skermoish, this will very soon fetch back a little loife into the plucky little beggar ag'in!"

I had no difficulty in finding the steward's pantry and a breaker of water, with a tin dipper attached, speedily carrying some back and, by our joint ministrations, and with it bathing his face and hands and pouring some between his lips, little Mr Johnson at last opened his eyes and began to breathe.

After a time and a certain amount of patience he opened his eyes wider, and became conscious, and later on was induced to swallow down a mixture out of his own special bottle that Garry carried, and we were at last delighted to see quite a broad grin spread over his round good-natured and somewhat comical face.

"By Jingo, sir!" said he, after a pause and rather long silence, and after he had drained off the last drop of the elixir, with a sigh of gratitude that evidently came from his heart, "you've saved my life this time, and no mistake. I never thought I should taste a drop of good brandy again in this world."

WE PART COMPANY

While Garry O'Neil and I were attending to the two French sailors who, though they had been a good bit knocked about in the course of the protracted struggle, were not seemingly very seriously hurt, suffering more, indeed, from want of proper food and rest than from the slight wounds they had received, we heard loud cries and a sort of dull moaning that appeared to proceed from the after part of the saloon.

Going thither at once, Captain Applegarth knocked with his knuckles on the panel of the closed door of one of the larger state rooms, running athwart the ship from whence the sounds proceeded.

"Hullo, within there!" he shouted, "what's the matter? What's the row? Come out!"

A shrill scream was the only response to his inquiries.

"What's the matter?" repeated the skipper, speaking in a gentler tone. "You have nothing to fear. We're all friends here!"

The cries and confused noises continued, however, and the skipper thereupon resumed his knocking, this time more forcibly, and with his fists aided by a kick from his heavy boot against the lower part of the still closed door.

At this imperative summons the shrieking ceased, and we heard a feeble voice within, calling out in French— "Mercy! for the love of God!" we could distinguish amidst a plentitude of sobs and violent groans in a deeper key. "Ah! brave Haytians! Have pity, and spare our lives!"

"Hang it all, you cowards, we're not those cursed Haytians, and I wish you could have been left to their mercy! It is only what you deserve!" roared the skipper, infuriated and out of all patience at the Frenchwoman's mistake and her appealing in such terms to the murderous scoundrels of whom we had made so summary an end. "We're Englishmen; we're your friends, I tell you, true-hearted British sailors, who have come to rescue you, so open the door!"

But Madame Boisson, who, of course, was his interlocutrice behind the door, remained obdurate.

"Ah! the false English," she cried, "down with the pigs!"

At this the skipper laughed grimly, and all standing near him were much amused.

"She's a good specimen of her race," cried the captain. "They always abuse other nations and cry out that they are betrayed when ill luck comes to them, instead of trying to help themselves, as we perfidious Englishmen do."

Finding it impossible to persuade her, though, to open the door of the cabin, which was bolted and barred within, the skipper sang out to me to go on deck and ask Elsie Vereker to come down and try what she could do, thinking that the obstinate prisoner would doubtless recognise the girl's voice and so, through her means, be made more amenable to reason.

No sooner said than done.

Up I went and down the companion-way. I returned anon accompanied not only by Miss Elsie, but by the colonel as well, Garry O'Neil, who hurried up the ladder after me with that intent, insisting on his coming below so that he could the better attend to his wounded leg, which had broken out again and needed fresh dressing, and after some little difficulty Garry got him down in safety.

Thanks to Elsie's pleadings, Madame Boisson at length capitulated, promising to come out of her retreat as soon as she had had time, "to make her toilet."

"By George!" exclaimed the skipper, overhearing this and turning with an ironical grin to the colonel, who had his leg upon a chair, and Garry bustling about him, busy with bandages, "she's a true Frenchwoman, as I said at the first. Fancy, after being imprisoned there in that stuffy cabin for four and twenty hours and imagining herself and husband might be murdered every minute by a lot of pirate scoundrels, thinking of nothing but titifying herself, instead of thanking God for their escape and rushing out at the very first opportunity, eager to be free. Strange creatures!"

"Heavens!" exclaimed the colonel, smiling at the other's outburst. "It is true, but they're all alike, and I've seen a good many of them, my friend."

Presently out sailed Madame Boisson, who I noticed was a middle-aged and well-preserved woman, attired in an elaborate dressing gown with a profusion of bows and ribbons fluttering about it, and with a good deal of pearl powder or some other cosmetic of that sort on her face, and her cheeks tinted here and there with—well, colour.

Despite her screams and hysterics, however, there was no trace of a tear in her twinkling black eyes, although her fat little husband, who ambled meekly in her train, betrayed signs of great emotion, his red face all swollen from crying, and otherwise looking like a whipped cur.

Madame made a most gracious salute to us all, and, glancing at me with a spice of coquetry, to which she was evidently not unaccustomed, was pleased to observe, that I was "un beau garçon."

In returning the skipper's polite bow she happened to notice the poor wounded sailors lying on the cushions by the companion, and the blood all sprinkled about—a sight at which she turned up her nose, declaring very volubly that the place was like a "pigsty," unfit for any lady to enter, and expressing her surprise at those "common seamen" being attended to and allowed to remain in the saloon, she having always understood that that apartment was only for "the use of the first-class passengers."

The skipper, who understood her well enough, as I did too, having learnt the language at a French school near Rouen, was very angry at her remarks.

"Those men," said he in his best Parisian, "are your own countrymen, all that are left of those who died to preserve the lives of you and your husband there, who ought to be ashamed of himself for skulking below while they were fighting on deck."

Monsieur looked foolish, but said nothing in reply to this. Madame sniffed, and flashed her glittering black eyes, as if she could annihilate him at a glance.

"My brave Hercules!" she cried indignantly, "be easy. You have been out in the Bois and have established your reputation as a hero and have no need to notice the insulting remarks of this Englishman. But for you," she added, turning angrily to the colonel, "this would not have happened."

"I? Good Heavens!" exclaimed Colonel Vereker, greatly astonished at her turning on him thus. "Why, it was I who did all in my power to prevent Captain Alphonse from allowing those cursed blacks on board the ship in the first instance, but you and Monsieur Boisson, both of you, persuaded him to the contrary."

"My God! dear Hercules, see how we are calumniated," said the irate Frenchwoman, rather illogically, turning to her miserable atom of a husband, who gesticulated and shrugged his shoulders in response, and looking over the skipper and Colonel Vereker as if neither existed, she went on to remark to Elsie, who, however, did not appear to relish very much her conversation or endearments, that, "some persons whom she would not condescend to name, were, of monsters, the most infamous and ungrateful—men, indeed, of the gutter—but that she, the little one, was an angel."

Here the skipper put an end to the interview. He had evidently seen and had enough of the Boissons, husband and wife, and, ascending the companion-ladder at the same time as Garry and myself, I heard him muttering to himself as he went along and just caught the following words: "To think—brave men—lose—valuable—save such—theirs—too dreadful. She frivolous—he—a—damned coward!" laying a rather strong emphasis on the last words.

We afterwards went down again, Garry and I, and managed between us to bring up little Mr Johnson, the brave fellow having picked up wonderfully after the attention we had given him, and the knife-thrust he had received from the negro was found to have only grazed his ribs, and he was anxious for fresh air, after his long imprisonment below, and to see and judge for himself how things were looking on deck after our scrimmage.

Here the light was waning and there was a good deal to be done.

"I think, Fosset," said the skipper to our worthy first mate, who had been ordering matters forward while the former had come aft, "we had better muster the hands first so as to know who's missing. I'm afraid several of our poor fellows have lost the number of their mess in the fight."

"Aye, sir, they have," replied Mr Fosset. "Poor Stoddart's gone, for one!"

"Poor fellow, I am sorry," exclaimed the captain with much feeling. "We couldn't have lost a better man, for he was about the best we had on board, poor fellow—a good engineer, a good mess-mate, and good at everything he handled, besides being the finest fellow that ever wore shoe leather. How did it happen?"

"He was knifed by one of those black devils, sir, as he led the boarders forrad!"

"Poor Stoddart! I am sorry to lose you! Well, there's no use crying over spilt milk, and all my words will never bring him back again. Mr O'Neil, just muster the men in the waist and let us know the worst at once!"

"Faith, ye're roight, sor; we'd bether count noses an' have the job over," returned Garry, sotto voce, singing out in a louder key to the survivors of the fray, who were grouped in the waist about the mainmast, where the remaining Haytians who had not been killed outright were tied up feet to the wrists, as the skipper had told Colonel Vereker when he came up. "Now all you Star of the Norths that are still alive come over here to starboard; the chaps that are d'id, sure, can shtop where they are!"

The hands laughed at this Hibernian way of putting the matter to them, and answered their names readily on Garry proceeding to read out the muster roll from a paper he had drawn out of his pocket—all, that is, save those that had fallen, eight in number, including poor Stoddart, our energetic second engineer, and one of his firemen who had volunteered to swell the boarding party, as well as six of our best sailors amongst the foremast hands.

Of the rest of the crew four were badly hurt and a few slightly wounded. Spokeshave was one of these latter, having, unfortunately, the end of his nose—that prominent feature of his—cut clean off by a slash from a cutlass; but the majority, we were glad to find, mostly escaped unscathed.

Seeing old Masters all right, I thought of his morbid forebodings before we came up with the ship, and determined to take a rise out of him.

"I'm awfully sorry about the old bo'sun," I said with a wink to Garry, right behind his back. "He wasn't a bad seaman, but an awful old grumbler, and so superstitious that he funked his own shadow and daren't walk up a hatchway in the dark. Poor old chap, though, it's a pity he's dead; I shall miss him if only from not hearing his continued growling over things that might happen."

"Well I'm blessed!" cried old Masters, completely flabbergasted at this exordium of mine; "I never thought, Mister Haldane, to hear you speak ag'in me like that. I allays believed you was a friend, that I did."

I pretended not to see him, and so too did Garry O'Neil, "tumbling to my game," as the saying goes, while I went on with my chaff.

"How did he die?" I asked. "Was he killed at the first rush?"

"Faith, I can't say corrictly," replied Garry in a very melancholy tone of voice. "I'm afeard care carried him off, somehow or other, as it killed the cat, for he war the most disconsolate, doleful, down-hearted chap I ivver saw piping the hands to dinner. An' so he's d'id! Poor old bo'sun! we'll nivver see his loike ag'in."

"Lord bless you!" cried old Masters angrily, stepping up nearer and confronting us, "I'm not dead at all, I tell you—I tell you I'm not—I'm blessed if I am. Can't you see me here alive and hearty afore you? Look at me."

"Ah, it's his ghost!" I said, with an affected and tremulous start. "He told me, poor fellow, he felt himself doomed, and nothing could save him; and I suppose his spirit wants to prove to me he wasn't a liar, as I always thought he was, the old sinner!"

This was too much for Garry, and he couldn't hold in any longer, and both of us roared at Masters, who looked scared; and, though angry and highly incensed with us at first, was only too glad at its being but a joke, and not a fact that he was dead, to bear us any ill-feeling long.

We were horrified when we were told later on, while we were committing to the deep the corpses of those slain—negroes and white men impartially sharing the same grave beneath the placid sea, at rest like themselves, the breeze having died away again soon after sunset—that Etienne Brago and François Terne, the two wounded sailors we had left below with the Boissons, and little Mr Johnson and the colonel and Elsie of course, that these were the only ones left of the thirty odd souls on board the Saint Pierre when she sailed from La Guayra a fortnight before!

After all the bodies had been buried in their watery tomb, not forgetting that of poor Ivan, who we all thought merited an honoured place by the side of his biped brethren of valour—well, after all this had been done the skipper had the pumps rigged and the decks sluiced down to wash away all traces of the fray.

A council of war was then held between us all on the poop, the skipper of course presiding, and the colonel coming up from the cabin to take part in the proceedings, as well as old Mr Stokes from our ship, where he had remained attending singlehanded to the duties of the engine-room, denying himself, as Garry O'Neil remarked, "all the foin of the foighting!"

This conclave had been called for the purpose of deciding what was to be done with the Saint Pierre and the captured black pirates from whom we had salvaged her, and without much deliberation it was pretty soon decided, on the colonel's suggestion, to send the ship to her destined port, Liverpool, taking the negroes in her, so that they could be tried before a proper court in England for the offence they had committed. "It's of no use your fetching them up to New York," said the colonel, "for though I'm an American myself and am proud of my nationality, I must confess those Yanks of the north mix up dollars and justice in a way that puzzles folk that are not accustomed to their way of holding the scales."

The skipper was of the same opinion as Colonel Vereker; so, the matter having been settled, a navigating party was selected to work the Saint Pierre across the Atlantic, with Garry O'Neil as chief officer. The skipper was unable to spare Mr Fosset, and Garry was all the more fit in every way for the part, as he would be able to look after the wounded French sailors, who would naturally go in the ship as they were the principal witnesses against the blacks on the charges that would be brought against them of "piracy on the high seas."

It was dark when all these details were finally arranged, and all of them went back aboard on our vessel for rest and refreshment, the colonel and his daughter, of course, accompanying us.

Madame and Monsieur Boisson, however, could not be made to leave the ship, saying they would not do so—Madame, that is, said it, and the brave Hercule, following her lead as usual, "would not leave," said she repeatedly, "until they once more touched terra firma," and not wishing they should be starved for their obstinacy, the skipper ordered Weston to look after the happy pair and provide them with food at the same time as he did the wounded and prisoners.

The two vessels remained for the night, still lashed alongside for better security, all hands being too tired out besides to be able to do anything further beyond "turning in" and getting as much rest and sleep as they could after the fatigue and excitement of the day.

Next morning at sunrise Garry O'Neil went back to his ship with his crew of eight men—all the skipper was able to spare him—and by breakfast time they had made her all atauto, bending new sails, which they found below in the forepeak, in place of the tattered rags that hung from some of the yards, and otherwise making good defects, preparing the vessel for her passage home.

We were all sorry to part with Garry even for the short period that would elapse before he would rejoin the old barquey, for he was the life of all us aboard; but the same regret was not felt for Master Spokeshave when we saw him go over the side to accompany the Irishman, the skipper having so decreed, as his assistant navigator, the damage to his nose not necessarily affecting his "taking the sun," though it might interfere with the little beggar's altitudes of another character.

By eight bells all the details necessary under the circumstances were satisfactorily arranged, including the transfer of the effects belonging to the colonel and Miss Elsie, these two preferring to voyage with us, unlike their whilom passengers, the Boissons, who remained in their old quarters, going with "Captain Garry," as we all dubbed our mess-mate on his promotion to a separate command; and half an hour or so later a splendid breeze just then springing up from the westwards and flecking the still blue water with buoyant life, the two ships parted company amid a round of enthusiastic cheers that only grew faint as the distance widened them apart, the Saint Pierre sailing off right before the wind, with everything set below, and aloft, across the ocean on her course for Saint George's Channel, while we braced our yards sharp up and bore away full speed ahead in the opposite direction, bound for New York, which port we safely reached without further mishap four days later.

I Go to Venezuela

"You'd better stick to us," said the skipper to Colonel Vereker, who talked of taking the next Cunard steamer, which was advertised to leave on the morrow, as the Star of the North was being berthed in our company's dock on the East River. "I'm only going to stop here long enough to discharge our cargo and ship a fresh one; which is all ready and waiting for us; and then, sir, we'll 'make tracks,' as our friends the Yankees say, right away over the 'herring-pond' to Liverpool as fast as steam and sail can carry the old barquey. Better stick to us, colonel, and see the voyage out."

"All right, Señor Applegarth," replied the colonel, who could not drop his Spanish phraseology all at once, though otherwise gradually returning to his and our own native tongue and becoming less of a foreigner in every way, "I will return with you."

Both were as good as their word, he and little Elsie coming home with us, and the skipper making the passage from Sandy Hook to the Mersey in eight days from land to land, the fastest run we had ever yet achieved across the Atlantic, whether outward or homeward-bound.

But, quick as we were, the Saint Pierre managed to reach Liverpool before we did, the pilot who boarded us off the Skerries bringing the news that she had gone up the river a tide ahead of us.

This piece of intelligence was confirmed beyond question by Garry O'Neil coming off in the company's tug that sheered alongside as we dropped anchor in the stream later on, midway between the Prince's landing-stage and the Birkenhead shore, the manager of our line being anxious to compliment the skipper on his successful rescue of the French ship, the percentage on whose valuable cargo for bringing her safely to port, and thus saving all loss to the underwriters, would more than repay any damage done for the detention of our vessel when engaged on the errand of mercy and justice that took her off her course.

In addition likewise to the thanks of the company and the underwriters, the skipper was also presented with a handsome gold chronometer watch by the committee of Lloyds, besides participating in the amount awarded by the charterers of the Saint Pierre for the salvage of the ship, though in this latter apportionment it was only fair to mention that we all shared, officers and crew alike, I for my part coming into the sudden possession of such a tidy little sum of ready money that I felt myself a comparative millionaire.

When talking with Garry, whom it is almost needless to say all hands were glad to see again, the men cheering him lustily as he crossed the gangway from the tug, he told us that though otherwise they had had a fairly pleasant voyage after parting company with us off the Azores, the Boissons gave him a good deal of trouble.

Madame, he said, worried his life out by "making eyes" at him when he went below at meal-times, while on deck he was never safe for a moment from her embarrassing attentions unless, in desperation, as he was often forced to do, he went aloft to get out of her way.

"Faith, an' sure, that warn't the worst of it nayther," complained Garry in his humorous way. "Though the vain, silly ould crayture bate Banagher for flirtin'—an', indade, bates ivviry other of her sex, God bless 'em, that I've ivver clapt eyes on yet—that quare little Frenchy chap, her husband, he, the little sparrow, must neades git jallous, an' makes out it's all my fault, an', belave me, a nice toime I had o' it altogether. At last I said to him, afther havin' been more than usual exasperated by him, 'If you want to foight me, begorrah, ye can begin as soon as you loike,' at the same toime showin' him me fists."

"Ah, non, non, mon Dieu, non, note yat vay!" sez he, joompin' away from me whin he caught soight o' me fists. "I was mean ze duel and ze rapiere."

"Not me, faith," sez I. "If it's duellin' ye want you'll have to go to another shop, Monsieur Parleyvoo, for it ain't in my line. Allow me to till ye too, Monsieur Boisson, that if ye dare to hint at sich a thing ag'in whilst I'm in command of this ship, the ounly satisfaction ye'll ivver have out of me in the rap-here way will be a rap on the h'id wid this shtick of moine here, you recollict, joist to thry the stringth of y'r craynium, begorrah! Faith, that sittled the matther, the little beggar turnin' as pale as a codfish and goin' below at onst, lookin' very dejecthed an' crestfallin. He nivver s'id another word afther that to me as long as he remained aboard, nor did Madame trouble me very much more wid her attenshins. On the contrary, bedad, from the day this happened till yestherday, whin she wor set ashore at the landing-stage yonder, she'd look moighty saur at me if we chanced to mate on deck—aye, faith, as saur as a babby that's been weaned on butthermilk."

"Why," inquired the skipper, when we had both a good laugh at Garry and his account of the Boisson episode, "have they left, then, the ship for good?"

"Faith, yis, sor, bag an' baggage, the blissid pair of 'em, an' moighty pleased I wor to say the backs of 'em!"

"But how about the trial of those black devils, those pirates, then; won't they be required as witnesses against the murderers?"

"No, sor," replied Garry. "The polis officers that came aboard whin we got into dock sid they didn't want monsieur nor madame neither, as they didn't know a ha'porth of the jambolle, worse luck, they bein' below all the toime. The magistrates think the two French sailors, who're goin' on foine by the same token, and the colonel, all of whom were on deck an' saw everything that went on, would be sufficient witnisses aga'n the Haytian scoundrels."

"Oh!" said the skipper, "have these men been brought up before the magistrates?"

"Aye, yestherday afthernoon, sor, an' they've been raymanded, whativer that may mane—it ought to have been rayprimanded, I'm thinkin', an' a cat-o'-nine-tails, if they had their desarts - till next Tuesday! The magisthrates belayvin' the ould Star of the North wid you, cap'en, wid the colonel aboard, to give ividence ag'st the mutineers, that they wouldn't be in from New York afore then, not knowin' what the ould barquey could do in the way of stayming as you an' I do, sor, an' that she'd arrive, faith, to-day!"

All happened as Garry O'Neil informed us, the Haytians and mutineer blacks of the Saint Pierre's crew being brought up again before the magistrates the week following our arrival home, when, after hearing the additional evidence against them given by Colonel Vereker and the skipper, the six black and mahogany-coloured rascals were committed for trial at the next assizes, which we were told would not be held for another month, on the charge of "piracy and murder on the high seas."

The colonel took advantage of the interval that would necessarily have to elapse before his presence would again be required in court to escort Miss Elsie to Paris, and place her under the care of the sisters at the convent at Neuilly, where, I think I told you before, he said her mother had been brought up and educated; while the skipper and others of us belonging to the Star of the North, being compelled to remain within handy reach of the authorities, in case our presence at the trial might be required, the opportunity was seized to lay the old barquey up in dry dock and give her a thorough overhaul within and without, though the engines, as proved by our rapid passage here, were none the worse for our breakdown in mid-Atlantic, thanks to the skill and exertions of poor Stoddart and the rest of old Mr Stokes' staff.

Most of us in this way got a short holiday while awaiting the assizes, which I spent with my mother and sister, taking home with me the money I had been awarded as my share of the Saint Pierre's salvage, which had made me fancy myself a temporary Croesus.

Alas, though, the sum, large though it was for a young fellow to find unexpectedly in his pocket, went but a very short step in satisfying the rapacious wolf I found at my mother's door when I reached the little cottage, where she lived with my sister Janet, in one of the suburbs of Liverpool.

A bubble company, whose directors had all been selected for their religious bias rather than their business qualifications, burst at one fell coup, almost in the very hour of my return home, dissipating into thin air, as the Latin poet has it, all the savings of a lifetime which my mother had invested in the swindle—the provision left behind by my father, when he died, for her use, and the subsequent benefit of my sister and myself. The devout rogue who had "managed" the concern to his own worldly interest and that of his fellow religionists, carried on the same, so they said, in a pious and eminently "Christian way," no doubt, respected alike in the eyes of God and men, according to the loudly-voiced tenets of the particular sect to which he and his co-directors mostly belonged; but he managed, all the same, to carry off to a remote and friendly land outside the pale of international law and where dividends need no longer be paid to clamorous creditors, a considerable amount of portable property of a valuable nature, amongst which, probably, was our inheritance, my mother's capital!

Under these circumstances it behoved me to consider how I could best aid my poor mother and sister, then left suddenly destitute through no fault of their own.

Fortunately, I had the means ready at hand.

In our constant association on board the Star of the North after his rescue from the drifting boat, in which he greatly exaggerated the help I was able to render him, Colonel Vereker was kind enough to notice me much more than my subordinate position on board would have seemed to warrant; and in a conversation we had together during the voyage home from New York, after asking me what my prospects were, he made me an offer to accompany him back to Venezuela on his return, promising me, should I accept, a good salary to start with, and a fair chance of ultimately making my fortune.

Loving the sea and my profession, however, with all a sailor's love, besides being attached to my old ship and her officers, I felt no inclination then to give up what I had learnt to look upon as my legitimate calling, and turn landsman; so, although I had the highest admiration for the colonel, coupled with more than a liking for his young daughter, between whom and myself there seemed such a mysterious sympathy on the evening of my sighting the Saint Pierre, when the captain declared we were some hundreds of miles apart, I reluctantly and, so it seemed to me, ungraciously, declined his proposal, telling him I preferred "sticking" to the skipper and the old barquey!

But the colonel very kindly would not take my refusal at first as final; and, when setting out for Paris to take Elsie to her convent school, she taking leave of me with many tears and assurances that under any circumstances she would always remain mio amiquito (my little friend) pledging herself, too, to be, if allowed at the school, a constant correspondent if I would write to her sometimes to let her know where I was. Well, the kind, good-hearted man, taking, as he said, a deep interest in my welfare for Elsie's sake as well as for my own, assured me that he would keep his generous offer open until the period arrived for his ultimate departure for South America, on the termination of the trial of the Haytian pirates and their mutineer accomplices.

So, recollecting all this, in my hour of need, I naturally turned to the colonel and told him of my trouble on his return to Liverpool for the assizes, at which, by the way, the black scoundrels and their allies were sentenced to five years' penal servitude, the judge regretting his inability to impose a heavier punishment from the fact of proof being wanted of the active participation of the prisoners in the atrociously cruel murder of Cato and the other diabolical work perpetrated on board the ill-fated ship.

We were all glad when this matter, with the examination and sickening details that it entailed, was finally settled, and we were at liberty to go where we liked.

Colonel Vereker more than justified my confidence in him.

"Heavens! my boy, you must and shall be as my son," he said, wringing my hand in a grip that I knew would be faithful unto death. "Come with me and I will make a man of you, and a rich one, too, Dick Haldane!"

"But how shall I manage about my mother and sister, sir?" said I hesitatingly. "How shall I manage about them during my absence?"

"You can make over your salary to them, for you will not want anything while at Caracas, as you will live with me as my private secretary," he replied, with another hearty shake of my hand. "The money shall be paid to your mother regularly by my agent here, so that you need have no fears on that score as to her support. But I do not want you to decide such an important change in your life without proper consideration, and the advice of your friends, my boy. Go and consult Señor Applegarth, who I know is an old friend of yours as well as being your captain; and then, if he and your other friends advise your acceptance of my offer, and your mother and sister are willing to part with you—why then, Dick, you may consider the matter settled, and you, some day, will be very thankful you accepted my offer."

The skipper did not hesitate for one moment in giving his opinion, though, like most of my mess-mates, he was good enough to say how sorry he would be to part with me, and how he would miss me.

"Go by all means, my lad," said he. "By George! it's a chance that doesn't come twice in a fellow's lifetime, and you may consider your fortune as good as made!"

Mr Fosset and Garry O'Neil were equally enthusiastic.

"Faith, now, sor!" observed the latter, with a comical air of assured deference at my future dignified position, as he imagined it would be, "I hope ye'll remember ye'r humble ould fri'nd Garry whim ye're Prisidint of the Venezuelan Raypublic, mid a lot of yaller divvles for lackeys, an' so many dollars that ye won't know what to do wid 'em. Begorrah, it's wishin' I am, I stood in ye'r shoes, alannah, an' I wouldn't care for to call the Pope me ouncle, God bless him!"

Spokeshave, though, sneered at my success in gaining so good a friend as the colonel; but owing to the accident to the top of his nose, which being still bandaged, or rather court-plastered up, and not tending to add to his beauty, he was not able to turn it up and sniff in his former irritating way that always exasperated me so much.

As for old Masters, his face became the picture of woe when I informed him I was leaving the ship and the company's service.

"You mark my words, Master Haldane," said he in his most sepulchral manner, "many a one afore you has throwed up the sea, and what good has it done 'em? No good! Them that goes to sea oughter stick to the sea, that's what I says; and if they throws it up, though I hopes you won't, they allus live to repent it. I be truly sorry you be goin', and ah, Master Haldane, I sed as how summet 'ud come of our seein' that there blessed ghost-ship!"

"And so something has happened, bo'sun, and a precious lot too, my hearty!" said I, jokingly, as I stood on the gangway preparatory to going over the side. "But never mind that now, old shipmate! Good-bye to you, men, and thank you all for your kindness to me from the time I first sailed with you as a youngster."

I really believe I could see a tear in the old bo'sun's eye as he wished me farewell with the rest of them, the crew manning the rigging to give me a hearty cheer and "send off" that could be heard across the Mersey.

Thus it was that I took leave of the old barquey, and, my mother's consent having been obtained before I finally settled with the colonel, no further arrangements had to be perfected beyond obtaining and preparing my kit, and a hasty run to the cottage to pay a last visit to my old mother and sister Janet, and wish them farewell for a few years, when I looked forward to returning to England and finding them both well and happy, and in more comfortable and prosperous circumstances.

That same afternoon Colonel Vereker and I started off by train from Liverpool for Southampton, at which latter port we embarked in the outward bound West India mail steamer, sailing for Colon, en route to Venezuela.

During Seven Years

We reached La Guayra, and from thence Caracas, safely enough, in spite of the country just then passing through the acute stage of one of its periodical revolutions that had supervened on the top of an earthquake; which convulsions of nature and society are characteristic features of Venezuela, like as the chief products of its fertile soil are cocoa and "patriots," the latter being almost as great an article of export as the former, especially after a political crisis, and consisting of all sorts and conditions of men who, whether born subjects or alien intriguers, are all desirous of serving their natural or adopted mother country for a consideration!

Colonel Vereker was largely interested in an extensive gold mine in the interior, where he put me as his overseer.

This was not an unwise measure for his own sake, apart from any motive he had in advancing my welfare—his real reason for appointing me to the post; for, with the exception of the captain of the mine, a Frenchman, the majority of those employed were half-caste Spaniards and Portuguese, all of whom studied their several individual pockets rather than the interest of their employer, while the main body of workers were péons and mezites, bastard mulattoes, with a large intermixture of negro blood, who valued their own lives as little as they did the lives of those with whom they had to deal.

I had plenty of work to do here, looking after all these scoundrels, having to keep my eyes open as much as possible in order to prevent wholesale robbery as far as I could, although it was utterly impossible to prevent petty pilfering of the ore on its way from the mine to Puerto Cabello, its general port for transhipment to Europe, to swell the treasure chest of the exiled.

However, by adopting the old Latin maxim, Suaviter in modo, fortiter in re, treating all without hauteur, which some of the insolent half-caste Spanish creoles affected, and yet keeping my revolver ready, with "my powder dry," so as to be prepared for any emergency, I managed to get along very well with the mixed lot I was set over, winning golden opinions from every one but a few of the worst characters.

It sounds as if I were boasting, but this is something for a young Englishman to be able to say in a country which, though it is the veritable El Dorado of poor Drake's dreams, and has possibly a future of wealth and prosperity before it when it comes under the rule of the Anglo-Saxon race—whether of ourselves, or of our cousins in Yankee land it does not much matter, for we are all of the same race and enterprising spirit—can be better described in respect of its present condition by a shorter and far more expressive word.

Amongst my other duties I had charge of all the colonel's voluminous correspondence, he having a mortal hatred to all letter writing in any shape or form, and in addition to my good patron's business communications, was entrusted with the task of despatching a lengthy epistle every other mail—they went fortnightly from La Guayra to France—informing Miss Elsie of our doings, the colonel himself adding the briefest of postscripts to his pequiña niña, as he invariably termed her and always enclosing some remembrance for his little daughter, to show that his love exceeded any epistolary proof of the same, as well as a more substantial token of a handsome cheque for her maintenance and education, forwarded to the care of the mother superior of the convent.

Of all my manifold duties this was the pleasantest I had to perform, being as grateful as water poured on the parched soil of my exile amongst an alien people, antagonistic to me in everything, and with whom I had to shape a steady course, and preserve a "stiff weather helm," as sailors say, to avoid open rupture and assassination, the Venezuelese "sticking at nothing," especially when that "nothing" happened to be one whom, for some sufficient reason to their minds, they deemed an enemy and they chanced to be behind his back—and as I told you before, I steered clear of many enemies, but I could never learn to trust them as a people.

Yes, my happiest hours at San Félipe were spent in writing to little Elsie, who answered my own letters, as well as those I despatched on behalf of the colonel, with unvarying punctuality, holding to the promise she spontaneously gave in England when we parted on her going to school, at which time she had no idea of my ever accompanying her father to South America.

Similarly, the saddest task that could have been laid on my shoulders fell to my lot five years later, when the mysterious attraction by which I had been drawn towards her as a boy had grown into the most absorbing affection—a love that filled my heart.

And I had to write and tell her—I, who would cheerfully have laid down my life to save her a pang—to tell her of her dear father's death.

This occurred just as poor Colonel Vereker had arranged for my returning with him to the capital of the State, where another revolution—the sixth, I believe, since I had been in the country—had broken out, with the object, as the object of all these explosions of the mob invariably was, to depose the reigning party in power, and put the leaders of "the popular movement" for the time being, in the power of the deposed authorities.

The colonel, who had a good deal staked on the issue of the struggle, took up arms on the side of the cause he esteemed just—that to which the most respectable of the inhabitants to a man adhered—as he had taken up arms before for the party of law and order, amongst whom he was looked up to, not only as a skilled soldier and tactician, but a stalwart partisan, his very name being a tower of strength.

Alas! though, no opportunity was afforded him now to display his valour on the battlefield and lead his hosts to victory; for while we were en route for Caracas, a dastardly hound of a creole, whose blood was a mixture of the beast elements—part Spaniard, part Portuguese, part negro—well, this treacherous brute assassinated Colonel Vereker in the most cowardly fashion.

I was by and saw it all.

The vile murderer came up to my poor friend as we were resting in a posada on the road from San Félipe; and, while engaging him in an apparently friendly conversation respecting the political points of the rising, he suddenly stabbed the dear old man in the back with a long stiletto which he had hidden up his wide shirt sleeves.

Fortunately, I was there, and I had time to send a bullet through his brain from my revolver before the wretch could stir a yard from the spot; but this could not save my noble-hearted, kind, generous protector, a man who had been more than a father to me, and for whom I had the utmost affection and respect. No; the death of the scoundrel could not save him, for the wound the cowardly scoundrel had inflicted was mortal.

My dear friend and companion only survived long enough to confide his daughter to my care and give me his blessing ere he died, drawing his last breath in my arms, a smile on his face and dauntless to the end, as he pressed my hand and uttered the usual parting phrase he had learnt from his Spanish associates—"Hasta la mañana—Good-bye till to-morrow!"

It was a long to-morrow, indeed!

After seeing the last tribute of respect paid to the colonel's remains, the gallant fellow being buried close to the posada where he had met with his untimely end, and a cross which I carved myself placed above his lonely grave, sheltered by a noble palm that stood erect, as he had done when living, a monument of nature's handiwork, I resumed my journey to Caracas, in order to carry out my lost friend's last directions.

The alcalde, who acted as the colonel's agent and was largely in his confidence, being an acquaintance of many years' standing, produced a copy of Colonel Vereker's will for my inspection, assuring me that this had been drawn up during his last visit to the State capital, while all his affairs were in the most perfect order, "the poor gentleman," as the alcalde expressed it, "being under the opinion that he would not have long to live," a presentiment of death I have often found many people to have had.

Generous and thoughtful for others to the end, he had not forgotten me in this his last testament, showing that the regard he had already displayed for my welfare was no mere temporary fancy!

On the contrary, much to my astonishment, he had bequeathed to me quite half his fortune—all his share, indeed, in the Gondifera mine—while all his realised property, which was invested in good English and American securities, out of the reach of the grasping hand of the hungerful Venezuelan patriots—all this he left to his daughter Elsie.

From a codicil, too, appended to the document, more in the form of a sacred charge than a legal instrument, "reading between the lines," I could perceive that the large-hearted man had fathomed the secret desire of my heart, though secret it evidently was not to him, loving Elsie as he did, albeit in a different fashion; for after enjoining upon me to regard his little daughter's interests even as he had studied mine, he added that should fate bring us together in the future as had happened so strangely in the past, his dearest wish would be gratified, for he had already learnt to care for me and to look upon me as his son!

Of course nothing of this was mentioned when writing to tell Elsie of the awful event and dreadful calamity that had befallen her, although later on, before I was able to return to England, when her education was completed and the good nuns wrote to me, as her father's executor, to say the time had arrived for taking her away from the convent unless she wished to change her religion and join the sisterhood, to both of which courses I was, of course, bitterly opposed, and, as you may imagine, was delighted when Elsie herself requested to be allowed to leave.

I must, however, have accidentally have shown my feelings towards her and have "let the cat out of the bag" in the letter I sent home to my mother, in answer to the last communication from Neuilly, asking her to take charge of my darling Elsie until I came home to win and claim her.

I imagined this from something that leaked out afterwards, and from the somewhat altered tone of Elsie's letters to me from the date of her leaving France to live with my mother; for, though affectionate enough, they had a certain little air of constraint about them, and though she spoke of various objects of interest to both of us, and of different persons whom she and I knew, and places she went to, she never by any chance ever mentioned herself, never after the letters she sent me containing the passionate outpouring of her inmost heart on receiving the news of her father's death, albeit all this she would feel perfectly certain was to me a sacred confidence.

Slight as the change was in her subsequent correspondence, I noticed it and it worried me, and determined me to have the matter cleared up as soon as I possibly could.

Meanwhile, however, I had to fulfil the colonel's last trust, and as I knew what his intentions had been in regard to the crisis in Venezuelan affairs at the time when an assassin's hand prevented him from acting the part he intended to play in the existing revolution, I thought I should be only carrying out his wishes in putting myself in his place, as far as it lay in my power to do so.

So, soon after coming to Caracas and settling the details of the colonel's last depositions, making my own will in my turn in case of accidents, though in what way is best known to myself, I went to the headquarters of the Government troops and joined the army of General Gomez.

Under this able leader I fought in several engagements that were fierce and sanguinary as all such fratricidal contests are and ever have been in the annals of civil war, at San Sebastien, Carapana, Tarasca, and elsewhere, our guerilla struggle extending over the whole extensive country in almost every direction, where there was a town to sack or property to plunder, until at last the insurgent "patriots" were conquered and peace restored.

All this took a long time; and then, having had enough and to spare of fighting and bloodshed, and tired of mining too, I disposed of my interest in the Gondifera mine, and at last sailed for Europe, bidding a long adieu to Venezuela and everything belonging to it, my journey home being hastened by a somewhat tenderer letter than usual from Elsie, who had read a paragraph in the papers about my having been wounded at the battle of San Sebastien, though, of course, I had not mentioned anything about the affair to her or my mother, as it was a mere flea bite and of no consequence, and I feared to have alarmed them needlessly had I said anything about it in my letters to them at home.

Home at Last!

Fellows who knock about the world sailoring and so on cannot help coming to the conclusion that its compass is narrower than stay-at-home folk might be inclined to believe, for you can hardly stir a step without knocking across some one whom you previously imagined to have been miles and miles away, separated, perhaps, by an ocean from yourself.

I had scarcely stepped into the train from Southampton, bound Londonwards, en route for Liverpool, having only landed from the mail steamer that brought me direct all the way from Colon that very morning, when whom should I see looking at me from the opposite corner of the railway carriage but a big, bushy-haired, brown-bearded man whom I did not know from Adam.

"Faith," exclaimed this gentleman, after a moment's scrutiny, a broad grin lighting up his face and his eyes twinkling with a comical expression that would alone have made me recognise him, had I not heard his delightful, to me at any rate, Irish brogue, "ye're ayther Dick Haldane or the divvle!" stretching out both hands to grasp mine.

I was as pleased to see him, as may readily be believed, as the genial Irishman was to see me, I was sure, even without his telling me so.

"Well," said I, after we had pretty nigh wrung each other's hands off in friendly greeting, "and how are you all getting on aboard the dear old barquey? I want to hear about everybody."

"Begorrah, Dick, give me toime to recover me bre'th, me bhoy, an' thin I'll till ye ivverythin'," and then he continued in a bashful sort of way, unlike his usual off-hand manner, "I've lift the say for good, an' sit up for a docther ashore on me own hook, faith."

"Why!" I exclaimed in great surprise, "how's that?"

"Bedad, you'd betther axe y'r sister."

"What! my sister Janet?"

"Faith, yis; the very same little darlint of a colleen. Dick, ye spalpeen, jist lit me shake y'r fist agin, lad. I'm the happiest man in the wurrld!"

"Whee-e-e-eew," I whistled through my teeth. "This is indeed a surprise!"

Then it all came out, Garry telling a long yarn about his calling at my mother's house to ask about me some few months back, and meeting there Elsie, whom he had no difficulty in identifying, he said, as "the little girl of the ghost-ship," though she had grown a bit taller and was more good-looking than he remembered her at the time he saw her on board the Saint Pierre. But, good-looking as she was, he did not think her to be compared to my sister Janet, with whom he had evidently fallen in love at first sight and very deeply so, too!

On his subsequently declaring his passion, impetuous as usual, after a very short acquaintance, my mother insisted as a first step to entertaining his suit that he should leave the sea, as he had another profession by which he was quite capable of supporting a wife as well as himself, if he so pleased.

"Faith, and I wint an' bought a practis' at onst, havin' a snig little sum stowed away in the bank," continued Garry, "the savin's of me pay for the last five year an' more, besides that money we all got for salvagin' the French ship, sure, of which I nivver spint a ha'poth. But aven thin, Dick, ould chap, yer dear ould mother wern't satisfied, bless her ould heart. She sid that yer sisther an' mesilf wu'ld have to wait to git marri'd till you came home, ye spalpeen; an' not thin aven, if so be as how ye'd turn nasty an' disagreyable, an' refuse yer consint. Faith, ye won't now, will ye? or, bedad, I'll be afther breakin' ivvrey bone in y'r body, avic, an' thin have to plasther ye up ag'in."

To avoid such a terrible contingency I there and then gave my hearty consent to the arrangement he and Janet, with my mother's concurrence, had thus planned without my knowledge; although, really, if I had been inclined to grumble at not being informed previously of what now so unexpectedly transpired, I had only time and distance to blame, not the parties concerned, for the engagement was of so recent a date that the news of it, though on the way through the post, had not reached Venezuela when I left.

After I had answered a lot of Garry O'Neil's questions concerning myself and the time I had passed in South America, speaking, too, of poor Colonel Vereker, whose death he had learnt from my mother, I began again, asking in my turn all about my old shipmates, and, of course, his own also.

"Faith, the skipper is foine and flourishin'," he informed me, "an' the ould barquey as good an' as sound as ivver she was. Do you ricollict ould Stokes?"

"Of course I do," I said. "Is he still chief?"

"No, no; he retired a year ago or more on a pinsion which the company gave him for his long service; an' little Grummet—ye rimimber him?—well, he's promoted, sure, to ould Stokes' billet. The ould chap, though, is alive an' hearty, an' as asthamataky as ivver!"

"What's become of Mr Fosset?"

"Och, be jabbers! he's a big man now. He's a skipper on his own hook, jist loike Cap'en Applegarth. He's got the ould Fairi Quane, the sicond best boat but one to the line. D'ye ricollict that ould thaife of a bo'sun we had on the Star of the North?"

"Why, you must mean poor old Masters! I should think I did."

"That same, alannah. He wasn't a bad sort of chap, an' a good sayman, ivvry inch of him, though I used for to call him an ould thaife just 'for fun an' fancy'—as the old song says—well, he's lift the ould barquey an' gone with Cap'en Fosset in the Fairi Quane. But ye haven't axed me onst afther yer ould fri'nd Spokeshave! Sure, now, ye haven't forgot little 'Conky,' faith!"

"No, indeed," said I, amused at his query and the funny wink that accompanied it. "What has become of that spiteful little beggar?"

"Begorrah, ye'll laugh an' be amused, but he's marri'd to a wife as big as one of thim grannydeers we onst took in the ould barquey to Bermuda, d'ye rimimber? Faith, she's saix feet hoigh, an' broad in the b'ame in proporshi'n. They make a purty couple, bedad! an' they do say she kapes him in order. Do ye rickolict what an argufyin' chap Spokeshave was aboard?"

"I should think I did, indeed," replied I. "I think he was the most cantankerous little beast I ever came across in my life, either afloat or ashore!"

"Faith, ye wouldn't say that same now, Dick," rejoined Garry with much earnestness. "The poor little beggar's as make as a cat, for he daren't call his sowl his own!"

I asked after some of the other men belonging to my old ship, including Accra Prout, whom the colonel wished to accompany us to Venezuela, the mulatto refusing on the plea that, though he should always love his "old massa," he could not go with him for one insurmountable reason.

"Guess I'd hav' 'sociate wid dem tam black raskels daan thaar, massa, an' dis chile no like dat nohow. I'se nebbah 'sparrage my famerly by 'sociatin' wid niggahs, massa, nebbah. De Prouts 'long good old plantation stock, an' raise in Lousianner!"

This supercilious autocrat, it must be borne in mind, all the time being more than half a negro himself, though, for that matter, his heart was better and his disposition braver than many a white man who would have despised his coloured skin.

Some of the other hands about whom I inquired had left the old barquey and shipped aboard other vessels, so Garry told me; but at this I was not much surprised, sailors as a rule being fond of change and very unconservative in their habits.

With suchlike conversation my old mess-mate and I beguiled our long railway journey to Liverpool, which we reached the same evening, but before we had quite exhausted our respective questions and answers respecting everybody we had ever met or known during the time he and I had been to sea together.

My meeting with my dear mother and sister after so long an absence abroad can be well imagined, and so too my first interview with Elsie, whom I should hardly have known again, for how can I describe her beauty and grace, and though I had been prepared in some measure from accounts my mother had sent me, still they exceeded my expectations.

It would be impossible if I tried to picture her for "a month of Sundays," as Captain Applegarth used to say on board the old barquey when he thought a fellow spent too much time over a job.

So to make a long story short and to avoid all further explanation, it need only be added that one fine day last summer, when the trees were all green and leafy, and the flowers abloom, and happy birds filling the air with song, Elsie and I were married.

Garry O'Neil joined his lot with that of my sister at the same time, the two brides being given away respectively by the skipper, who managed to run the Star of the North home in time for the wedding, and old Mr Stokes, the chief engineer of the old barquey, who had only to cross the road, instead of the Atlantic, to get to our house, as he lived near to us now—he also was present. Captain Applegarth, who was a very old friend of my mother's and a kind one too, likewise, lived in a good substantial house surrounded by a lovely garden in our pretty, picturesque, old village.

To all whom it may concern, it may, in conclusion, be mentioned that this double-barrelled affair took place in the quaint, old-fashioned, non-ritualistic, semi-Gothic, and many-galleried old village church, of which so few remain now in England, situated close to our cottage, and where our widowed mother had, in our childhood, taught us to lisp our first prayers to heaven, our dead father resting in the ivy-grown and flower-adorned graveyard adjoining. The nuptial knot was tied by Parson Goldwire, as everybody called him in the neighbourhood, assisted by Matthew Jacon, the equally elderly parish clerk, without whose joint ministration on the occasion neither Janet nor myself would have believed the marriage ceremony had been properly solemnised, both my sister and myself standing in much awe of the learned divine and his inseparable "double," and holding to the creed that the austere pair represented the very quintessence of orthodoxy.

A Presentment of the Past

After Elsie and I got "spliced," to use the old familiar language of my boyhood, the expressive argot of the sea, for which I shall always retain a passionate love, only second to that I bear towards my dear wife, we set off for the Continent, having determined to spend the happy period of our honeymoon abroad, like the fine folk of the fashionable world with whom, though, there is little in common between us, their ways otherwise not being our ways, nor their thoughts, ambitions, hopes or desires in any respect akin to ours.

First we went up the Seine to Rouen, where I had passed a couple of years of my school life, studying French and teaching the young scions of the Gallic race with whom I was associated for the time the exigencies of football, as we play the game in Lancashire, varied by an occasional illustrative exhibition explanatory of the merits of la boxe Anglaise.

Time passed swiftly with so sweet and sympathetic a companion; our tastes were similar, both taking the greatest delight in ancient buildings and lovely scenery; the weather, too, was charming, and altogether we were as happy as two mortals can be on this earth.

Elsie and I saw all that was to be seen in the old city we first visited, which, in addition to its architectural beauties, should have a special charm for all Englishmen from the fact of the dauntless Richard Coeur de Lion having such an affection for the town that he bequeathed it his lion heart, and then we journeyed on through la belle Normandie, loitering here and there at those historic spots, woven into the life of our country, spots where artists of all nations love to linger.

We stayed anon at slow, sedate Caen, as still as the stone for which it is celebrated, and that furnished the building material of Winchester Cathedral; Bayeux, boastful of its antique tapestry; and Dol and Saint Servan, and away beyond, Sainte Michel, so like and yet unlike the like-named Saint Michael's Mount of Cornwall, in our own sea-girt isle that it might have been chipped out of the same block by its grand handycraftsman to serve as a replica; until, entering brighter Bretaigne, in the sunny south of France, where the landmarks of the past seem to stand out in bolder relief, we visited Nantes and other places of interest, and jogging on thence through Angouleme and Poictiers, halting a day at

Poictiers to fight our Plantagenet battles o'er again, we finally ended our pilgrimage at Bordeaux.

At this wonderfully picturesque port, whose semi-ancient, quaintly modern aspect strangely attracted us both, we anchored awhile, remaining many weeks in excess of the customary limit of the traditional honeymoon, ours being an indefinite one and only to be completed we trust, when Elsie and I cease to breathe.

Late in the autumn, when the leaves had begun to turn russet and brown, and the air of a morning assumed a crisper and more bracing tone, telling us plainly as these signs tell that summer had fled for good and aye, and winter was coming by-and-by, we bade adieu to dear old Bordeaux, and taking a steamer there bound for the Thames, having had enough of railways and land travel, we started to voyage home by sea, my native element.

On the evening of the second day that had elapsed since losing sight of Pointe de Graves at the mouth of the Garonne, towards sunset, we had weathered Ushant and were shaping a course up Channel, north east, so as to clear the dangerous Casquettes rocks of Guernsey, when I noticed a large ship, close-hauled on the starboard tack, steaming inwards for the French coast, as if heading for Brest, her nearest port.

At that moment the tired sun, which previously appeared to linger above the horizon, uncertain whether to go or to stay, dipped suddenly as we were looking at him, a pale, yellow radiance succeeding the dazzling beams that had well-nigh blinded us, shining straight in our eyes, while the afterglow, mounting rapidly into the western sky, became more and more vivid each moment, two purple islands of cloud which floated across this refulgent background having the lower edges dyed of a rich crimson that seemed to set the sea on fire and tipped the spars and sails of the passing ship with flame.

She was flying the French Tricolor, and as our steamer went by, saluting her with a couple of blasts from her steam whistle in friendly greeting, the stranger vessel as a return, in accordance with the time-honoured rule of nautical etiquette always observed on such occasions, dipped her ensign.

This action, coupled with the similarity of the scene and its surroundings, the ship in the distance with her flag half on the hoist, the sunset glow, and the fact of my being on board a steamer then as now, brought back to my mind at once the incidents of that memorable evening of the past, more than seven years ago now, the vraisemblance between the two being simply astounding!

"Elsie, dearest Elsie!" I cried with a start, as the strange coincidence of the presentment struck me, the date being even identical. "Do you remember what day of the month this is, querida mia?"

"Why, of course, Dick, I do," she answered, nestling up to my side as if for protection, for we were sitting in a warm corner by the taffrail, just abaft the wheel-house, and screened from the observation of the rest of the passengers who were walking up and down the deck as usual after dinner. "Why, Dick, dear, it's the seventh of November, your birthday, you know; surely you have not already forgotten the little present I gave you this morning, my likeness in a locket for your watch chain, a miniature done by that clever artist at Orleans, and you told me you would always wear it for my sake. Dick, my husband, where is your memory?"

"No, my little one, I have not forgotten it," said I, kissing her, thinking she was going to cry at what she thought was forgetfulness on my part. "Here it is next my heart, like yourself," said I laughingly. "But, Elsie, alma mia, I was thinking of another anniversary, and a Friday evening too, to make it all the more wonderful! Don't you recollect now?"

"Oh Dick, my dear husband," she whispered, seizing my arm and gazing out over the taffrail at the ship, all ablaze now from the reflection of the sky, and nearly hull down to leeward. "I see, I see. What a strange coincidence. It is really wonderful!"

"It is, my darling," said I. "But it was more extraordinary still that you should have seen me that memorable evening, now more than seven years ago, and when I too saw the Saint Pierre with you on her deck, and more wonderful still, when the captain and some of the crew even to this day insist we were actually several hundreds of miles apart!"

"Ah, but you are near me now, though, thank God!" she cried, looking up into my face with the most charming expression of delight, causing me to be foolish in bestowing another little kiss on her upturned face. "I don't know how it was, but whether the ships were as far apart as the captain and the others say, or whether they were not, I did see your ship and you on her, as I told my dear, dear father at the time, and he himself did not believe it. Dick, dear, it must have been the gift of 'second sight,' as the Scotch people call it. There was a nun at the convent who had it, and could tell, so she said, when anything was about to happen to any of her family, though she couldn't predict events concerning persons who were not 'blood relations,' as she termed them. Don't be frightened Dick, but I do think that I must really possess the same faculty!"

"Well, if that is the case, sweetheart," said I, "there must be some psychological affinity between us, and we are both endowed with the same weird gift, although the possession of the same has never been brought to the knowledge of us except on that one memorable occasion. That cannot be otherwise explained; but the fact of the two ships meeting afterwards may very readily be accounted for under the circumstances. The winds and currents of the ocean drifted them together, like as they did us, dear. Don't you think so?"

She did not answer for a moment, and, as our steamer speeded on her way, the glow in the sky gradually faded and darkness crept over the face of the sea, the flashing light of Ushant whirling its luminous arms round in rapid rotation, like some spectral windmill, away in the distance over our lee, where the French ship had long since disappeared.

Presently my Elsie, who had been looking down into the now gloomy depths alongside, musing over the bitter-sweet memories of the past, lifted her eyes to mine, glancing heavenwards.

"No, Dick, my dearest," said she, speaking at last, a certain hesitation and catch in her throat and a tear in the broken intonation of her voice, "Dick, I've been thinking and—and—it was a power greater than that of the winds and seas that brought us together. It was God!"

www.ingramcontent.com/pod-product-compliance
Lightning Source LLC
Chambersburg PA
CBHW030331180626
46810CB00003B/1312